A Vortex Tale

S. L. Wise

Dedication

For Finn, Hildi, Kestrel, Asher, & Sebastian

Remember, "Look to the stars".

Acknowledgment

Thanks to my readers extraordinaire: Dorothy Black, Christa Irwin, Nina Jablonski, Emily A Miller, and Lori Swanchak. Your ever present reflections, comments, and 'asks' for more, kept the pages coming.

And thank you Edie…for just about everything under the stars.

Contents

Prologue

She longs to rest in stillness,
Beyond the spiraled reach
Of whirling fragments, illusions & debris
She yearns to live
Where memory and body connect to a raw faith in being
And authentic seconds of healing pry open a closed-off heart
Rusted shut from tears, too many to count.

Within this sanctuary, extraordinary truth renders all things brighter
And love can spread its soothing magic.

The child,
Once lost inside the shadowed vortex of her mind,
Finds an ancient lamp, lighting the way to a trusted pair of outstretched hands.
The ageless darkness of despair
Now vanquished by a witness holding hope,
The young one now offered the will and wisdom
To reach for the embrace of a star and navigate her journey home
Returning to the settled shores,
Where wolf and girl may sleep.

PART I

Before

Chapter One

She savored the sensation of calm that always crept up her body as she'd stepped from the noisy hubbub of 8th Avenue into the quiet elegance of the pre-war building where she had lived for close to fifty years. The elevator up to her 7th-floor apartment continued her shift from contained public person (and all the expectations of behaviors and attitudes) to personal freedom (full-throttle private inner life, as outrageous as she chose it to be. It was nobody else's business). Occasionally, that sacred process was interrupted if a neighbor or someone delivering packages or food to another apartment unexpectedly happened to need a lift as well. She did not encourage conversation beyond minimal politeness.

Disruption was at its worst if the building superintendent, Curtis Cronkly, humming random show tunes, stepped into the elevator cage. He'd stare directly into her eyes, intent on holding her attention for the entire ride. She would try to look down, but there was no opportunity to break away from his gaze and (since he preferred to hum when he was alone and now he had a captive audience) non-stop chattering about lightbulbs, water leaks, and the rudeness of people who tossed household garbage in the basement recycle containers causing him endless hours sorting through disgusting refuse bins.

The worst was when he described in detail personal items of

laundry accidentally left behind in the public washing machines and dryers of the building. "Can you imagine someone left a perfectly good green sports shirt in my size in the tub? And the week before, I even found stained underwear (I'm not going to tell you what kind – ha!). My wife told me to toss them both into the garbage, but I kept the shirt. Of course, I can't wear it around the building in case its owner sees it. Now that can our little secret as well, right? I mean, shrinks keep secrets, right?"

When he stepped into the cage, the odor of grimy machine oil sticking to his thick fingers and rubbing into his faded work pants permeated the air. Trying to keep her breath even and steady, she felt like a child trapped alone in a tiny room with a dirty man. Her private self, exposed and invaded, sought protection from his presence. She'd stop inhaling for all seven flights while stretching a public-self smile of fake sincerity across her face so he would have no clue about her vulnerability, no way to enter into her.

She had no proof that he was a predator, no hard evidence whatsoever. A few times, she had actually researched the sexual abuser list for her block. His name never showed up. There was just something about him that made her feel hunted. She felt it in her gut. And she was in the business of trusting its messages.

Lately, when she returned home from her art therapy practice, she felt especially drained and had nothing left to give to other people. Socializing was out of the question. On those days, she noticed the boundaries she had honed so well between her public and private selves becoming feeble and less within her control. In the past, these two selves respected their lanes, taking appropriate turns to lead. Though occasional breaks through parts cropped up from time to time, she generally managed herself well and, like the outside of a mask shown to the world and the inside seen only by the maker, she could keep both halves of herself in order.

Losing control of her public and private personae terrified her. Curtis frightened her because, with him, she experienced confusion dominating the exquisite internal balance she had created for herself. When he was around, the odds of power changed in his favor.

Thankfully, for today, he was nowhere to be seen, and she had the elevator to herself.

As of late, traveling between art therapy sessions was causing her feet to swell, her left knee to stiffen and her back to spasm between the shoulder blades. Compression socks helped, but they were nearly impossible to get off at the end of the day, even though she had learned the trick of sticking her thumb as far down as it could go and stretching her leg to help it glide over her recalcitrant heels.

Arthritis had claimed victory over her aging fingers, which

for decades had pulled the weight of her rolling workbag up and down her dusky apartment hall and across the unpredictable streets of New York City. The art supplies inside seemed heavier and heavier with each passing year. The goal of the final part of her trek home was to simply reach her apartment door and let herself in with as little aggravation as possible. She'd counted the steps to the fire door for years and determined it was forty-five feet from the elevator. Her door, just a few short steps beyond, was on the opposite side of the hall

The fire door was a moldy grayish-green color which she imagined was covered in leftover paints from a prison or public-school building where institutional colors were designed to suppress spontaneity and rowdiness. The door was always propped open with a brick for easy access to the stairs, though she never really understood why.

Reaching her door, she'd briefly recite a clearing mantra, "Now I can let the world go," while pressing the cold brass key between her achy fingers. She'd try to steady her hands, which were a bit shaky with age, aiming intently for the key slot to let herself in. That key and lock meant the world to her.

Gratification these days comes from the little things in life. She rated the slick glide of her apartment key into the brassy security lock as one of them. The blade pins shifted into exact order (she liked to imagine there were tiny soldiers inside moving into formation and even considered buying a lock she really didn't need just to deconstruct and explore precisely how it functioned). She appreciated the jeweler-like precision of her fancy lock and the pleasing clicking sounds it made as the tumblers seamlessly lined up.

When she first moved into the building, her front door security was just a simple chain on the door trim fitting into a metal slot. Its lumpiness clearly showed it had been painted over multiple times in a kind of dirty white. A few years later, she installed a rudimentary deadbolt (it seemed like a step up in the world) that was stiff and awkward to turn but more reliable, preventing someone from breaking in.

As she became more financially successful as an art therapist, the niceties of daily life improved. She purchased a high-end 'amazing lock' from an equally super high-end hardware store in mid-town which not only provided security but effortlessly delivered an experience of releasing the deadbolt that she could only compare to finger ballet. She'd barely turn the key before the inner pins would initiate their pivots like miniature pirouettes, landing perfectly in each appointed slot. Then, joy spreading in her heart, she would open her front door with flair and finesse. Getting into her home had become smooth sailing, an event of pleasure. Life was pretty good.

She had been wearing a lightweight coat the past few weeks as the weather was getting cooler. Joking with herself, she'd think, "I am a person of 'bad habits'" because the coat never made it back into the closet to be properly hung up. Typically, her coat might stay out a whole season, continually being tossed limply on the back of a chair until she had one of her massive cleaning sprees when the apartment chaos got to be too much. Then, because housekeeping was not really her forte, she's straighten and clean her home superficially, not really rooting out the clutter accumulated over the years.

Studying the tweedy coat, she ran her hands along its nubby woven texture, admiring its rusty colors of burnt orange and maple leaf red. She loved the classic A-line pattern with double-breasted faux bone buttons. The way it smelled after an evening mist peaked her imagination. The sensation was rustic and homey.

She held it under her chin, stealing a glance at herself in the mirror and thinking, 'Not bad for 71.' Being a tinge overweight seemed helpful at her age to keep those pesky wrinkles 'poofed' (she was prone since childhood to making up words that painted an impression and were not found in any dictionary). Unsettled by her dubious relationship with the mirror, she vaguely reminisced about her body at different times in her life. How she thought of herself never seemed to coincide with what she saw in her reflection.

As a therapist, she was accustomed to encouraging people to

open up and explore their memories and did so herself with some frequency. On this particular evening, she felt a specific memory coming on and drifted straight into it.

She was a youngster, maybe around ten years old, standing with her mother in Hale's Department Store among clothing racks packed with spring coats. They found a few possible spring coats (a ritual that she reflected, sadly, no longer seemed to be in style) for her to try on. Her favorite, by far, was made from some sort of a new-green and ocean-blue cottony material woven in a stripy pattern. This was THE one. It was dreamy.

In the dressing room, the coat drooped from her young body, far too big for her, but her mother, being practical in matters of avoiding unnecessary expenses, assured her that it made the most sense to be a little too large for the girl because at the rate she was growing, by next year it would fit just right. Its' length was a different story, clearly needing immediate alteration.

Her mother sent word through the saleswoman from the coat section that the store seamstress was needed. While they waited for her to arrive, the girl was instructed to keep the coat on so they would not be asked to vacate the dressing room. Hale's had strict rules about how long customers could remain in the dressing rooms without adding more clothing to try on. If one was waiting to be fitted, it was understood the room was not being wasted. With all this waiting, the tiny space grew airless and warm.

After about fifteen minutes (though to the girl, it seemed to take far longer), the fitter arrived. She carried a small wooden circular step for customers to step up on for marking and pinning hems as she squatted to do her work. On her wrist was a giant red strawberry impaled with what looked like about a thousand flat-head pins. This seamstress was amazing. She could put a dozen or so pins in between her lips, pull one out and insert it into the hemline that she was chalking all in a flash of about 1 second.

The tricky part for the person whose clothing was being altered was to stand perfectly straight and still, only turning super slowly on command from the seamstress, and all the while, not fall off the step. The slightest mis-movement could completely wreck all the fabulous measuring and pinning that was required to perfectly hem the garment.

The process could also be dangerous. Little children had a tough time coordinating, balancing and turning, but it was more than understood that a 10-year-old girl, who was serious about her part in getting a great hemming job done, could manage the technique perfectly without failure. So, the girl intent on pleasing her, the seamstress (and therefore her mother) kept slowly turning, becoming more and more overheated.

Something was feeling off. The rules for being fitted included a prohibition against speaking. Everyone knew that speaking could totally shift the accuracy of a perfect hemline. So, the girl tried not to speak. Then she noticed weird happenings with her vision. Black and white checkerboard patterns began wafting in front of her eyes. She tried to blink them away, but this made matters worse, and the patterns only grew more intense, now spiraling and throbbing at the same time.

Mother (her daughter always addressed her formally from as far back as she could speak except under extremely challenging situations or just upon awakening) noticed the girl was not turning nicely. Now, amid the memory, the daughter recalled a sharp, blood-red thumbnail gouging into the soft center part of her girl-sized hand while simultaneously hearing a quiet but stern "Stop swaying" command. Softly, the 10-year-old felt her dry tongue stick to the roof of her mouth as her lips tried to whisper one word, "Hot." Mother snapped at her, "Shh. Don't make it take longer. Just be still," and once more dug her nail into the child's palm.

And so, in an effort to please the adults in the room, the girl tried to distract herself and enjoy the nifty patterns that were pulsing about in a more and more animated fashion. She tried to convince herself this was fun. She was lucky to have special visions. It was amazing.

But those mind tricks weren't really helping, and her thoughts soon wandered to her feet. Everything down there seemed all numb, and where her feet should have been, she sensed there was nothing, and she was filled with a strong urge to drop her head to her chest just to take a peek to be sure they were still attached; it was all she could do to ignore the impulse. Turning without feet was next to impossible, and she worried about being admonished for non-cooperation. Then her legs started feeling very rubbery. Things were definitely not going well.

Startling the girl, the fitter seemed to scream a sharp "turn" at her through a long, stretched-out hollow tube. The child wondered where the tube had come from and how sound could travel such a distance and still sound so loud. By now, the room had grown to be enormous, and she wondered how the fitter's arms reached all the way from a door to the hem of her coat. It all seemed incredible.

"Mummy, I don't feel so good." But really, the child wasn't sure if she had spoken those words at all because the light of the world was closing down, and there was no difference between her and the wall, which made her break out into a tremendous fit of laughter in spite of the consequences she was sure would follow. Mother responded, "Quiet. Just another minute or so, and she'll be done."

What was going on? It wasn't making much sense to the girl to stick to Hale's protocol or her mother's demands. Rules of decorum seemed to be melting off her body as rivulets of sweat cascaded down her back. Proper turning for the fitter became impossible.

But collapsing wasn't. Crumpling into a hot mess of a child made all the sense in the world to her. And so, the girl stopped making any effort to stand like a good soldier and, instead, flowed into a rapid descent of unconsciousness as her coat-laden body hit the floor. The rest of that memory was forever lost to her, but she imagined it was not a good day all around.

Her thoughts wandered aimlessly for the next few minutes, ultimately bringing her back to the present moment in her apartment. She saw herself standing in front of the closet mirror, eyeing her septuagenarian figure. She found herself incredulous thinking that two grown people who, in a small, overheated dressing room with a 10-year-old child wobbling while perched on a tiny step, failed to notice something was wrong seemed so negligent. She felt certain she would have been alarmed immediately seeing the pasty color of the girl's face and hearing her random mutterings about being overheated. The youngster gave plenty of clues that she was roasting inside that green and blue spring coat and was very dizzy from turning.

As she considered her mother's complete lack of attunement to her daughter, she confirmed to herself, once again, that it was no surprise she had been drawn to a healing profession. As an art therapist, she generally took her cue from the clients. She understood uncovering truths with her clients could be accomplished indirectly through images and metaphors, which often was more effective than poking about too directly or proffering heady interpretations that often missed the mark and fell flat. She believed clients risked being further traumatized if a climate of safety, caring, and compassion was not adequately present in the first place.

In her imagination, trauma was a spirited thing, wild and ready to pounce, willing to snatch and destroy what little hope may be present in order to feed its endless hunger. For her, this work was a calling, ready to try to calm whatever parts of the beast came forth. She viewed her job as temporary responsibility, a guardian to hold the hope until the client, gaining strength and confidence, was ready, able, and wanting to hold it for themselves.

Mulling all this over a few minutes longer, she shook her head as she had done numerous times before when her mind transported her back to her own childhood. In disbelief yet again, she tried to reject the darkness of abandonment that had cast its shadow so young in her life. But, like lovers in the dissent of a death grip, their declaration of love was toxic and unyielding.

Chapter Two

The bookish smell of her apartment was one of the first things she noticed when she entered her home. While she loved reading, her passion really was for collecting books, touching their spines and covers, and then imagining how the content might transport her into another world.

Perhaps she inherited this particular love from her mother, who, in her middle years, was the local librarian in their tiny town. Her mother always left her alone when she saw her with a book in hand. Books made things at home seem tension free. As an adult, she tried to read as often as she could. However, most of the time, the books she brought into her apartment ended up landing in colorful piles waiting to be opened.

Next, she would lug her work bag over to the mirrored closet in the foyer, depositing it between one stack or another of the unopened tomes. Her routine went as follows: Door opens, woman steps over the threshold, inhales deeply through the nostrils appreciating the odors of a home, then lugs the bag to a closet and stops. At the intersection of those two actions, the same thought always presented itself, "Thank goodness this bag has wheels," and she'd pause to admire her cleverness at having purchased just the right container for carrying and storing art supplies from home to clients.

She loved her bag and described it to herself as delicious, sturdy and swank. It was constructed from black vegan leather with rose-colored zippers and buckles defining pockets just right for harboring art materials and bits of creative odds and ends. She adored fussing over the larger pouches holding markers, paints, colored pencils, erasers, all kinds of crayons and textured papers. Glue sticks, scissors and tape all had specific places to be tucked.

The deeper middle section contained oversized items like cardboard and heavy-weight paper for more serious sessions where a lot of durability would be expected from the materials. There were ribbons and bits of fabric, even needles and thread and small amounts of pillow stuffing for making finger puppets or other small objects with felt decorations. If the clients were inclined to work 3D, she carried a five lb. package of air-dry clay though her preference was to not offer up that material unless it was really obvious it would be perfect for the occasion. She never carried glitter. It made such a horrific mess, got into everything, and would keep showing up months later. Glitter was so irritating, and she had convinced herself it somehow was demeaning to her profession.

Since the workbag was on wheels, all she really had to do was pull it along behind her though these days, the grip made her fingers sore and tingly, and she had to keep switching hands before they grew completely numb. Aside from the sheer beauty of the bag and its great utility, it was the ball-bearing wheels that really grabbed her fancy. Gone were the days of shoulder bags weighing her down, forcing her into an awkward gait to compensate for being lopsided from carrying supplies.

She tried Pilates one summer on the recommendation of the mother of one of her child clients, who had noticed her irregular posture. It was expensive and didn't help much, and she was informed there would be no realistic way the issue could be fixed as long as she carried the problem around on her body. The instructor barked, "Get wheels" at her as she left her final session. At first, she didn't know what that meant, but by the time she got home and into her bath, she got it. A bag on wheels changed her life.

Her first one came from a vendor on 14th Street trying to make a fast sale. It was basically a red plaid heavy plastic bag on wheels – the kind people take to do their marketing. The giant opening on top closed with a flap that zippered all the contents into one somewhat weather-resistant, rectangular space. Her art supplies were loose inside, and navigating before, during, and after sessions was a mess. Looking cheap and irritating to use, it did not make her feel very good about herself, though her shoulders felt some relief.

Next, she tried a spinner-wheeled suitcase, one small enough to fit into the overhead compartment of a 747 jumbo liner. This bag, more expensive than she had really wanted to pay, had small but effective spinner wheels and a hard plastic chartreuse shell that completely protected the inside contents from the weather. Her supplies could be stabilized with elastic tie-downs attached inside the shell by the manufacturer. She used this bag for almost a decade – it was that durable. But she was severely constrained by the shell itself, which could neither expand nor adjust to accommodate awkward shapes. Plus, the whole thing basically functioned like a clam and, to get inside had to be completely flat on the floor to get anything from the inside. Clients could easily see everything at a glance. She felt exposed and embarrassed when this happened, as if she were carrying her lingerie instead of pastels and oil crayons.

As the years went on, and she was doing reasonably well financially in her private practice, shedecided she deserved better. She made a comprehensive wish list of everything she would want in a work bag. It had to have possibilities. It needed lots of special spaces for the knick-knacks of her art therapy trade, including dedicated compartments for different types of papers and drawing materials and plenty of sections to support tools like brushes and paints. It needed to be easy to reach everything and safe against dramatic weather. Mainly (she would admit this to no one, but it was her basic truth), it had to be aesthetically lovely. No more traipsing around the city looking less than divine!

She liked to say, "The bag found me," when colleagues and clients inquired, "Wherever did you find such a glorious bag?". She wasn't sure why she kept its provenance secret, but somehow sharing that, she stumbled into finding it partially tucked under a computer counter at Office Pride seemed demeaning to the bag. From that happy accident, she felt certain the bag, and she had found each other.

For some odd reason, she definitely wanted people to believe the bag was exotic, one-of-a-kind. After she bought it, she checked the Office Pride website catalog for months. It never showed up. The bag's history was simply a mystery and, like many good mysteries, was to remain an enigma. She lied and told people who asked that the bag had been an anonymous gift and that she never knew from whence it came.

Telling lies was a relic of her past when she would speak in opposition to protect herself. In the case of her bag, the lie slipped out so easily that she never considered correcting it. So, the origin of the bag, the donor of the gift, was a non-truth that compounded with time the way most small lies do. She had observed that, generally, tiny lies grow exponentially faster than really huge ones. That is because giant lies take more planning – they often are mapped out in advance. The little, itty-bitty ones, those that really don't matter much at all, are free as a lark to spin and fly about gathering more untruths without much thought at all.

The mirrored coat closet was stuffed with coats and boots, hats, all sorts of tall cleaning items like brooms, and a six-foot feather duster pole that needed new feathers. The clutter prevented it from fully closing. There was also that Deluxe ReNovo Porto-Vacuum cleaner she bought about twelve years ago.

It was a big expense at the time and came with so many parts she had no idea how to use. It was intimidating, but she believed she was dedicated to making excellent use of it. And at first, she did. Every Sunday afternoon (for the first few months), she'd run it through her apartment, picking up the tiniest of debris and dust. Then she convinced herself it was doing such a good job that she could go longer without using it. The weeks turned into months and then longer until she randomly used it only a few times a year. It got shoved into the back of the closet. The vacuum accouterments, including an extra-long hose, a couch attachment, and other items for getting into hard-to-reach corners, were nowhere to be found in there (where on earth could they be? No one else cleaned her home – a decision she made from the very beginning of living on her own. It felt too invasive to have someone take on those tasks for her).

Over time, her suitcases and odd boxes were stuffed into the back on the floor. The spaces they occupied prevented longer hanger items from fitting properly into the cramped area. She couldn't remember ever truly clearing things out or organizing them.

Lately, she'd felt a mounting pressure to do so and get rid of the remnants of things she no longer used or even really remembered she owned. She knew she had too much 'stuff' and figured a deep clearing was in order. Musing to herself out loud, she muttered, "Aging has a way of pushing humans to put things into simple order," only to realize she was teetering towards the kinds of feelings she always associated with old people.

She dropped her coat onto the diminutive antique piano stool (she never had a piano but loved the stool that twirled when she sat on it). Loosened spindles rose on the back into wooden joints fitting like pegs into assigned holes that had dried out some time ago. She kept meaning to reglue all of them to the seat so it could be useful as a sturdy little chair for pulling on boots or, in the off chance a child came to visit, a suitable sized place to sit. But this repair kept getting postponed and never quite made the urgent 'to-do' list. She made do with the couch for doing such things, and no children came to visit.

She enjoyed kicking off her shoes at the end of the workday, though in truth, she was ashamed of her feet and thought her toes were stupidly short and had never been very good for running. She tried not to care, especially since she was the only one seeing her toes these days, so it wasn't such a big deal. Shoes off, she'd curl her legs up under her, though recently, she noticed her left leg was more cooperative in curling under than her right one, which seemed stiff and made a creaky sound. Aging wasn't fun.

Settling in for the evening opened her up to personal contemplation. In general, when she considered on a macro level how things had turned out in her life, she felt pretty good, rather accomplished, and satisfied that she had done some really good work over the years. On the micro level was often wracked by what she had or had not accomplished from her most current 'to-do list'. Some days she could tick more items off more than others.

She tried not to become hyper-self-critical about her personal failings, but old habits die hard. Her mother's voice could easily intrude, robbing her of joy by shaming her as a failure – pointing out all her unmet expectations. It was a lifelong battle to keep that woman out of her brain. In spite of all the work she had done in therapy over the years, she still felt her mother's claws grabbing into her, especially in the early years when she was still relatively new to New York and so desperately dark from the trauma of her past. The grip wasn't nearly as tenacious now, but it also wasn't entirely vanquished. She exhaled deeply in an effort to release the toxicity.

Looking around, she noticed the low heatless autumnal sun softening the defined edges of her paintings and photos in her living room. The pale umber-like walls appeared to glow through fusions of previous paint jobs - colors layered on top of each other over the years. Throughout her five decades living there, she had selected wall colors inspired mostly by whim, each time with the intention of altering the feel of the place and harkening new beginnings. She remembered dusty sage walls from about twenty years ago with particular affection because that was the first time she could afford to pay someone else to paint her entire apartment and not have to do the job herself.

Next, her mind drifted to thoughts of her professional life, appreciating how her financial outlook had improved over time.

Early in her career, she made decent enough money working much like an itinerant therapist roaming from grants to gigs. But there was little income consistency leaving some months financially shakier than others.

The range of art therapy experiences that came her way was varied as she was hired on limited grants in shelters, schools, prisons, and agencies supporting all kinds of human needs. The variety of people partaking in what many people referred to as "this new field called 'art therapy'" really helped her hone her therapeutic skills. Boarding the Staten Island Ferry, riding the subway to the furthest reaches of Queens, working on the waterfront of Brooklyn, and catching Metro North to the Bronx and beyond left her feeling like part of the heartthrob of the city. None of it tired her out. She likened what she did to a calling. The work was inspiring.

After a few years, she was ready to break out on her own, away from dependency on the world of grants, and opened a small private practice in a tiny office off Union Square which she shared with a newly licensed chiropractor. They alternated days and evenings using the space (neither could afford the full rent on her own). As her practice grew, her time for external art therapy gigs shrank though it would be years before she completely gave that kind of work up.

As she took on more clients of all ages, she saw trauma as a common thread running through the histories of most clients and at the core of so much suffering. Trauma had certainly directed much of the course of her own life. Trauma generated vital adaptations for survival that often functioned way past their usefulness. This dynamic created layers of new problems and difficulties in its own right. The unconscious internal adjustments meant to sustain life became distorted ways of living, disrupting relationships, capacities and meaning. To simply endure was marked by deep personal ruptures in continuity and connection. Such problems made themselves evident in most diagnoses but were often miscast as one mental illness or another.

She believed there was a central truth to it all; the brilliant mechanisms that helped sustain life in the face of trauma needed to relinquish control back to the survivor after the threat was gone. Trauma wants to terrify and hijack as much of the person as possible, keeping these mechanisms locked in place, ever greedy for power and highly insecure about banishment. Unlike humans, who can transform and grow, trauma mechanisms want to remain forever at the same developmental level as they were created, ready to keep the territory they saved in the first place. The therapist partnering with the client is on a mission to return the territory to the survivor. Therapy is an act of justice. It is a noble calling.

Intellectually and politically, she identified as a feminist with her professional roots deeply embedded and nourished in the soil of empowerment, personal agency, dignity, equality, and human rights. For her, art therapy was the medium, the tool that made possible uncensored access to memory, the revelation of story, the capacity for the imagination to make meaning, the engagement in play, and to envision possibilities for the future. The blending

With her own therapist, she learned about compassion, attunement, and healthy boundaries. She felt, in real-time, a kind of collaboration between them, but she was never subsumed. She never told her small lies or any lies at all. She came to learn that children lie because they are afraid. She felt only safety in her therapist's presence.

It was her therapist's support and encouragement in forging an unexpected alliance between art and psychotherapy that ignited her own curiosity about dedicating much of her life to helping others through art therapy. She was hungry to learn as much as possible to be of service to others and found herself seeking knowledge from experts in the profession – ultimately getting her master's degree in art therapy simultaneous to a certificate in trauma studies.

So she went from being a small-town artist in Perryville, Ohio, to a highly competent, certified art therapist in New York City. This was the backdrop for her on one exquisitely beautiful late summer day when so many lives were tragically forever changed.

Chapter Three

The morning of September 11, 2001, happened, and nothing was ever the same again. There was just 'before' and 'after'. The events of that day were imprinted as flashes of memory, fragmented moments, and incomprehensible devastation.

No single event in her lifetime was as catastrophic. Every day norms disintegrated the moment the towers were struck and fell, the Pentagon was attacked, and an open field in Shanksville, PA, became ground zero for Flight 93. It can be said that even in the briefest moments of terror, the spirit struggles against all odds to reconcile the psychic impossibility of the trauma witnessed or experienced with the harsh reality of its truth. The inescapable certainty is there can be no resolution or outcome that makes any sense until possibly way after the dust has settled. It takes time to restore meaning.

On that shocking day in September, her personal demons were gorged whole by a monstrous invasion of unbearable disruption. Life felt like the tiniest point of light, just on the other side of tragedy, wanting to cast hope into the darkness but fearful of being snuffed out.

Her work as an art therapist, verbal therapist, crisis interventionist, and provider of psychological 1st aid during the next two years put her trauma training to the test. She was hired by insurance companies and given assignments to work with large groups of personnel employed in buildings surrounding the Trade Centers. Proximity to circles of impact determined the approaches she took. She ran group art therapy sessions with children and families from different agencies throughout the city. She helped provide debriefing sessions with first responders mandated to debrief after their shifts on the 'Pile'.

Every therapist she knew was working just as hard. There developed a sense of kinship among her peers. Therapists looked out for each other. They shared ideas, techniques, and resources. The goodwill didn't last forever, but for the first year or so post-9/11, she experienced real generosity across the helping professions.

However, her private practice was nearly shot to hell. Initially, some clients could not navigate the transportation disruptions in the city – just getting around was a nightmare. For others, 9/11 compounded the chaos in their personal lives, making coming to sessions too complicated to arrange. At times other clients committed to appointments only to find themselves emotionally immobilized in their homes. She did the best she could to accommodate chaotic schedules, but it became quite unmanageable to constantly shift sessions around. So she gradually cut back on private work and took more group art therapy gigs.

She thought it would be good for her own sanity to memorialize her observations, interventions, and thoughts through journaling. At the same time, she captured her own emotional life through imagery created on a daily basis. She certainly would never call such casual drawings 'art,' nor were they sketches for some larger works to be developed later. They were just more or fewer expressions in real time, moments pushing from within to be recorded for no purpose other than to be.

Everything she did in those days was in an effort to help her make meaning and maintain some semblance of control in her life. The weeks and months passed. Her appreciation of the innate resilience of human beings, the crucial importance of safe and caring relationships (especially in childhood), the healing potential of creativity, and the significance of meaning for contextualizing trauma inspired her to write poetry. She did everything she could to try to keep from disappearing.

As life settled into a new normal, she lectured and published about trauma art therapy. She was invited to travel, teach, and lead art therapy groups across the United States, the Middle East, the Far East, Europe, and South America. Where a crisis happened, be it from a natural disaster, interpersonal violence, or other tragic events, she was one among many asked to lend expertise to training trainers. And all during those years, though she needed it less and less, she held on to her office because it helped her feel grounded, rooted in the profession which had been so good to her.

As she entered her fifth decade of life, she began missing the more intimate work with individual clients. She was tired of all the travel and short-lived relationships. Most of her previous clients had moved on with their lives or found new therapists, and her contacts had dried up in the ensuing years after 9/11 when she had been so busy. So she reached out to a guidance counselor colleague, who was well-placed in a fancy Upper East Side private school, just to see if she could get any referrals.

As the adage goes, timing is everything, and hers was exquisite as the school counselor had a number of parents seeking therapy for their children, and while she had not considered art therapy (because so often it is a 'forgotten' profession), this counselor was grateful for the opportunity to have yet another means for the children to get help. The only hitch was the children would need to be seen after school, which meant the art therapist would have to travel to their homes.

And so, toting all kinds of art supplies to help inspire her young clients, she traveled to their homes rendering mobile therapy to them all. These young people renewed her spirit. She felt useful and enjoyed seeing them where they actually lived. It gave her a rich understanding of the familial structure. It all seemed quite natural to her, and somewhere between instinct and expert, she believed she was well-suited to assist their lives in their homes.

In addition, the money she was earning was compelling. For

the first time, she could really plan ahead and make decisions to improve the quality of her life. She socialized a bit more though she was happiest in her apartment, making art. She took small vacations every once in a while, primarily to the beaches on Long Island or the mountains of Vermont. She hired house painters to spruce up her apartment. Most of all, she enjoyed feeling competent in helping the children (and thus the families).

Bit by bit, she cut back on seeing clients in her office by not taking new ones in and, when it was time for termination with current clients, preparing them for the change of circumstances in her professional practice. It took about a year, but eventually, she completely dropped the office lease.

For over two decades, the work was exhilarating and profitable. Referrals came not only from school counselors but from numerous parents of children who had benefitted from their art therapy experiences. The reasons for therapy varied, as one might expect. Death, divorce, moving, bullying, and so many other issues impacted children and families.

Her own biases surprised her as she erroneously had it in the back of her mind that super-rich people could more easily conquer these sorts of challenges since the worry of money wasn't really there. Instead, she learned that money did an excellent job of masking troubles and dodging truths. Certainly, it was better to have money than not. But it did bring its own problems that could severely complicate the healing process.

On a personal level, she had a growing realization that she actually had very few adult interactions in any one week. She often felt isolated from her friends and peers because of the secrecy involved in treating children from *high-profile* families. Confidentiality (which naturally was paramount to observe no matter who the client) aside, she could not even make the slightest comment about the famous parent(s) when they appeared in the news, on Broadway, in the Congress, museums, medical facilities or anywhere whatsoever. She could not ever remotely share an opinion or feeling about any of them, even though her colleagues could comment as much as they wanted because they were not in the same boat as she. The collegial isolation drove her further and further into her own head until there was little psychic income left to socialize outside of work.

Chapter Four

She squinted her eyes to better define the play of forms in one of her favorite paintings hanging close to the windows. Abstract colors, fiery hues of red and orange, fragments of tiny clusters of pigment twisting as a synchronized murmuration of exotic birds swelled across the canvas. An impenetrable moss-green shape floated randomly near the edge as an interference, blocking the cyclonic dance from escaping the stretchers. Satisfied by her art, even after all the years she lived with her creations, the entire collection of her work still seemed inspired.

For her, color was energy wrestling currents and headwinds to be liberated from the confines of the rectangle. While she was painting, she tapped into a kind of freedom she unconsciously felt driven to create. She never completed the leap into celebrity as other truly famous artists did because the cliff frightened her too much. But she had been a good enough painter in her youth to get some traction with her friends and social acquaintances. They liked her art and were very supportive in their comments. She sold a fair number of pieces but certainly not enough to make a living. She thought, "It's funny how things turned out."

As the last of the daylight dwindled, she stood and walked into her kitchen, opening the refrigerator to figure out dinner. Mealtime growing up was always somewhat apprehension-inducing. She and her mother weren't poor, but neither did they have the kind of access to choices she had as a grown-up later in life. Mostly, meals came from boxes and cans, and it was a point of excitement when some vegetable or meat had been converted into a new instant food product. Her mother would decree, "The best recipes always come from the back of the box".

She recalled macaroni and bean foods were ok, but processed meats from the can leave her teeth itching and her mouth tasting metallic. TV dinners were pretty good, especially because you could choose which one you wanted for dinner. The one with turkey and bread stuffing, succotash, whipped potatoes, and cherry cobbler was her favorite. Her mouth started salivating, even now just calling up the memory. She laughed, thinking, "Some things never leave you," and kind of wished she had that to choose for dinner tonight, though she would leave out the succotash, which was mostly chewy with its rubbery mouth-feel to it. In those days, her mother never considered all that processed food disastrous for her kidneys and cholesterol.

Mealtimes could be wracked with anxiety because of the tension her mother had around actual 'made from scratch' cooking. As a child, on high alert to please her mother with compliments about the food, she frequently choked in the middle of dinner but knew better than to let her mother find out. She had to pretend she was *not* gagging, so her mother wouldn't feel insulted or angry. She spent her lifetime struggling with making good eating choices because she gravitated towards easy-to-swallow soft foods like ice cream and melted cheese sandwiches, which likely contributed to her weight problem.

She remembered from one of her therapy sessions a million years ago that the daily stress of living in her home had not only severely inhibited what should have been normal ease of swallowing but also extended to her not breathing properly. Until therapy, she hadn't been aware that, at times, she actually did not breathe at all or, at best, in shallow gulps. Her therapist frequently synchronized her inhale and exhale along with her in session. She learned there were reasons people stop breathing, and hers, it seemed, involved being completely terrified of her own mother combined with a fierce longing to become invisible - which was hilarious when she thought about it because she was pretty sure she was invisible to most of the world much of the time.

The impact of her mother's abuse hit her like a pile of bricks.

Chapter Five

Peering into the fridge, she really did have some pretty good food options. Gone were the days when unfinished meals became rotting leftovers shoved into the back of the refrigerator. That habit, a childhood relic of trying to avoid second rounds of already mediocre food, changed for the better after living with Jenna for 3 years and 6 months. Jenna was fanatical about eating leftovers the next day before germs could destroy the appeal of eating whatever, as she called it, was on the 'refuse' plate. She also was a wizard at reinventing new dishes from the old. Jenna used to say, "Give me a frying pan, some olive oil, herbs and whatever you've got, and I can transform it into something really interesting."

Jenna worked odd jobs when she needed cash. For a few months, she drove a taxi. Another time she erected sets in a well-known bar for singers in the West Village, which is where they initially met one night after a folk concert when they both were waiting for the bathroom stall. It seemed likely Jenna maintained a small trade selling various kinds of pills because people seemed to randomly come and chat, hand her some money, take a small envelope, and leave quickly. Jenna claimed she never used it, but she had no problem with people who did.

Their first romantic encounter was the first night they met. Jenna was lithe and somewhat androgynous, unlike her soon-to-be lover, who had curves and flesh and turned a rosy color when Jenna said something funny or touched her lightly with the confidence of someone who no doubt had a good deal of experience. She never imagined kissing a woman anywhere, let alone in such a seedy environment, but Jenna wanted to, and so did she, and they did. And that was that.

When they first started living together, Jenna took over making the meals. Her cooking involved aromas that seemed exotic and sexy. It was fun to come home from a long day with art therapy clients and try to guess the ingredients Jenna combined into a newly invented recipe.

Jenna was also highly skilled in the art of intimacy. Their sex was exceptional and had an air of mystery – one wasn't certain what was coming next. She found herself doing and feeling things with Jenna that she never experienced with the men she dated. Even Vic, who was dear to her heart, was predictable and fun but not nearly as imaginative and engaging as Jenna. In fact, most of the men she had ever been with were nice enough, but she never found herself lost in passion the way she was with her girlfriend. As Jenna would say, "No part of the apartment was off limits when it came to their 'arousal games'".

One summer evening, when she returned from working with clients on Staten Island, she was met at the door by Jenna, who was insistent it not be closed completely. Jenna also demanded she not speak a word. The house smelled of cinnamon and curry. Dinner was going to be incredible. Jenna seemed commanding and in charge. She would do as she was told.

Living in an old apartment building with thick walls did not preclude neighbors from knowing a bit about each other's lives. Sometimes she could catch the smell of her neighbors' cooking or hear muffled conversations through walls or uncarpeted floors above hers though specific words were difficult to understand. So, when Jenna whispered, "We're going to leave our front door open just a crack, so don't make a sound. Just stand still", she obeyed.

Carefully, stealthily, Jenna began softly petting her lover's head. Such head caressing was so relaxing, as were her shoulders and arms being stroked. She started wondering where Jenna was leading her and worried slightly that the neighbors might hear something intimate if things built up too much. The door being partially open felt both risky and enticing. Jenna stopped (as if she could read her girlfriend's mind). In a whisper, she instructed her, "Let it go. Let me take you where *I* think you should go. Forget the neighbors," all the while loosening the straps of her lover's dress, watching intently as it slipped off her rosy shoulders and dropped to the floor in a loose pile around her ankles.

Jenna's eyes looked electric. She was on a mission. This was definitely sexy. Then, in the midst of her turning all control over to her girlfriend, she saw Jenna pull out a pair of shiny stainless-steel scissors. Briefly astonished, she thought that was something new for them for sure. Jenna clearly had a plan as she breathed ever so softly but with complete authority, “Forgive me. Stand still.”

The next moment was transformational as Jenna, without a moment’s hesitation, cut her lover’s last remnants of clothing. She snipped through her bra and panties until nothing was left except the nakedness of her blushing round-bodied woman standing on the threshold of their home with the front door cracked open. “Be still,” and she was while Jenna admired her handiwork and took in her beauty, though, for her girlfriend, there was something reminiscent of the past that was unsettling for her.

Jenna then laid down the rules for their lives moving forward and asked, “Shall we try some new things? It would certainly make me happy.” Jenna then told her to respond only with a thumbs up or down. “Thumbs up? Good. I think you’re ready for dinner. Let’s eat.”

The kitchen was small, but there was room enough for a café table and two parlor chairs. Jenna had set a beautiful table with tiny votive candles in mirrored holders, black napkins folded to hold their forks and knives, white wine on ice in an unused stainless asparagus steamer, glass goblets, and dinner plates with sides high enough that the curry would not slip over the edges. Jenna was up and down, serving the food, pouring the wine, and chatting about her day.

On the other hand, *she* was still undressed, prohibited from speaking and told to rest on her seat, which was covered with another black napkin. To eat a special curry meal and not talk while one is naked in the kitchen is harder, one might think. But Jenna regarded this scene as a progression into the new phase of their relationship. So as not to have her woman feel awkward or discouraged, she periodically added, "You're doing great. Keep it up. Have some more wine." It was a pep talk as if she were coaching someone on a swim team.

All these years later, in spite of the disastrous end to their affair, her thoughts raced to the highly erotic moments of that evening. She recalled standing against the front door, but this time it was closed. She was commanded to touch herself while Jenna sat on the piano stool, watching. There were other orders to follow that night, and while she had never experienced the risk and trust needed for this type of lovemaking before, she felt an indescribable tenderness each time she complied which made the desire to please Jenna that much stronger. Jenna was shaping her in preparation for more and more.

This was the beginning of a powerful new kind of bond

between them where possession and ownership became the currency of their love. Jenna made her promise to belong to her. She had a pretty good sense of what that meant and felt swept into going along with it. She guessed it was a phase, albeit a super enjoyable phase for sure. Over time, their 'arousal games' became more intense and consequential.

By day, when she was with clients, she recognized herself as the same person she had been before she ever met Jenna. Evenings and weekends were another story. Their games were so real. She was never certain what to expect from her lover, although the 'vanilla' lovemaking seemed to no longer be part of their repertoire. She longed for those times again and was getting tired of the constant gameplaying but did not know how to make her needs known, important, or essential.

By now, she and Jenna had been together for about 3 years. What she initially had thought to be a phase had basically become a lifestyle. She tried to figure out when and why she slipped away, disappeared and how and when Jenna shifted from lover to captor.

As she thought about it, she realized she had given away her power, her agency, in the tiny details. Asking Jenna, "Do you like what I am wearing?" she would be told, "This is what you will wear. And tomorrow, you will wear that." It wasn't erotic. But she was rewarded when she complied, and so she did. "Yes, of course, I will wear that". "My sweet love. Your Jenna is so happy when you do as you are told". One would think as a therapist, she would recognize her descent into utter dependence, but her own trauma history left her bereft of any self-protective skills.

Their sex was mostly about being watched, which was how Jenna liked it though her girlfriend usually left her feeling lonely and sad. She felt like she was lost in a maze with no way out.

Then one evening, she arrived home, really tired from a long subway trip from the Bronx. She wanted a bath and a meal. She opened the front door, and Jenna came towards her with that soft "you're mine" smile on her lips and caressed her head while kissing her throat. She felt a tingling. Even though she was tired, she was inclined to perk up.

Jenna unbuttoned her lover's blouse, and her fingers drifted lightly across the lover's bra, lifting her breast out and over to her mouth. Her other hand raised her skirt and slid into her panties. (Nothing voyeuristic about this! This was great!) She was joyful that Jenna was really participating, and she recognized this sex from before their games. And, as traumatized people often do, she instantly forgave her partner for all the loneliness she had caused her to carry in her heart.

Jenna gently pulled away. "I have a surprise for you. Close your eyes." She put a sleep mask over her lover's eyes to block her vision, and though they had used this prop often during arousal games, she felt slightly disappointed things seemed to be taking a turn in this direction.

Jenna caressed and gently squeezed her arms as she led her down the hallway to the bedroom. She whispered, “Don’t speak”. It was such a gentle command that she still felt hopeful about the evening. But she had an aching feeling she was still in the labyrinth in spite of silently trying to convince herself, “Jenna is so sweet. We’re good. It’s going to be good”.

She heard spa music and Native American flutes against the sounds of ocean waves filling the bedroom. The music surrounded her and was a little louder than usual. Some kind of flowery incense, perhaps honey suckle (she wasn’t sure), permeated the air. Jenna sure could always set a scene perfectly.

In a huskier than usual voice, Jenna told her to stand still while she finished undressing her. This was such a predictable order from Jenna that, at this point, she expected nothing different when they started to make love. But this time, there was an edge to Jenn’s tone that left her feeling uncertain and vulnerable.

Jenna stood behind her, running her hands gently all over her body. It was delicious, and she felt herself beginning to swoon in her arms. Jenna firmly told her to “keep relaxing, open up,” and being the obedient partner she was, having been shaped to be her perfect submissive. She completely turned herself over to Jenna's influence because, at this moment, that was the very demonstration of love, and she wanted Jenna to know how deeply she loved her and how willing she was to commit all she had to be what her lover needed. Jenna, filled with the power of her control, kissed her lover's neck and pulled her lover's arms behind her back.

And then, like a seismic wave stretching across the earth, she felt a different pair of hands, thicker and rougher, toying with her body. She was confused and shocked. "How did Jenna do that? How could there be another pair of hands touching while her arms were grasped behind her back?" Jenna tightened her grip as her lover instinctively tried to move her legs together. Above the ocean sounds and floral scents, Jenna reminded her, "Just go with it. Remember, you're mine and mine to share. You're gonna love this. You're making your Jenna so happy. We can see how much you love this. Now tell us how happy you are."

And so, the traumatized child who couldn't tell 'yes' from 'no', who was lost in an impenetrable forest of abuse, who desperately longed, as she never had before, for the father who denied she was his to come now and rescue her, lied through her tears and body's betrayal. She acquiesced to the predator, "I'm happy," which was what Jenna needed to hear more than anything.

For 6 more months, she went with whatever arousal games

Jenna wanted to play while her heart was disintegrating. It took that long for her to get over her embarrassment about calling her therapist after an almost five-year hiatus. She wasn't surprised when Dr. Fine answered, listened and then responded in her usual direct way, "This is not love. This is abuse. Let's find out why you got caught up in this mess. And Beatrice, throw her out."

Chapter Six

Beatrice Pons grew up in Perryville, near Ashtabula, Ohio. She hardly had any recollections of her father (that she had ever shared with anyone because she didn't trust the feelings it brought up inside her gut), but she did share his surname even though he left when she was just shy of four years old.

She was her mother's only child and, from an early age, was frequently reminded by her, "I knew when I gave birth to you, you were going to be all mine." And then, with arms pushing down into her belly, her mother would form the fingers of both hands into a closed circle as if to underscore her possession of the little girl. The gesture felt menacing and void of air, as if those fingers were trying to strangle her.

Sometimes the child tried to convince herself that she didn't need air at all, which was ironic because when she tried to sing out loud in school chorus or swim underwater at day camp, her heart would pound against her chest so fiercely claustrophobia would set in, and she'd have to stop whatever she was doing to just catch her breath. It wasn't until she, as a twenty-something young woman in therapy, had it pointed out by her therapist, Dr. Fine, that the prodromal constriction in her throat and shallow breathing in her chest and gut likely were critical warnings that she was about to choke or faint from fear.

Beatrice always assumed no one noticed anything about her, like she was invisible. Being truly seen by Dr. Fine pushed up new feelings in her for which she had no words. They were sort of sweet and sort of desperate, which at first made it difficult to look the doctor in the eyes for more than the briefest second.

Beatrice's mother was demanding, unpredictable, hilarious, and at rare times, loving. The erratic behaviors terrified young Beatrice, keeping her confused and constantly on guard growing up. One time her mother brought home a dozen mixed donuts, including jelly, which, for a six-year-old, was ecstasy. Playfully, her mother declared, "Let's scrap dinner and eat til we burst." They had so much fun picking who got what, and everything was going great until later that night when Beatrice threw up in her asleep.

The next morning when her mother came in to get her ready for school, she found her daughter sleeping with vomit stuck in her plaits of hair. The bed sheets were soiled from the bile of being sick. Enraged, she shrieked at Beatrice (a terrifying way to be awakened), "God damn it to hell, why didn't you wake me up if you were going to be sick? Now you've ruined my whole goddamned day. Get out of bed NOW." The little girl was bewildered. She was barely awake and didn't know what she had done wrong.

As always, when her mother terrified her, the child deferred her own needs and completely obeyed the command. This time, while her mother was raging and pulling off the violated bed sheets, an extremely bad thing happened. The little girl knew, as sticky warm urine started trickling down her leg, that she was losing bodily control, that there would be even more hell to pay. She stopped breathing. If only she never needed to breathe again. She tried to disappear. If only wishes worked.

Strangely, before her mother actually noticed, the urine was sort of feeling good and defiant against the girl's thighs. She did try to slow it down, but that wasn't working. Then her mother noticed a growing wet spot on the pink shag carpet and proceeded to fly into a total frenzy, grabbing Beatrice by the upper arm and dragging her into the bathroom and onto the toilet. "Finish and take a goddamn shower. And don't you dare cry? I should cry for all the work you've stuck me with. Next time you better wake me BEFORE you get sick."

Beatrice longed for her father. When she was born, he gave her the nickname Birdie because when he first cradled her in his arms, she felt like such a delicate bird. He was around until she was just under 4 yours old. She had a few very faint memories of him, like the time he played her some tune on his guitar, his dark, sad eyes, and hairy forearms. They used to play with water at the kitchen sink. He'd stand her on a step stool, and together, they would make the soap foamy, try to shape castles and clouds, and then watch the faucet water swirl their creations down the big center hole of the sink. He would tell her stories about the water traveling all the way to China right there from their little house. Together, they imagined what it would be like to ride along the flow of the current, all the places they would visit along the way and the animals they would see.

He often seemed sad to her, and she wanted to make him happy, so she would twirl around the house and make him drawings of all kinds of interesting things. One time she drew a portrait of him which caused him to burst into belly laughs. He tried to share it with his wife, but she seemed disinterested and impatient. “I suppose you think she’s got talent, right? Well, I wouldn’t bet the farm on it.” Which squashed all the good feelings in the house but brought a slim smile to her mother’s face.

He promised to take his daughter to the wire factory where he worked. They would put his portrait in his locker so he could see it every day. She waited for that day to happen, but it never did arrive. Things were changing at home in ways the little girl could not understand. Lately, she would wake up in the morning to be told by her mother that Papa went “somewhere” for a few nights, but he’d be back. No one ever explained to her why he left, and though she missed him horribly, she knew he was coming home.

When he’d return, he would bring bits of thick colored-wire strands, and they would make imaginary animals and line them up on the kitchen windowsill. He would carry her around the room, pretending to talk to the animals. Sometimes her mother would wear her prettiest dress, the one with the white eyelet collar, and her hair would be super shiny and styled. She smelled sweet as if she had come to some exotic place where smells were like that. She wanted Papa to be cozy with her, pulling his arms and talking baby talk to him, but he seemed uncomfortable and kept moving himself away from her reach.

This time, too many days had gone by without papa-daughter bubble fun and songs and being called "Birdie". Her mother looked messy. Her voice was flat and low. Even though the little girl was scared to do it, she asked her mother where her Papa was.

In one long breath, she told the little girl, "Beatrice, your father is not coming back. He has a new family. I am your only family, so let's be good soldiers and get on with the tasks of life." The girl heard the words but had no idea what her mother was talking about. The verbiage was all jumbled in her head. It was mixing her up. Why was Mother speaking nonsense? How could Papa have a new family? Is he making foam clouds with another little girl? His eyes, who does he see with those dark eyes? He'll be too sad without his Birdie. She kept him happy. What was going on?

A few days later, Beatrice could explain everything. She told any adult who would listen and any child in the neighborhood who asked her where he was, "Papa has gone to the store". That was the only explanation that made sense to her for the next few years. It was odd to her, so many years later in the throes of her own therapy, that no one at that time gently disabused her of that narrative, including her mother, who she once heard telling a concerned neighbor, "If she wants to believe that crap, who cares? It keeps her satisfied."

Her mother wanted no part of Beatrice wasting her energies grieving over the loss of her father. Her policy about her daughter having contact with her father was if she wanted to see him and he wanted to see her, she would not stop it. But the child would have to figure out how to find her father and make those arrangements for herself. Mother would say, "I will not stand in your way, but I won't help either."

Beatrice, fearful of losing both parents and being sent to an orphanage (a threat her mother liked to make when her child was too demanding and needy), convinced herself that her mother was being reasonable and fair. She had to consider how her mother was feeling and didn't want to add to her burdens by being a difficult and selfish child. Her mother needed all her strength to be two parents rolled into one.

Intent on eradicating any residual affection and longing that her daughter might still have for her father, her mother pondered ways to eradicate all of her nonsensical yearnings for all time. Like a snake hiding in tall grasses readying itself to release its deadly serum into the unsuspecting prey crossing its path, she waited for an optimal moment to attack.

Eventually, the opportunity presented itself seamlessly, without much struggle or resistance from the victim. In a fleeting moment after months and years of patiently laying the groundwork for pure betrayal to infect the very spirit of the child, where the setup was to undermine truth so much that it had no means to fight deceit, a rather eloquent process was enacted by the mother to permanently disrupt the father-daughter bond.

Her mother began by insidiously pretending to validate whatever reasons Beatrice came up with about her father's disappearance. She would lean into her daughter's ideas (maybe he was kidnapped – "Can we call the police?", maybe he got lost – "Can we put up signs with his picture on it?") and concur, "Who knows, you may be right. Let's let it brain-simmer for a while," and she strung her along until the next round of rationalizations erupted from the girl.

Then one day, as her mother was finding the ruminations of her daughter more tedious than usual, she decided to put a stop to all the child's imaginings. Enough was enough. Almost 8 years of her nonsense about her father was driving her crazy. The time had arrived to put an end to her daughter's fussing on this topic.

Which is when she initiated the TALL TALE, designed to end the irritating inquiries and explanations forevermore. She was ready to resort to the motherload of explanations to put a stop to it all.

One week before Beatrice's twelfth birthday, her mother approached her with a surprise. She pointed her into their tiny dining room and announced, "Twelve is a big deal, so we are going to officially call this your 'birthday week' and celebrate today *and* on the real day this coming weekend. Let's have some fun!"

They walked past the non-funtioning mahogany grandfather's clock, standing like a tired soldier in the corner of the room. It had come from a Sears mail-order catalog some 11 years earlier with instructions on building it for use in "the elegant homes of couples young and old". Beatrice's father not only put it together, but he took fastidious care to make sure the pendulum worked properly and the time was accurate. Winding it every three days was one of those family rituals that Beatrice mistakenly thought her mother loved as much as she did. The clicking sound of her father winding the mechanism, counting the chimes on the hours and the monthly moon (painted silver against a royal blue background filled with shiny golden stars) that appeared far too infrequently in her opinion, held pleasant memories she'd recall now and then across her lifetime. Sadly, once he was gone, the clock was no longer attended to and completely stopped functioning. By the time she moved away from Ohio, she had lost all interest in the relic clock taking up space in the entirely too-small dining room.

Her mother had set the perfect scene at the table. Both their place settings had two oversized devil's food chocolate cupcakes (their favorites) from Lawler's Bakery. Both had the most perfect crunchy white sugar icing. Beatrice's had a single, lighted red and white striped candle standing right in the middle.

Her mother encouraged her, "Make your wish and blow it out.". The girl always wanted the same thing, silently praying, "Papa, please come home." As she grew older, her wishes felt more and more like hollow habits that had lost any meaning because they were always ineffective and pointless. But magical beliefs of childhood could not be wished away, and well into adulthood, she was still unable to leave the habit behind.

She softly uttered thanks to her mother for the thoughtful surprise. Their relationship was happiest when they plunged together into food that was fattening and generally considered subversive. Cupcakes from Lawler's to celebrate a birthday that had not yet arrived definitely fit the bill. This particular festivity, unheard of amongst their usual repertoire of excuses, made her suspicious about what was really going on. She was drawn into her defense of opposites, wary about what was coming next while pressured to appear festive and joyful so her concern would not be noticed.

Her mother's tone suddenly shifted like an unexpected sharp left turn (Beatrice's body temperature was rising), and she looked steadily into her daughter's eyes, saying, "Now that you are about to be twelve, I think it is time for you to know the real, honest-to-goodness truth." The girl's tongue, in the midst of swallowing the bit of devil's food chocolate cake with white sugar icing, found the un-birthday treat sticking to her palette, lodging in her mouth. Her throat dried up so quickly she had to force the cake down with milk which then temporarily blocked her breathing, leaving her with a familiar choking sensation. The only route past this predicament was to force a cough to get it all down, causing her eyes to well up from the effort.

Her mother ignored her daughter's irritating disruption and continued. "The truth is, my girl, he did not believe he was your father. Never really did. So, he finally left. So, there you have it."

Beatrice was struggling to get the words to make sense. They were jumbled in her mind as crossword puzzle parts come to life. The words were moving all over the place, but none of them fit together correctly, and she had no idea how to begin planning what to put where.

The room was warming up – a clue Beatrice recognized, now that she was older, as prodromal. Something was about to happen. And with the delicacy of a feather caught in a thermal, she weightlessly drifted towards the ceiling rafters of the dingy old dining room. She imagined her body had morphed into a big balloon that still looked vaguely human but surely could not be because she understood in real life, people cannot float toward the center of ceilings.

While she was up there, she took a peek down and saw the festive table, the remains of her half-eaten Lawler's cupcake, and the red and white striped candle resting next to the cake remnants on the plate. The table setting did look pretty, and she appreciated her mother's good taste in doing such things.

At first, all she could see of her mother was the top of her head. Then Beatrice looked more closely and noticed the oddest thing. The silent gape of her mother's mouth opening and closing looked mechanical and seemed ridiculous. It was like a soundless cartoon which made her want to giggle, but she figured that might give her away, which was not a good idea.

Her mother's teeth flashed sharply against the darkness of the dining room. Funny, she hadn't noticed her mother's teeth before. She looked away lest her cringing at the sight of them interrupt the calm of her flight.

And then, as the silver moon moved into place and the old clock chimed for the first time in years, she imagined she had wings on her back, ready to transport her out of the dining room window into another universe with stars a billion years away. She dreamt she was riding the light back to its source when starlight first began to rush through the cosmos all the way to her little house in Perryville, to the time when her tiny hand was in his, and she believed in their world and felt safe enough to sleep.

At that exact moment, she realized that her new secret wish, the one for her real birthday, would be for a pair of wings to make possible some sort of journey toward the love that once had been and no longer was.

Beatrice slowly settled back down to earth, sitting consciously on the old dining room chair. She'd lost all appetite for cake. Her mother's voice concluded, "And so, my darling, as hard as this is to accept, being twelve means facing reality head-on. He just doesn't think you're his and never really did. He certainly felt affection for you. But you don't belong to him the way you do to me. He's moved on and probably has a whole new family."

That day, Beatrice swallowed her mother's entire tale meant to explain everything forevermore. If Papa wasn't her father, why would he even think about her at all? He probably had a real daughter in his true family, and she was making him so much happier. Sure, he had been kind to her as a baby. Birdie was loved in a certain way, but not as if she were his own. It all made perfect sense.

Her mother was relieved that her daughter was taking the new truth so well. She no longer needed to keep up with the child's mood swings and longings around holidays and birthdays. She was pretty confident that this lie would finally keep the girl satisfied.

Chapter Seven

Beatrice's mother shared scant information about her past with her daughter (and nothing at all about her father). She did learn her mother was from the Abelmeyer family, originally of Ashtabula (and before that somewhere in Bavaria, which was in Germany) and was of the third generation living in the same house on a piece of land near a road reaching Cleveland.

The family built a small garlic farm on a fairly large tract of land that abutted the dusty path to Port Ashtabula that eventually became part of Route 90, clearing the way to get to Cleveland in no time at all.

Great Grandpa Abelmeyer had won the land fair and square in an ax throwing contest held outside the Venture Bed & Bar on the 4th of July in the late-1800s. He was a young man looking for adventure (having crossed the ocean in steerage to find his way on a new continent) and had not known much about farming but knew quite a bit about cooking and eating.

When he won the land, his life became all about homesteading and growing garlic. Being handy and resourceful, he built a simple three-room cabin that remained the family home until the whole property was sold off decades later. Since he knew he was going to grow garlic, he set hook after hook into the wood-hewn rafters creating a means to hang the product to dry.

The tasty *Allium sativum* came in many varieties of colors and strengths, long necks with delicate white flowers, short necks with juicy bulbs, and red ones that were spicy on the tongue. He'd stand on a chair and sling them over the hooks to dry in robust tied-up bunches. Later, when children came along, the hooks were useful for holding the various switches he whittled to the thinnest diameters possible because they were more effective that way for miscreant children.

Great Grandpa's house reeked of garlic though the truth is told, he was completely desensitized to it and had no idea folks could smell him coming a mile away. He even made garlic soap which he claimed kept the bugs off him in the languid days of summer when every kind of stinging thing flew right from Lake Erie to the mainland, hungry to feast on whatever flesh was available.

He earned a good living selling to customers just outside the port. They looked forward to his deliveries of packaged fresh garlic that came in tan paper bags bearing the Abelmeyer name written in peacock blue ink diagonally across the front. At first, he did the writing because he was more educated than his wife, but when the growing season set in, she took over that responsibility.

Bags of full-bodied bulbs were sent east and sold by vendors who had customers in other towns wanting the small-farm sweet-tasting garlic produced near the shores of Lake Erie. There were profits to be made for all sorts of folks in the garlic trade, including real medical doctors and charlatans the same. Stories about the healing attributes of the allium herb on soothing nervous dispositions, its power to ward off evil just by hanging somewhere in the house, and its ability to purify the soul went a long way to keep garlic popular for a large swath of the population.

Great Grandpa farmed enough of his land growing garlic to live a modest life supporting his family. Aside from all the other people with an interest in the herb, his very favorite customers were the owners and cooks working in the many restaurants in the Port town of Ashtabula. On those delivery days, he was assured of some outrageously delicious meals. He'd try to stagger the garlic drops over a number of days so he could enjoy all kinds of dishes specially prepared for him to try. Once he got married, it wasn't so easy to get away for too many days in a row. He did the best he could.

He married young. There was no real personal information about his wife Eunice, Beatrice's Great Grandma Abelmeyer. One evening when her own mother was in a talking mood, she told the story about hearing that Eunice (her mother's grandmother) was mostly distant and preoccupied, like she was expecting to see a giant wave that never came cut across Lake Erie. Apparently, Great Grand Pa Abelmeyer kept admonishing his wife,. "Don't go borrowing trouble, Eunie," which seemed to calm her down.

Grandma Abelmeyer bore her husband three boys and two girls. With the exception of the youngest boy, Jake, the other offspring seemed to be in a hurry to leave Ashtabula for work opportunities or to start families in faraway parts of the country. It seemed they'd had enough of getting the switch and harvesting garlic.

Jake was known for his heft, hard work, and quick temper. Rumor had it that he grew extra big from eating all that garlic raw while working the crops, as he was always hungry. He avoided being around people mostly because they irritated him, and he couldn't stand the inevitable small talk and bragging that came with socializing. As far as anyone knew, Jake never attended school or made friends or had buddies. People called him a "loner'. Eventually, Jake took over the property when both his parents died from the influenza pandemic of 1919.

He lived alone on the farm on the outskirts of Ashtabula and became quite set in his ways with no one around to disagree or challenge his thinking about this and that. In the evenings, a kind of dark mood would set in that left him feeling uneasy, and he began to wonder at times if he was real. He'd stare at his hands, noticing every crease and hair, but he did not recognize them as his. He'd try to convince himself that he must be alive because he could see the smoke waft from his pipe. He could smell the garlic hanging overhead. He grew worried about dying in that house and no one finding his corpse for weeks or months. What would happen to the garlic?

Jake determined that to become real again, he needed a wife. He married a local girl, the daughter of the owner of the Rooster Spoon Restaurant on Ridge Rd in the Port. He had sold garlic to her family for well over a decade with his father and never really noticed the girl, who now was looking more shapely and interesting to him. Jake, wanting to do things properly, spoke with Angela's father, who, thinking strategically about the farm and his own potentially free access to garlic, was agreeable for him to taking his daughter's hand in marriage.

The arrangements were very businesslike and quickly accomplished. Angela and her belongings were speedily moved into Jake's house in a matter of days. Angela actually was numbed by the swiftness of change in her circumstance, and it wasn't that she didn't like Jake, but she was far from certain she wanted to spend a lifetime with a man growing garlic on the outskirts of Ashtabula even if he did own one of the largest plots of land around. And, as she immediately learned, he smelled of garlic, even when he was naked.

Apparently, Jake's appetite for food was matched by his appetite for Angela. He wanted her as often as possible in as many ways as he could imagine. She was not nearly as interested in his needs or fantasies and was frankly terrified of having his baby and giving birth made by such a big man. So, shortly after they married, when she did get pregnant, she vowed to herself that one child would be the sum total of any she had. She would never give birth to a baby from him again, even though the baby they made, Beatrice's mother, was no bigger than most babies that come into the world.

Jake didn't know what to make of his wife's resistance to sex. She told him she was in too much pain from the baby, and the doctor indicated her suffering would end no time soon. It was, of course, a lie. And, as the man of the house, Jake believed he was entitled to have easy access to her body. So, Angela, wanting to keep the peace yet avoid the act, offered her hand as frequently as needed, day or night, which seemed to settle the issue and keep everyone satisfied.

Beatrice knew next to nothing about her mother's childhood except through some mutterings about it being "no picnic" as the only child of those people. Her mother hid herself through books borrowed from the Ashtabula Central Library. She consistently won the class spelling Bs from 1st grade through 8th , and she had colorful ribbons to prove it. One warm sticky spring morning, foretelling of a long hot summer to come, Beatrice's mother, who was just ready for high school and wanted the ribbons to decorate the wall in her room, asked her mother about where they might be.

Angela Abelmeyer told her they got lost in some box or other. Her daughter kept going through the house, upending clothing, drawers and kitchen items with no luck. Finally, Angela, not feeling guilty in the least, admitted to her daughter they just got thrown out and she should stop acting so 'high and mighty' about a couple of ratty ribbons.

Beatrice was informed during one of her mother's fun donut binges that her name was inspired by winning all those spelling B's as a kid (it's not the same as having my prize ribbons, but it's a good screw you to the old lady). Plus, in the summer between 8th and 9th grades, out of boredom, her mother read the entire *Divine Comedy*, which she didn't understand all that well, but it kept her in the airconditioned library during the dog days, and she really liked the formal way 'Beatrice' sounded.

The summer she turned sixteen, her mother noticed a handsome young man busy with non-stop loading and unloading merchandise on one of the docks in the port. Drawn to his dark eyes and hair, his upper body strength, and tired from reading so much and being slightly bored, she started a mild flirtation with him. His smile seemed genuine. They exchanged hellos. His voice had a softness about it. He also had a truck.

As the days rolled by, he paid more attention to the girl hanging around and noticed his skin warming up when he first spotted her walking toward him. They'd talked a bit and then began eating lunches of bread and baloney she brought along as they strolled along the docks. Something good was happening between them. Eventually, they ventured off the boardwalk, heading into a dead-end ally, and kissed.

Beatrice's mother, certainly in the throes of a giant crush on this young man, was also cognizant he might be her ticket out of life on the garlic farm. He was a good worker, kind, and had a vehicular means of getting far away from Ashtabula. She started to think seriously about leaving.

He enjoyed her company and found her humor a relief against the dead-end job he was stuck in. Loving the lilt of her voice, he imagined there might be more to life than the docks. She challenged him to think big and imagine the impossible. He figured she thought that way because of all those books she'd been reading. Plus, kissing in the alley was fine, but he had a definite itch for more.

He wasn't much on books, though he did love to read *Astronomer Monthly,* which was a short column in the local paper that talked about stars and time and how everyone is made up of bits and pieces of things created billions of years ago. Every time he read that column, it seemed as if he heard soft sounds like frogs singing in the night. He would tell her, "You can never find the one frog singing. It's just a chorus that comes up all around you, and you're inside it with no beginning or end. That's what reading about the stars does for me" to which she'd respond, "You've got quite the imagination fella".

Eventually, after plenty of her teasing and numerous promises and one big fight where she called him a coward while she scratched through the skin of his arm and threatened to dump him, she convinced him to pack his bag. Late in the evening, when her folks were asleep, and the stars were at their brightest, looking so close he could touch them, he picked her up in his broken-down truck. He swore he would get her somewhere far away where they could start a new life together.

They got as far as Perry, Ohio, about 17 miles east towards Cleveland, before the truck completely broke down. In those days, it might as well have been 100 miles away since there were only back roads and country paths crisscrossing the landscape. They left Ashtabula behind and set up a home in the tiny village by the lake. And this was where Beatrice was born and raised. It was all she knew as home.

Beatrice recalled she and her mother returned to the Abelmeyer homestead just outside Ashtabula exactly one time. She was just a little girl, no more than 4 years old. They went to visit Grandpa Jake and Grandma Angel (a name the child insisted on calling her) in the old family home where water was still pumped water from an outside well, and the bathroom really was an outhouse complete with a thick stick to shake inside the black hole to scare away any lurking critters. Beatrice wondered why there was a quarter moon carved on its door.

The grass around the house was tall and brown and scratchy on her little legs. Inside, she remembered seeing thin, willowy branches stripped of their bark tied up against the open rafters. Grandpa Jake seemed huge and scary to the little girl. He told her those branches were switches which confused her because she knew switches were for turning on lights. Chomping down on his cherry-smelling pipe, Grandpa Jake hissed at her, "Those are for keeping young children, like your momma once was, in line. She'd get to choose which switch she wanted, but she always had a hard time choosing." And then he started laughing and turned first to his wife, who kept her eyes low and vacant, and then to his girl, who was now a momma herself, and challenged her, "Go on now, pick your switch; what, cat got your tongue?"

Even at her tender young age, Beatrice didn't like his kind of fun and sensed it would be best if she pretended she was invisible in this house. Her mother just stood there, looking as mad as she'd ever seen. She was more than familiar with this bully.

In the early 1960s, after her grandparents died, Beatrice learned the old house was torn down when the land was purchased by the Wright Rubber Company. They made tires for export to Canada just across Lake Erie and needed land near a good road to building a factory. The proximity of Ashtabula Harbor, only a few miles from the old homestead, made access to the water direct and profitable. Apparently, she still had living cousins spread out throughout the country because they were all named joint beneficiaries of the sale. Beatrice's mother always liked to say, "Rubber set me free" because the small monthly income she received from her share of the sale kept a roof over their heads and food on the table.

As a child, she always loved making things out of scraps of paper, shoe boxes, aluminum foil and anything else she could get her hands on. She would lose herself in a painting by numbers and making outfits for her troll dolls. She found clever ways to incorporate art into homework assignments with opportunities to make amazing maps rich in detail and clever shading. Art-making helped her breathe and set her free. Her mother never really understood her daughter's passion for art. And that was the point.

Years later, as Beatrice commuted between Cleveland and Ashtabula to attend professional art school, she depended wholly on her summer job money saved from years of serving food in the diner, ticket taking during park carnivals, being a day camp counselor, and working as a mother's helper for a family of four children who lived in the fancy end of town all helped pay for her transportation and food. The school was covered by a scholarship.

In her final year of art school, Beatrice's mother became seriously ill. During her visits home, she witnessed her mother steadily wither away from pancreatic cancer. Mother and daughter were entrenched in a silent standoff of lost opportunities. Their relationship suffered from words not being spoken and sentiments not being. Her mother, after a lifetime being incapable of mutuality or empathy, was no closer to her child in her dying. And Beatrice, in the magical thinking of a suffering child, still hoped her mother would somehow become someone she was not.

The young woman painted fiercely during the final months before her mother died, relying on canvas and paint as her only refuge. She created image after image of doors that were either closed or opened. In many, the thresholds were brilliantly lit, casting a burst of light onto walls of extreme blackness. In others, the portal was like a gaping hole steeped in hues of black and deepest blue while the walls glowed with angry reds and yellows as if on fire. The scenes were other earthly with no references to place or time.

She was unsure which side of the wall she was on. In her most desolate moments, when the world seemed reduced to a meaningless speck of matter casting about through the universe, she dared not look at her art for fear the Sirens on the other side tempted her to join their call, which would have been forever and irreversible. Many years later, when she went into therapy and then became a therapist herself, she reflected back on those days and recognized her bleak mindset for what it was – colossal depression catching up with her defenses and nearly ending her relationship with reality.

The finality of her mother's death stunned her entire being. She dared not let on to the few people who came to bid farewell or give condolences at her loss. Actually, her mood was lifted. While she could not say she was happy, neither was she sad. What she did experience was the deadening of a relentless pounding in her brain that she always believed was simply tension. But, in its absence now, she understood it was her mother's persistent aggression that had shaped her whole life and forced her into a private world of opposites. As soon as her mother was buried, she made plans to get out of town forever.

Beatrice inherited her mother's share of the garlic farm money. Though the illness had drained much of her income, enough money remained to get her to New York and pay for her share of rent in a dark, unfinished loft in Soho (well before it became untouchably chic and expensive) with three other women artists, who had placed a 'roommate wanted" ad that was posted in her art school. She figured she had enough money to last a year, though she actually stretched it out even longer.

There, in the newness of her life in New York, the epicenter of her dreams, she continued to make art, went to a ton of openings, and worked two jobs - by day as a receptionist in a small gallery in the Village and by night waiting tables at a famous restaurant in Little Italy. The owners loved to feed her before her shift and made sure to send her home with doggie bags filled with all sorts of goodies. Her roommates were thrilled with whatever food she brought back. She started feeling good about life. Things were going well. She had friends u*ntil she did not.*

Chapter Eight

Four women artists living communally in an old mattress-making loft in what eventually became to be known as Soho at first seemed like an ideal, albeit adventurous, situation. Each woman had a private cubby space set up in the four corners of the loft – all four spaces were big enough for a single bed. Four excellent mattresses (each with a tiny flaw that no one would really notice or care about, but the defects prevented them from being sold) had been left behind when the factory moved to Jersey City. This saved the women a lot of money, not that they would have considered buying new ones, but these mattresses had never been used, were pristine, and firm.

The four women celebrated how lucky they were to start out fresh on something as intimate as a bed, though they had to be stacked on a few cinder blocks as none came with box springs. Squeezed between the bed and the sheetrock wall in each cubby sat small wood-colored Formica bureaus with two drawers adequate enough to keep underwear and other personal items out of sight. Each cubby also had room for a narrow metal clothing rack (more treasures were found when a high-end fur factory down the street closed, and they were left out for garbage collection. The best stuff often came from the streets in those days).

Each space had a real door though the walls of the rooms did not reach all the way to the ceiling, which typically was 11 feet high in raw lofts those days. Sound traveled pretty swiftly into the general space in the middle, which was why the ladies always kept a radio playing at a low level from the kitchen to mask most noise.

The 'Ladies", as they became known and were called by friends and strangers alike, shared a joint studio area in the middle of the loft. The divisions of that space were not equal. Depending on who was making what, the dimensions of the space could shift as they were separated by pieces of sheet rock balanced upright on dolly wheels that could easily be moved to accommodate changing size needs. The Ladies shared a common understanding that as the art evolved, so should their spaces.

By comparison, Beatrice worked fairly small, so her studio space was the smallest. Plus, she was the 'newcomer', and though all things were supposed to be equal, they really were not. But this was something she would not completely understand until her third year living there.

There was a tiny, crudely designed kitchen area just off the door to the loft. It had a slop sink doubling for cleaning paintbrushes and cooking utensils. The electric stovetop was a street treasure that had belonged to a well-known artist a few buildings over. He painted in an encaustic method on those burners but now needed a reliable set of rings to melt the wax and pigments. His was a dangerous process for painting, and on more than one occasion, he ended up in the emergency room with wax burns on his fingers. He was now 'doing well' having been taken into the 'stable' of a highly respected art dealer, which meant he needed to keep making more of those wax works to keep the money rolling in, the dealer happy and allow him to install a real stove and oven without risk to burning the place down.

Their refrigerator functioned though the freezer needed to be defrosted way too frequently as crystals seemed to grow on the food overnight, and the whole thing made an irritating buzzing noise pretty much all the time. The Ladies shared everything in it, which made Beatrice uneasy because she could never be certain what food might have rotted. Because she brought home so many meals from the restaurant gig, she did feel like she was a big contributor to this part of their communal living.

She was troubled detecting she was excluded by certain comments or jokes from not knowing the references. She tried to pinpoint what unsettled her the most, basically coming up with that she was just 'uncool'. They all were casual and easy with themselves, while she struggled with identity and self-acceptance. Her life had been small, and theirs worldly and expansive. Socially they were miles apart, which left her feeling embarrassed and lonely much of the time.

The table they ate off of was actually an unfinished hollow

pine door propped on top of two metallic sawhorses. It was super sturdy but aesthetically lacking, so one day, they all decided to divide the surface into four sections and each painted in acrylic, whatever came to mind. The result was pretty terrible, and the surface was dizzying to look at. No one wanted to cover the images with plates or food, so they all agreed to cover the images with black and pretend that the exercise had never happened.

That was when Beatrice first appreciated at a cellular level that paint could hide all sins. Things painted over no longer exist. And if they once did, the memory was all that remained, and that would end with the last person who had the memory to know it existed in the first place.

It stirred up something old, and she briefly thought about her father, who wasn't her father; therefore, who was he? Since she remembered him, did that mean he existed? These queries lowered her mood despite the energy and fun, and creativity that surrounded her New York life.

The bathroom in the loft left much to be desired. In it was an old toilet with a round black seat that squirmed from side to side if one didn't land perfectly in its center. The hinges were weak and creaky. The stained sink was tiny – barely big enough room to wash both hands and the mirror above it had corroded over time, so she could only see only half of her face at a time though she rarely bothered to look. But the worst feature was the folding gray vinal panel door, which, when pulled closed, clicked shakily into a plastic groove. No lock. Thin. No privacy. She tried to convince herself that this aspect of her living condition was very Bohemian and to be expected in raw lofts such as theirs.

Oddly, there was a fully tiled stall shower built next to the toilet area. Admittedly, it was not all that appealing as many of its old green tiles were cracked and chipped, and the shower spout was located only about 5 feet from the floor. Using it was an ordeal requiring a lot of bending for rinsing hair. None of the women could figure out why there was a shower in an old bed assembly factory, but they made a lot of wisecracks about workers testing the mattresses etc. Years in the future, as Soho became chic and it cost a fortune to live there, these kinds of impoverished bathrooms were converted into high-end bathroom spas with every conceivable bathing option as a standard part of their renovations.

It was while she was living in the loft, trying to have the time of her life hanging out with her roommates, and working two jobs that were sort of fun and paid well enough that, combined with her small inheritance, that she could put a few dollars away every week into an interest-bearing savings account at the Fellows Bank of New York, located just east of the Westside highway near the Brooklyn-Battery Tunnel.

She was painting on her days off work. Her art had no doors or thresholds. She was experimenting with abstract oil colors. Vibrant flecks were strewn across small canvases and heavy-weight cold press paper. The explorations were pigments searching for a form while carrying along a current of movement. While the meaning of them had not revealed itself to her, she was driven by the pure flow of hues undulating within the private world of the stretcher edges.

Her canvases were small compared to those of her roommates. Beatrice was content with feeling larger than what she was creating, like some goddess willing the colors to evolve and submerge themselves on her command. The paintings, pristine and jewel-like, really came to life for her while she was making them, though no none of her roommates gave her any of the validation of accomplishment she longed for when the pieces were completed.

The lack of external validation left her solitary and concerned that the art held no meaning for anyone except herself; this was a problem because as soon as she admitted to herself she really loved an image, she had a strong urge to deny the right of that good feeling to exist. Contiguous love and hate for her creations developed into a steady state of mind, leaving her bereft of fulfillment. Crushing anxiety would set in, and it was all she could do not to destroy what she made. Because she didn't trust herself with her own art, she hid it away under the mattress or behind clothing - out of sight and safe from her impulsive demise.

Even though she worked part-time in a gallery, it never occurred to her to show her work to the owners to get their opinion or ask to be considered for a group show. The gallery was near 1st Ave and 1st Street and was called *First on First*. They specialized in 3d installation pieces with a political bent, which was nothing like what she did.

Truthfully, that job was much more boring than the restaurant, which at least had customers who came in for a good meal and a good time. The gallery visitors were super smart, somewhat angry intellectuals who spoke about things like existentialism, the human condition and a book called The *Magic Mountain*. There wasn't much foot traffic, and the artistic niche was so rarified it had limited interest except on the nights there were openings. Then the place would be packed.

Her responsibilities included answering the phone and watching over the gallery at all times so none of the art was stolen. She was also charged with making sure the guest book was signed, addresses transcribed onto Rolodex cards, the bathroom was clean and stocked, the front desk had fresh cut flowers, there were water bottles chilling in the fridge in the back behind the desk, and run whatever errands the owners might need tending to.

The owners were a pair of self-assigned avant-garde

philosopher leaders transplanted from Port Jefferson, Long Island, who had graduated from the same high school twenty years earlier. They belonged to the art history club in school, which was part of their attraction to each other and eventually led to their serious personal and professional relationship. They were desperate to move to the City where they would not have to be so careful as a couple.

On the Manhattan side of the river, they lived together without arousing strong glances or even scorn. They adored the flavor of the lower-east side, the cheap cost of space, and the diversity of the population. No one paid much attention to anyone on those streets. They could reinvent themselves and build a business.

Inspired by the immense suffering they had experienced as a gay couple in their early years together, their gallery was born in the spirit of pursuing political awareness, critical art appreciation and rebirth. They made quite a lot of money over the years from their niche market, including museum collaborations and high-minded buyers hellbent on supporting meaningful causes. They were living out their dream of exposing oppression through art expression.

Beatrice found them by responding to a help wanted ad in The City Call for a "Gal Friday" to work one day a week in their gallery. She wasn't sure what a gal Friday did but figured she'd give it a shot and went for the interview. The owners skipped quickly through inquiring about her background in art. Then, clearly well-planned in advance and more important than finding out what she knew about art, they probed more personally, asking her to share the most important thing she felt she'd ever done. Beatrice stated flatly and without hesitation, "I escaped Ohio". This was something the owners could completely relate to as they had escaped Port Jefferson. They need to go no further and end the interview. After a fifteen-minute interview, she was offered the job on the spot with the proviso that she worked the rest of the day.

Chapter Nine

Since life appeared to be falling into place, Beatrice started dating. The Ladies' loft was known for its spontaneous Saturday night parties, which would often be going full blast by the time she got home from the restaurant around 11:00 pm. She was beaten, but there was no way for her to go to bed and curl up with a good book. In truth, she was torn between partying and sleep. Socializing usually won out.

That was how she met Craig, a loose end (which did not come with a date), a fairly silent, attractive guy. He was an artist welder whose studio and bed were in a three-story white brick building near the entrance to the Holland Tunnel. He showed real interest in Beatrice, which was the first time she could recall getting attention from a guy that made her curious and feel a little sexy. He had super tight curly hair (she called them 'locks') and piercing blue eyes, and his sculptors' forearms drove her crazy thinking about how strong he must be.

The first time they had sex was the first time she went to his place. As they headed towards his place at dusk, he looked peered around her to see if anyone was coming and then s put his arms around her waist, lifting her into the air. "Whoa, I didn't think you would be so easy to pick up!" as he lowered her to the sidewalk. That felt weirdly like an insult and left her feeling uncertain like she had been the brunt of a joke that she didn't know about, but maybe others did. She even imagined her roommates in on it, making a bet with Craig even though that seemed way too sinister to be possible.

Against her better judgment that evening, she went along with having sex with him in his white brick building near the Holland Tunnel because her shame about her body pushed her into choices that often have glaring defects. As can happen with people living in 'opposites', she convinced herself that maybe his mighty forearms really *were* hungry for her in spite of his crummy comment.

Half an hour later, they walked back to her place. By then, the party had dispersed, and the three other ladies were in their cubbies with their guys, and there seemed to be a lot of sex happening in the loft. Craig grabbed a beer from the old fridge and gulped it down. She was about to ask if he wanted to stay when he turned his back to her as he strolled out the door and said, "See you around, kiddo," and he vanished into the night.

A few days later, during a slow night at the restaurant, a local cop comes in. He was young, cheerful, and chatty. The owners always offered their cops a free meal, so he sat near the door and ate a bowl of spaghetti and meatballs Marinara, napkin tucked neatly into his collar. He had no intention of getting any of the red sauce on his uniform.

She was working his table, so they shared some small talk and gentle banter. She noticed a rosy blush creeping out from under his collar and up towards his earlobes. He was so nice and friendly like she imagined a younger brother might be. She didn't think about him as dating material. She was still shaking off the unpleasant feeling Craig had stirred up in her the other night, and so the distraction of this mild flirtation came as a relief. By the time he had finished eating, she got the sense that they had the potential for more and her view about dating shifted. Then he left, and she let it go.

Her shift ended. Beatrice left carrying a giant white paper bag with food for her roommates. As she walked out to the sidewalk, Jimmy, the cop, appeared. He assured her he was not stalking her (which made her wonder for a moment if he was), but now that he was there, off duty, might he carry her bag for her? She adored his manners and briefly considered how her mother might approve of this young gentleman.

Together, they walked well past her loft, talking deep into the night. They strolled over to the Hudson River and sat on a cement bench under the silver moonlight. Softly laughing and whispering. They behaved as if they had been partners for many years. This was delicious and real romance seemed to be stirring between them. Craig was fading away.

Jimmy walked her back to her place, and at the door, he

asked if she would like to go out, maybe to a movie, on her next night off – which happened to be the next evening. They agreed to meet at the Waverly in the Village. There was a romantic comedy playing. This was a good and natural start.

It was so late that all the roommates were asleep, which was a good thing because she had forgotten the white bag with the leftovers somewhere between the restaurant and home.

She didn't work at the gallery or the restaurant the next day, so she had lots of time to get excited. She thought about what she would wear – casual yet with a bit of artistic flare, like her peasant blouse that had tiny mirrors and her black jeans. Her hair needed to look soft and full, maybe up, maybe down. She'd have to see what worked best with the blouse.

Her red sandals would be good, but she couldn't afford to get her toenails done. Maybe that didn't matter. She had a small black velvet jacket that was the one piece of clothing she kept from her mother's closet after she died (the rest was packed for Goodwill). Velvet brought out the best in her complexion. She was giddy! Could a person fall in love that quickly? She was feeling just crazy about him. The velvet would be perfect.

Jimmy and Beatrice met at the movie house for the 6 pm show. She wasn't entirely sure, but a few times, she thought she felt his leg grazing hers. Once, in the middle of a particularly romantic moment in the film, she heard him sigh, and he moved his hand from his lap to the armrest between them. Naturally, she did not touch it, but she was pretty sure it was a gesture towards her. She loved this date.

After the show, they grabbed some pizza slices - eating and chatting as they headed back towards to river. They went to 'their' spot – the cement bench by the entrance to the dilapidated old Cunard Line peer. They spoke of small things that amounted to intricate intimacies about how amazing it was that they had so many feelings in common. In a moment of silent reverie, he grasped the fingers of her left hand with his right and lifted them to his lips, kissing their tips and commenting that they tasted delicious. Beatrice was feeling warm and relaxed and desperately wanted to lie down with him, but the bench and dock were not lying down kinds of places, so she suggested perhaps it was time for him to walk her home. He no longer exuded that younger brother type of energy she had felt when they first met. And that was a relief since her intentions were far from sisterly.

The loft was dark when they got there. That was almost never the case, and she felt relieved not to have to introduce Jimmy and subject him to the chaos of the ladies. For once, she wished she lived in a less Bohemian environment, something more traditional, with predictable furniture and decorations that exuded stability and permanence.

She had told Jimmy about her cubby room and figured now was the right time to show it to him. They stepped inside, and since there was no other furniture, both sat down on the bed. She expected he would make a move on her, and then they might embrace and make love before everyone returned. She imagined it would be quick but deeply meaningful and filled with the promise of more meetings of lovemaking leading to becoming inseparable all the way to engagement and then marriage.

Her mind was flying, inspired by the passion of fantasy mixed with proximity. She could feel his breath on her neck. He was kissing her ear, her cheek. She was getting very warm in the tiny space, and for a fleeting second, an ancient passing memory was awakened. She was collapsing from the overwhelming heat. But actual details evaded her. "Jimmy, I need to take off my jacket and blouse." He was such a gentleman helping her shed her outer layers of clothing, including her black jeans.

He asked if they could lie down together, which was just so endearing! Permission granted, they lay down, Beatrice in her underwear and Jimmy fully clothed. Once again, he kissed her fingers though she wished he would kiss her elsewhere and kept waiting for that to happen. He seemed to really love doing that, and it briefly occurred to her that maybe he had some sort of finger fetish because she could tell he was pretty excited, and it was definitely doing something for him.

He told her he had never met anyone as beautiful and kind as she was. He wanted to get to know every square inch of her (which was sounding pretty good to her by then), and she took his hand that had been holding her fingers and moved it delicately onto her belly. Her body movements indicated she was ready for the next level. His hand, still perched upon her belly, became rigid. As he removed it from her body, he kissed her lightly on the lips and said, "I think that's enough for tonight."

With that pronouncement, he edged off the bottom of the bed and straightened out his shirt that had become untucked during their tryst. His fingers, which only moments ago had been holding hers to his lips, flattened his dusty blond hair down in an effort to look well-groomed.

She started to get up. "Please don't get up. I want to think of you just like this when I leave. See you after work tomorrow night?" "Yes Jimmy. Please pick me up. See you then." With that, he let himself out, and she took a moment to let the evening sink. In order to stave off any puzzlement about how the evening ended, she needed to take action. And so, in the darkness of her cubby, before sleep stole her away, she took care of her own needs in the safety of herself.

Chapter Ten

The women decided to hold a huge bash the following month. As all four of them sat around the table planning, they discussed expectations about the evening. There would definitely be some other artists, a good number of art dealers, a few professors from a local art school, some realtors (they were always looking for art to stage apartments) and a couple of bankers with connections to wealthy investors all of whom would either be bringing dates or looking to hook up.

The three women (Beatrice silently referred to them as the Troika) had already decided which easels or movable sheetrock walls would best suit their work. It was already arranged, which apparently had been predetermined some other time. Beatrice inquired about where her work would be shown. The Troika agreed that since her work was small, a nice card table near the kitchen would be an ideal spot for people to see what she had made.

This felt neither completely right to Beatrice nor completely wrong. Lately, she was ambivalent about the quality of her art, and a more modest display matched her insecurities. On the other hand, something about this arrangement seemed sneaky and embarrassing. But she acquiesced without a fuss, as was her habit since childhood.

The intention of the party was to move their art out into the world, so the real focus needed to be on the dealers and bankers. They should have plenty of food and booze. All four women chipped in $100.00 to buy what they needed to set up the dining table. It was going to be fantastic to see the loft transformed into a gallery for the evening.

They decided to get dressed up – do it like a major opening. One of them made a poster they hung downstairs at the entrance to the building. She did calligraphy so each of their names was listed for the public to see. Beatrice offered to get an entire sheet cake from the restaurant the night before. Everyone thought that would be fantastic, and one of the Troika, likely in an effort to seem magnanimous, even offered, “The could be the centerpiece of the food, Bea. What a great contribution!”

Chapter Eleven

Beatrice had been seeing Jimmy almost on a nightly basis since they first met. If she were working, he'd meet her when she finished and see her home. Sometimes they would take a detour and head over to the Hudson for some private time by the river. Sometimes they would just go straight back to the loft and get cozy in her cubby.

The Troika had met him and were polite enough, but she never got the feeling that they approved or thought he was a 'catch'. He was a cop, which for them, had its limits. They would joke with her about how "Ohio" it was of her to date a cop. She never really understood the reference but, to avoid confrontation, just laughed along with them and made it seem more casual and insignificant than it really was.

She and Jimmy spent their time in the cubby exchanging details about the lives each had led before meeting up in New York. Beatrice stuck to a semi-sanitized version of things – leaving out whole swaths of detail about her absentee father and cruel-tempered mother. She only offered up a simplified, "I was an artistic country girl longing for the heartbeat of the city" version of her life.

She did not fully understand her need to hide so many parts of her past, but she was certain she didn't want her boyfriend to know much, if any, of it. The history she shared with him was sanitized because telling the truth made her feel damaged and unworthy of him. He was such a good guy. In fact, she did not want to dredge up any of her past that could potentially mess with the current joy of her life. She was living an amazing adventure in the heart of New York. Jimmy didn't need to be a part of that other stuff.

Jimmy was crazy about his mother and wanted to talk about her now that things were getting more serious with Beatrice. He loved how warm and welcoming she was with his friends. She could also cook an incredible chicken fricassee with a side of baked onions. She was always remarking about her weight and losing that extra 20 - 30 lb. she got after becoming a mother, but he loved her soft roundness and how she smelled like fresh laundry. He'd tell her, "Mommy, (even as a grown man, which sounded odd to Beatrice, making her twitch slightly at the sound of it) there's more to love. Don't lose an ounce!" and he would pull her to him hug her extra tight. His friends used to gently tease him about finding a girlfriend to squeeze that way and how he'd know she was the right one if she could chicken as well as hers.

His dad, intensely shy, wasn't as open and warm as his wife, but he was polite and attentive, which lent an overall impression of not caring as much as he actually did. However, he had a short fuse when it came to frustration and was prone to blaming himself mercilessly when things went wrong.

Jimmy confided to Beatrice about how frustration could push his dad into serious rages. Once when he was trying to teach his son how to ride a two-wheeler, explaining to the boy about balance, little Jimmy just couldn't get it. Then the bike chain came loose, and his father, irritated because he couldn't get it back on the wheel properly, flew into a fit of anger, calling himself all sorts of names but, most of all, a failure.

They were outside on the sidewalk. Jimmy was aged eight, and his father, a grown man, was cursing and crying about how stupid he was that he couldn't even teach his little boy to find his balance and learn to ride a 'damn' bike. And the child, who couldn't tolerate his father's pain, tried to console his father with comments like, "I can just try harder, Dad," or "Something wrong with a bike whose chain jumps off so easy."

Jimmy's mother, hearing the commotion from the kitchen window, had a very good sense of how the next chapter of this drama would be playing out and was willing to do just about anything to bring that curtain down. "Cookies, boys?" she offered as she emerged sweaty from the kitchen with a fresh batch of warm snickerdoodles (his dad's favorite). They both reached for the tray. "Why don't you two fellas come on inside now and have some cold milk to wash those down!"

His mother was always anticipating and rescuing, which, as

a child, made Jimmy feel secure, as she would never let him fall off a cliff. He loved her all the more each time she averted catastrophe and knew from an early age that he wanted to do the same for others, and becoming a cop seemed to fill the bill.

Jimmy really was a blend of both parents in interesting ways. When he was in uniform, he was genuinely warm and helpful to everyone he encountered unless, of course, there was something unpleasant going on that needed intervention. In those moments, he would make his voice deeper and louder and pump his chest out, and a spotty redness came onto his face, which was certainly not like the blushing redness that Beatrice found so endearing and moderately sexy when they were getting heated up. His professional persona made her think of a comic book character going from mild and meek to manly and menacing to fight whatever foe crossed his path.

One night, when the couple had been ambling along the river, an unkempt guy leered out of the darkness of the evening and tried to touch Beatrice's hand. He was clearly intoxicated and no real threat, but Jimmy exploded about it, shoving the guy off the sidewalk where the man because he was drunk, tripped as his foot got caught on the uneven cobblestones of the street. Jimmy cursed the guy while pulling Beatrice by her elbow hurriedly past the fellow who looked bewildered. He had suffered an abrasion on his left hand from trying to break the fall. She had never seen that side of her boyfriend before, and it frightened her.

Later, when they were snuggling in the warmth of her cubby, she asked him about it. “What happened out there?”. He was hesitant to say much other than, “I wouldn’t be a very good boyfriend if I didn’t protect you, would I?” which caused her to feel a combination of uneasiness and pride, which left her in a confused state of mind.

In the weeks they had been dating, the sex seemed to have stalled. They would be highly emotionally intimate and loving, and she would be mostly unclothed. He would be clothed and definitely be “ready” but always stopped short of all-out lovemaking. He said he wanted it to be perfect. The loft was certainly not perfect. He lived in a cops’ dorm, so intimacy there was out of the question. They needed to get away to somewhere special so he could make the kind of love with her that he imagined about day and night.

He filled her with his fantasies about things that would happen between them, the lives they would share together, and what he would do to give her pleasure. He was such a gentleman. Waiting for him was kind of a dream carrying an excitement of its own.

One evening after he picked her up from the restaurant, he surprised her with an invitation. “A friend of mine has a house in Salt Aire, Fire Island. It’s going to be empty next weekend. You wanna go?” This was two weeks before the big bash was happening in the loft. She was ecstatic. “Yes!!!! This will really be our time.” And he agreed this would be their golden opportunity to be fully with each other for an entire 48 hours. It would be like being married, and he winked in his adoring way and added, “In every sense.”

She informed her roommates about her trip, and they were genuinely thrilled for her. They had already gone through all the reasons they thought Jimmy had not had full-on sex with Beatrice, including he must be gay. This new development squashed that thought. Jimmy was not gay; he was excited about being with her. He just needed a place to feel more natural about it. Things seemed brighter to her, like when they first met.

Chapter Twelve

That Friday night, they took the Long Island Railroad to Bay Shore and then hopped the Salt Aire Ferry across the bay. The night air whipped across their faces as they stood on the outer deck of the ferry. They brought food for 2 days so there would be no need to shop. They brought bathing suits even though it probably would be too chilly to go into the ocean. They brought a few books, a jigsaw puzzle, a camera, and clean clothing. When the happy couple disembarked, they grabbed one of the little red wagons waiting for visitors on the dock and listened to the click clack click as they pulled their belongings along the wooden boardwalk to one house short of the dunes and ocean.

A rope fence marked the path to the front door of the house, where the name, *Island Cove*, was burned into a plank mounted above the entrance. On the wood deck, they located the key hidden in a fake rock next to a ring of seasoned firewood, exactly where his friend instructed Jimmy to look. Everything was going as planned. They went inside.

The house smelled musty, as homes near the beach often do, so they opened the windows to let the night breeze air things out. There were 3 bedrooms and one oversized bathroom with a faux red brick vinyl floor that creaked underfoot. The worn-out white towels (perhaps they spent time doing double duty at the beach) were folded according to size in open shelves lining the wall opposite the sink.

The art on the walls was of a nautical theme depicting seashells and buoys, and water birds. That subject appeared throughout the entire house, including the lamps, bed covers and tableware. Fishermen's netting was decoratively draped under the raw-hewn wood beams of the ceiling. Beatrice was amazed that so many objects came with maritime designs. This place sure had an atmosphere.

They had been invited to make themselves comfortable in the bedroom with the queen-size bed, which was where his friend's parents usually slept. At first, they felt funny about that, like they were intruding on private space even though they were alone in the house. The sheets were folded neatly at the foot of the bed and smelled clean and piney with a hint of ocean. A laminated index card with a little poem and an anchor adorning it was perched on top. "Enjoy your stay, but we pray, leave clean sheets, nice and neat! We don't want to seem mean – before you leave, please use the washing machine!!" That would be simple enough for them to do.

Beatrice giggled as she stacked their food in the refrigerator because there was a giant anchor magnet on its door with faded notes sticking out of the edges. It was so charming, so romantic. All this attention to theme and décor. She was just so happy keeping house with Jimmy. They were a couple.

And they were hungry. Because it was close to 10 pm, they decided on sandwiches that were fast to make, and almost magically, they simultaneously asked each other about walking to the beach to eat them. The coincidence was charming, causing Jimmy to gently pull Beatrice to him as he squeezed her just enough to feel he was really holding on. They left the house barefoot and arm in arm, walking down the dark path onto the boardwalk. When they reached the end, they stepped onto the cool sand, skipping up the short flight of stairs that crossed over the dune onto the beach proper. They were surrounded by the sound of the ocean pounding endlessly like a heartbeat in the night.

Forgetting to bring a blanket, they just sat directly on the sand, eating and listening to the breaking night waves. The moon looked like a toenail hanging in the sky, and it was a pretty clear night. So many of the stars (normally obscured by the lights of the City) were visible though neither of them could name what they were looking at. After a few minutes of snuggling and eating in this ideal setting, they both looked at each other and admitted to being cold, causing them to laugh at how, once again, they were so connected by what they felt. They returned to the house.

Jimmy found some kindling, a compressed log, and a box of matches in a copper pot by the fireplace. Voila, there was a cozy fire in no time. There was wine. It was lovely. They were in love. And alone on a couch in a house by the beach.

Jimmy made the first move while declaring his devotion to Beatrice. He would stay with her always. He loved her in ways he never could have imagined. He would cherish her, respect her, and fill her with joy. All during his amorous proclamations, he was helping her out of her clothes. His fingers trembled as he began exploring her in ways that were certainly more intimate than in the cubby.

Beatrice was trying to encourage him to also get as naked as she was but was meeting some resistance until she finally admonished him with, “Come on, Jimmy, no one’s around!”. She was trying to make light of his shyness, but she was starting to feel vaguely self-conscious and slightly predatory in pushing him, which was odd and somewhat creepy since she thought they were supposed to be in this, naked, together.

Jimmy pulled away, turning his back to her and methodically removed his clothing, placing his pants, shirt, and underwear in a neat stack on the rocker next to the couch. When he turned back around, she finally beheld him in his naked glory. She let out a deep sigh and smiled. He was quite a feast for his girlfriend’s eyes. She was pleased with what she saw as the glow of the fire danced across his skin.

However, his face bore an expression she had never noticed before when they were together in the loft. His eyes grew intense, seeming to fixate on parts of her body as if she were not a whole woman but rather an amalgam of arms and legs and breasts and vagina. In certain angles, the flickering light made his face appear gnarled, cunning, and sort of hungry like a stray dog which made no sense given they had just eaten and he talked so tenderly.

"Beatrice, lie down, please, my love," so she lay the length of the couch as he stealthily lowered himself down on top of her in one seamless movement. Body-to-body warmth and the heat of the fire stimulated them into an undulating movement that held the promise of ecstasy. They were almost as close as two humans could be.

She kept assuring herself this was divine. She kept expecting the next wave between them would lead to full-on sex. Or at least begin the process.

But nothing was actually happening, and though she knew he was ready (she could feel that), they were suspended in an endless dance, like tracing a Mobius strip and never arriving anywhere. But what *was* going on? She felt her body get jumpy the way a cat needs to get away when it's stroked too much.

"Jimmy, I'm ready. Please honey, please…" He just kept moving his body against hers without making any progress. "Jimmy, what's wrong?" His eyes were staring beyond her head, now looking distant and broken. A frightful thought came to her, so she whispered, "Jimmy, you haven't ever done this before, have you?" He remained silent as he lowered his chin to his chest, all the while rubbing harder against her thigh.

The wetness of his tears trailed down her breasts. He was heaving against her, crying with abandon in the same moments that her love for this man trickled out of her body, descending completely beneath her. She felt her head pounding with the weight of responsibility that she was to be his first which did not feel sexy to her because she feared his need for her would be too great, and she could not bear the consequences of giving him what he most wanted.

She imagined she would become 'all his', belonging to him, and he would need her forever as the one and only person in his life to fulfill his needs. Old images of hunting traps dripping with the blood of recently captured prey, not knowing how to get free without injury, raced through her mind. Her mother's face played faintly as an image on his torso.

She started gagging (though he chose to ignore it), and her breathing was growing desperately short. And as the scale of his needs was enlarging, it was sinking in that she was growing feather light and more invisible, which was a relief, as she was floating upwards towards the netting on the ceiling, and she did not want his body to weigh her down.

From her hovering perspective, she peered down at Jimmy, but he was nowhere to be seen. In his place was a young girl, gripping her knees in her small hands and sitting stiffly against the arm of the couch.

Then Beatrice noticed her mother, who dressed in a light rose-colored chiffon nightgown, the kind she remembered seeing her wear when Papa was around, glide across the floor and sit down lengthwise, propping her legs up so her bare feet landed in the little girl's lap. With that, she commanded the child, "Tickle my feet".

At first, the child hesitated. Her ears grew crimson, and her eyes appeared to be tearing. But her mother was insistent, and the girl, having no power of her own, did as she was told. Her mother murmured, "That's good, that's good." It was clear to Beatrice the child hated to touch her mother, and she imagined the disgusted child might want to stick something sharp into those feet if she had the chance.

Beatrice felt her own tears well up as she wept for the child who was imprisoned by her mother and wanted to flee. She wished with all her might that she could teach the little girl how to drift upwards to find sanctuary, but this was something she did not know how to do. Instead, she figured she'd return herself to the couch and the man, which could possibly liberate the girl from her mother.

She closed her eyes and took slower breaths, which miraculously helped waft her downwards and drive her mother completely from the room. She was not sure where the child had gone, but she was not worried because she knew she likely was not far away.

Now, in a puddle of mixed-up tears, all that was left between Beatrice and Jimmy was a terror they both experienced for different reasons. Because, while she had traveled to the safety of the ceiling, he had been left alone with a girl-child on the couch.

And with the entitlement of a conqueror grabbing his prize, he had managed to lose his virginity with the woman-child, and though he may not have fully understood that the person he assumed he was with had disappeared into the woman-child, he certainly sensed something was wrong because he was fully a grownup and he saw that she moved and spoke like a child and therefore, what they did could not be considered a consensual act. However, in the midst of completing his needs, he convinced himself it was.

Though she could breathe now, being near him left her confused and furious and disgusted that she failed to rescue the child from the man who had crossed love with satisfying his needs.

They agreed to stay the rest of the weekend because neither could quite face their lives in the City though they spoke little and did less together. There was no 'working through' what each thought had happened, no energy to put things back together. Their relationship was fractured beyond compare. By the time they reached Grand Central Station, they were both relieved to get lost in the crowd going their separate ways.

Chapter Thirteen

The Troika was completely up to their eyeballs in loft cleaning and getting the art ready for display as the party was happening in less than a week. When Beatrice walked in, no one asked her about her weekend or whether she had sex with Jimmy or took any interest in her at all, which was fine by her because she wanted to avoid all of it. She was dying to focus on the bash.

She gathered some of her favorite art (admittedly, she had been less productive since dating Jimmy because her painting time had been occupied mostly by their together times). Of what she had, a series of six color-field painting studies was what she chose for the card table display. They were done on 300 lb. watercolor paper using acrylic paint in layers to build up a surface that pushed colors into one other, hard edges challenging softer forms in a dance across the picture plane. She was inspired to title the series, *Fugues 1-6* though she did not quite understand why. She felt good about the work in spite of the small scale. Hopefully, someone would notice them and lay down some money to buy one.

Each woman focused on tidying her cubby as best she could, and then they worked together, making the loft resemble a home for empowered women artists. They mopped the floor, threw out things that had been relegated to “maybe I’ll use this sometime” status that never happened and stashed stuff they wanted to keep in nooks and crannies covered with curtains.

By Friday evening, the place was transformed. Beatrice had managed to get the sheet cake into a taxi to take back to the loft. The booze was set out, food was in the fridge, clothing for the party was ironed, and they felt like racehorses at the gate. They were ready to run.

The party was supposed to start at 8 pm, but the buzzer began ringing at 7 pm, which her mother had always said was rude because guests should never arrive early. Beatrice did not want to think about her mother and internally scolded herself for letting her have any opinion about this bash which was going to be fantastic and a tremendous distraction for her from all the crazy stuff of the previous weekend with Jimmy. She was feeling strong.

At first, guests trickled in, making generous comments about the beauty of the space, the drama of the giant paintings and the excitement of having a finger on the pulse of this generation of women artists. A number of people asked if the *Fugue Series* was a study for one of the more monumental artists whose work stood mightily in the center of the loft.

Beatrice sneaked back into her cubby and quickly improvised a label for her art on the card table, indicating her work was studied for her paintings yet to be. She still wasn't sure if the label was enough explanation, but it was all she had to ease the confusion and her irritation.

She admired the skill with which the Ladies took up conversation with this lawyer, that dealer, their partners, and other guests who, by 9:15, filled the loft to capacity. At that point, it was close to impossible to actually see the grand paintings but quite simple to hold hers in hand to see. A few people showed interest and asked her questions about motivation and process.

Meanwhile, the Troika schmoosed the crowd. Clearly, they were making headway as business cards were pressed into eager hands. Knowing smiles were exchanged. Some hyper-jovial laughter permeated the air. Appointments were made for studio visits. There was talk about group shows. One dealer mentioned the three joining his stable with a promise of potential individual shows to come. He was one of the dealers who stayed for some socializing after the party petered out in the wee hours of Sunday morning.

Beatrice notices one fellow lingering at the card table, apparently taking the time to appreciate her images. He introduced himself to her as Victor. He was a realtor who covered the upper Westside for residential and mid-town for commercial spaces. He was invited to come by a lawyer friend, Phil, who had heard about this shindig and was looking to rent art for the lobby of their new office space. Phil had disappeared into the crowd.

Victor was kind of a twinkly person. He seemed easygoing, a good conversationalist and very direct. He had a bit of a paunch and was thoroughly enjoying the sheet cake Beatrice had brought to the party. She guessed he was fairly successful by looking at his Omega watch and pinky ring embedded with some sort of gemstone that flashed in the right light. He was so comfortable in his skin which was such a relief and change from the *other person* (Jimmy had been relegated to past history even though only a mere week had passed). "You mind if I hang out at the party for a while?" She gave him a thumbs-up sign, to which he added, "Good. I'll see you later."

By the time the loft emptied out of guests, some intimate partnering appeared to be taking place. Two of the ladies of the Troika peeled off with one of the older art dealers. He owned an enormously important art gallery in midtown that catered to the millionaire crowd. He could make or break the future of any artists in his 'stable'.

He was also notorious for expecting loyalty from his artists, and in return, they could expect group shows first and then the holy grail, a solo exhibit with all the glory that comes with it. He believed he was taking all the risk and so, from time to time, expected to be amply appreciated with threesomes from the artists who hoped to get ahead. Male or female, he was open to it all.

The other lady took the art dealer's banker into her cubby. He had tipped her off earlier in the evening that he was a good guy from a big bank, and maybe she should get to know him. She didn't mind being friendly to him because he seemed sort of nice, and it got her out of spending the night with the dealer, who was more than twice her age.

Beatrice was alone, standing by Victor in the kitchen, when her roommates left for their corner cubbies. She stood there feeling awkward and unsure about what to say or do next.

Victor spoke up, "I like you. I like your art. Feel like fucking?" and though the invitation was abrupt and crude, it was just what she needed to get back to feeling grounded and real. They went to her cubby and had a wild time romping on her excellent mattress, neither loving each other nor making promises nor being devoted. They did agree it would be fun to repeat doing this again.

In his direct and refreshingly crude way, he asked her if she were interested in being "fuck buddies," which was exactly the right thing to ask of her, and she was delighted, and she did not float to the ceiling that night or any other of the many times they buddied up over the ensuing months and years.

Chapter Fourteen

Beatrice arrived for her Friday therapy session in great spirits. Her mood was infectious, and even though Morgan had something interesting she wanted to run by her, she knew better than to advance her idea before attending to what her client needed from the hour. So, the doctor waited for the patient to begin.

"I'm moving". Morgan was genuinely relieved to hear her news because she had long thought that her living circumstance, those women, the horrible loft, and the generally depressive atmosphere contributed to Beatrice's depression and feelings of entrapment. "Tell me about it, please."

Beatrice explained the entire scheme to her (she had heard about Vic and had a modicum of affection about his role in her life because while he sounded rough around the edges, he seemed to be a genuine friend. He helped steady Beatrice'ss anxieties about being swallowed whole by intimacy gone wild). Morgan saw the move to an apartment as a step away from drama and loneliness. "When's the move?"

Beatrice had given the Troika a month's notice. She was going up to the apartment (she still hadn't seen it) with Vic this Saturday to get the keys and paint it. She figured she would move in the following weekend. Aside from her meager belongings in the loft, she had a small storage unit across the river in New Jersey, which housed unopened boxes of her things, including a few of her mother's that she hastily packed before she left Ohio.

These years later, she had no idea what was in them, but there was no more need for storage costs. Unpacking everything held a great appeal for her. Vic would be renting a van to transport everything from there as well as the loft. She would start moving into her new home on Sunday.

Morgan decided to put her own interesting idea on hold for now because, in the face of witnessing her client's apparent reconnection to life so stimulated by the impending move, she wanted nothing to disturb her feelings of joy and anticipation.

Bea and Vic met in the lobby of the apartment building Saturday morning. There had been a misunderstanding about painting the apartment because she didn't realize she was entitled to one free paint job as owner of a new lease. So, when they took the elevator up to the 7th floor, walked down the long hall, past the fire door on the right, and made a left turn opposite into what was to be her new home, the smell of paint permeating the air surprised her.

Painter's tarps covered the floors, and buckets of opened eggshell white paint were strategically placed around the rooms. A-frame ladders were near cans. Basically, it was impossible to get a feel for the place because so much was covered or blocked during the painting process.

Nonetheless, Victor wanted to show Beatrice as much of the place as possible, so he shoved tarps aside, "This is your kitchen. Check this out. You'll have room for a small table and a couple of chairs." In the foyer, "Hey, Bea, there's a mirrored door to this storage closet!" From the living room, "There's enough room in here for you to do your small paintings *and* have a couch. Look at the ceiling. It must be 9' tall!"

The bedroom was down the hallway. To the right, before it, was a full bath with one of those extra-long porcelain bathtubs where the water came out from a spout near the middle of the tub. Over the toilet was a sliver of a window. The medicine cabinet looked worn out, but this was all so much better than the bathroom in the loft. Directly ahead in the hall was a linen closet so deep that she could stretch her entire arm in it and barely touch the rear wall.

Turning left into the bedroom, in spite of the painter's equipment draped over the floor and windows, it was possible to get the feel of the room. It was a large square, maybe 14 x 14, with windows lining one wall. The walls were interrupted here and there by columns that Vic explained to her no doubt held heating pipes and plumbing lines for other apartments in the building. She could fit her bed easily between those spaces (she planned on taking her incredible mattress from the loft when she moved).

After they completed their rounds and were about to leave,

Victor took out a single key hanging from a gold ring. He handed it to Beatrice, and she noticed a small charm hanging next to the key. Etched on one side of a gold disc was the letter "B". On the other side was a "V".

In the elevator descent to the lobby, he said, "Don't worry. You've got the only key."

For Beatrice, the ensuing weeks were spent settling into the new apartment, working at the restaurant, and therapy. In addition, there was the celebratory breaking-in of her excellent mattress in the new bedroom with Vic. Their playful inauguration took place on the first Sunday after the move. The mattress, supported by neither box springs nor frame (a few months later, he bought a box spring and frame to complete the setup of her bed), was plopped in the middle of the bedroom floor amongst all her loose belongings, cardboard packing boxes, and wrapped paintings. A year later, Vic surprised her with a carved teak and mahogany headboard he bought in an open-air market when he was on holiday in Bali.

Vic knew the headboard was an over-the-top gift. The beauty of the carvings with their birds in flight, some sort of pond with grasses and reeds surrounding it, and low bas-relief clouds dancing across the upper edge of the panel struck him as so marvelous that he could not resist buying it for Bea.

He imagined this might be just the thing to bring back as a

gift for her. It was truly artistic. There was also a nagging recollection of one of their post-midnight chats in the loft when she mentioned her father's nickname for her when she was little, "Birdy", which filled him with a certain non-specific sadness and a hollow feeling in his gut. He never forgot the name her father gave her, and though there were times when he wanted to whisper that name to her that himself, he knew better than to ever utter it.

The bird wings were made of mother-of-pearl shells, and the sky had swirls of copper etched around the edges of the cloud forms. The grasses and reeds were carved in a wood resembling mahogany, accenting the ring of water the birds were playing above.

All the wood was well oiled and smelled vaguely of painters' oils, so familiar to Bea from the studio. For years to come, she marveled at the sensuality of the wooden basrelief, which she would often run her fingers over when she was lying in bed. Her headboard and mattress were as close to heaven as she could imagine.

The night Vic attached the headboard, Bea placed red votive candles on the windowsill and on top of the other furniture in the bedroom. It turned into a quasi-romantic night as they spoke more deeply about things of the heart, which pushed them into making a sharp turn towards silliness to avoid what was actually very confusing for them both because this was not where their friendship was meant to go when they started their play dates so long ago.

Without exactly planning it, they fell into a yearlong hiatus (the first of numerous departures, reunions and then departures). Unspoken, they understood the natural hallmark of what made their intimacy tolerable was knowing, for sure, exactly what emotional depth would spare them from potential wounding.

In a unique fashion, their love flourished through absence, like air plants that thrive without water. This pattern of coupling briefly and then stepping apart developed into longer and longer periods of separation. Thinking about each other became their truth as the actual reality of being together needed more and more distance.

And the years carried this arrangement along until after one visit. Victor declared, "Bea, the lease is fully in your name now. Just sign it every few years and keep your payments regular," whereupon he shoved off into his world while she remained in hers.

Chapter Fifteen

Beatrice continued her therapy. She never planned ahead about what to talk about because she observed early on that her mind would turn blank on any plans she might have made for topics to bring up. As she crossed the threshold into Morgan's inner office, all bets were off for what may be discussed. Even when she brought art to a session, she did not determine ahead of time what to say.

Once, when she appeared agitated that her thoughts had all scrambled, Morgan calmed her by saying, "It's ok to just be," which made her want to cry because some harsh voice inside her said she had no right to just 'be'. She got confused between hearing her own words and other words that seemed to take over inside her head, so often she kept her mouth shut and eyes down.

Morgan initially viewed their work together as if she were at a vast archaeological dig uncovering delicate artifacts with a toothbrush. She knew there was much safety need to develop for Beatrice to make the slightest progress. It was going to take much time and a feather-like dismantling to uncover what was valuable below the earth and not traumatize the landscape above in the process.

Beatrice recounted her life in Ohio. She felt that as a child, she lived without, as she would say, "really touching the walls." She believed she had the power to become invisible and that she could breathe without taking in air. As an adult, she understood none of that was real, of course, though naturally, she wished it to be so.

During one session, she recalled sitting on a bit of lawn in the front yard of their modest home. Scents of purple lilac blossoms and fresh-cut grass merged with memories of playing intensely with her dolls near the lattice-covered crawl space under the house. She loved her dolls with the full heart of a seven-year-old and devised endlessly intricate games with them on themes of running away to a horse farm or being rescued by some super tall person in a long flowing robe whose face remained hidden in shadows.

On that afternoon, her mother had had enough of her daughter dilly-dallying in play. She stood directly over the little girl and scoffed, "You know Beatrice, one day you won't want to play with dolls any longer," which shocked the little girl to the core and severed some part of her insides connected to innocence and trust. She knew better than to show any tears. She did, however, know how to pretend.

She entered into her opposite world, and smiling, she looked up and responded, "I know, Mother. I will put them away." And then the girl got up, gathered her dolls, and ran inside her tiny bedroom. Placing them lovingly in an old shoe box, she stuffed the whole thing into the back of the closet. There the dolls remained, hiding, never to be exposed to her mother's view of reality again but also to never again be cradled in the arms of the child.

Periodically, even into her teens, Beatrice would check to make sure the box was still in the back of her closet. Without opening it, she would shake the contents, feeling secure when it rattled with the familiar sound of doll bodies rolling around - evidence they were still safe. She would put the box back into the darkness and, at the same time, imagine tearing her mother's tongue right out of her head while she'd hit her thigh with great force and whisper into her room, "I don't feel a thing."

Chapter Sixteen

Beatrice drew weary of the commute to the restaurant, and, in truth, the job itself no longer held much appeal for her. She started reading 'help wanted' ads in search of something that would provide a bit more money and a lot less time traveling to get there. After attempts at employment opportunities as a receptionist, another gallery position, two diners in her area, a salesgirl in a high-end lingerie boutique and a veterinarian's assistant, she landed a job four nights a week as a proofreader in an administrative law firm about 20 blocks south of her apartment. The pay was good. The hours were from 5 to 10 pm, which, leaving her days free, suited her just fine. The firm provided night employees with dinner food and free car service home for anyone living within a forty-block radius.

Her first paycheck was big enough to pay for her to repaint her apartment. The original cheap white paint had aged poorly and turned a sour mustardy color. She opted for a soft salmon pink and spent a weekend covering her walls and thinking about Vic and wishing he was there to spread the workaround.

Several paychecks later, she was able to buy some much-needed furniture, a little café style kitchen table, parlor chairs, a couch covered in dotted aquamarine fabric, a comfy matching chair and other home furnishings.

She had a folding table set up in the living room for making art. During the day, up until the point of going to work, she moved between the couch for reading and the table where she made art. Her mother, who had been an avid reader and librarian, criticized her daughter constantly for 'toying around with those paints and things' rather than 'falling into a good book'.

When Beatrice was young, she struggled with reading. She found concentrating difficult as her brain would shut down because the words would get all jumbled. When her mother insisted she read recipes or other directions to her, she would get lost on the page, mix up numbers, and feel ashamed to the core for being so inept. She believed her mother's admonition, "You really can be so stupid. Better fix that, my girl."

For a while, the few friends she had from her days living downtown would occasionally visit and keep her updated on the remarkable careers of the Troika, their exhibitions and love lives. It was uncomfortable hearing about their successes, and she fought off feelings of embarrassment that she had somehow betrayed her vows of artist hood by leaving the loft and highbrow attitudes of downtown. "One even acquired a summer house with a studio in East Hampton. Didn't she miss the scene?"

While they lightly complimented her watercolors and oil pastel drawings, no meaningful conversations emerged from their observations, leaving her with the impression she was 'less than' and no longer to be taken seriously as an artist. Her work had become too personal for them. Their reactions humiliated her, making her wish she had, once again, hidden everything in a portfolio under the bed. She quickly bolted the door after they left, feeling a heaviness wrap itself around her chest, squeezing her ribs as she imagined, for the millionth time, she did not need air to breathe.

Chapter Seventeen

Morgan had no expectation that this Friday's appointment with her client would be much different from most sessions of the past few months. Together, they had cautiously excavated stories about her childhood in Ohio. Most themes revolved around Beatrice's mother. The topic of her father never got the kind of traction that Morgan sensed was lurking in the background, and she took Beatrice's avoidance as a defense not ready to be peeled back. She understood her mother was a predator, cruel and self-serving. The girl had clearly been robbed of the right to feel safe in the world, to be treasured, and loved unconditionally.

Morgan also had her suspicions that her client's mother might have crossed some intimacy boundaries with her daughter. Beatrice's effect seemed numb and disconnected. Speaking flatly, she would recount in barely audible whispers the humiliations she helplessly withstood under her mother's barrage of verbal and emotional abuse. No wonder Beatrice convinced herself she was invisible and had no need to breathe. At times, Morgan found herself hating that woman who had been so vicious to her little girl, occasionally imagining trying to choke her.

Morgan's supervisor warned her that she was treading a fine line of countertransference in fantasizing about killing the woman. "Work through that, Morgan or it will suck the life out of you and leave your client feeling abandoned once again." So, Morgan renewed her dedication to remaining within the therapeutic frame and not ending up being another selfish female in her client's life. It was all about self-discipline, not getting overly caught up in her client's vulnerable child state that needed shielding and nurturing, and good boundary-keeping.

A while into their work, she hoped that Beatrice would begin to feel safe enough to start probing a bit more about her father. What really went on there? How could he just disappear even in the face of his belief that she was not his own child? Had he loved his 'Birdie' and then one day just abandoned her to live alone with this selfish, narcissistic, and vengeful woman? Why didn't he at least try to see her? Morgan wrestled with feelings of confusion and anger about the father, who seemed to have just given up, skipped town, and erased her in ways that appeared as heinous as her mother - a child abandoned and forgotten as if she never existed.

Beatrice's complex childhood trauma had driven most of her life behaviors. In some ways, she was feral – the product of raising herself into a human hood, where survival was the prime motivator for action. She learned early on that her imagination helped quell the dangers and put distance between herself and the person she most needed for survival but was most lethal to her wellbeing.

Art-making became her weapon, her collaborator helping

her evade the ravenous gaze and vicious words of her mother. She hid behind her talent, masking her true thoughts and intentions with images that were dismissed as colorful fantasies – something to chortle about. The metaphor was her intermediary between sheer terror and basic survival.

Practically from toddlerhood, she did her best, at all costs, to never let her mother know who she truly was, what she truly felt. Beatrice developed her powers of protection so well that by the time she was old enough to be more or less independent in the world, she had perfected the skills of becoming both invisible and visible at the same time. She studied how to react by watching television as well as the reactions of others, especially her few friends when she went to their houses to play.

When absolute panic paralyzed her, she'd imagine her way into weightlessness, floating past the petrifying impasse as she drifted above the fray. The view from up there always empowered her, driving the noise from her mind and protecting her body from feeling further intrusion.

So, on that particular late fall day, when the cool sky darkened early, and the leaves no longer crunched underfoot but began to stick to one's boots because the dampness of winter was just around the corner, Morgan's office felt especially cozy. Beatrice, cheeks reddened from the pre-winter chill, had arrived holding a rolled-up drawing under her arm, which she placed by the side of her chair as she sat down.

As the two of them settled into the beginning of the session, Beatrice surprised her therapist by mentioning she had a dream about her father. The therapist remained silent as she edged forward slightly in her seat. The feral girl was given the space to share without interruption.

"He never really said goodbye to me. I remember my mother telling me Papa and I could find each other. I just had to ask. That permission terrified me. She said I could make my own arrangements to find him, but I didn't know how to do that. I didn't know where to begin. And I didn't know if she was tricking me and that I'd get my hands and feet caught up in the jaws of a giant metal thing that looked like a big metal animal trap that would bite into me, causing blood to run from my limbs and I'd be forever crippled, and then I even had thoughts of gnawing off my hands and feet to get out of it. More than anything, I thought if I were crippled, I could never get away from her, so I better not try to find him now so I could get away one day when I was a grown-up." Beatrice paused briefly to catch her breath.

"Last night, I dreamt I was sleeping in our old dining room, and I could see the Grandfather clock from the bed I was on, and it was near midnight and about to chime the hour. I noiselessly kept calling out for him, 'Papa, where are you?' and it made me more and more angry that nothing was coming back to me. Not a peep. Fucking silence. How the fuck was I supposed to find him? And then I heard a tiny voice coming from the bedspread that started soft and then went to screaming 'You are so stupid, dumb, stupid girl, stupid girl' and I made a fist and started to pound my thighs so hard til there was no such thing as pain, and I was screaming nothing resembling any words, but filling the room with all the hate in the world."

Beatrice stopped dead still. Her body began to shiver. In a voice as young and innocent as Morgan had ever heard, Little Beatrice uttered, "I am four years old. How am I supposed to find Papa????"

The therapist followed every nuance of the client's words, body language, and intonation. She understood she was shifting between her dream and reality like mercury in a clown toy – ever moving, breaking apart, rolling, merging with itself only to jiggle into a new shape as it never attains the stability to stop wobbling.

Her eyes were fixed on her client. She remained breathless in her chair as if her very inhale-exhale movement might intrude into the moment. Morgan's insides were filled with pure, kind love, an emotional embrace that was touchless, non-demanding, nurturing, holding, and still.

She also absorbed Beatrice's terror lingering in the room like a heavy hanging mist blocking any possibility of focusing sharply on the details, dulling perceptions so that up and down became obfuscated as the regular orientation of things disintegrated before her eyes.

Beatrice kept repeating "how, how, how" as she lowered herself off the chair onto the floor. She found the carpet she had stared at silently for so many wordless sessions, becoming grassy and smelling green. Lower, lower, she descended into the softness of the grass, inhaling the earth beneath the newness of its roots. Her head and hands formed a triangle, with her body and legs splayed to the side. She ceased using words because they held no meaning.

But sounds did. The soft whimpering of a wounded animal began to fill the room.

She was crying because she could see her arms and fingers becoming furry, and she knew from some nameless place within that she was becoming a wolf. She had fought this inevitability all her life, and now it was happening, and she mourned for herself and the little child within who she had always tried to protect, and though she thought she had succeeded in keeping her hidden, now she had to admit she had failed her.

Amidst her despair, a less familiar low-level howling sound emerged from her, and she was startled. She felt for her arms, which had definitely become more animal than human. This bodily change inspired curiosity in her, so she felt her face which had taken on a shape entirely different from the one she normally had. Her noticed sense of smell provided so much more information than when she was merely human, and the green of the floor barely masked the scent of the other animal in the room who appeared to be part wolf and part human much as she was.

The wolf-girl disappointed that the little child had been exposed, grew furious with herself for forsaking her vow of protection. Clawing at herself, she believed she might be able to release the little one so she could run for freedom.

She began hissing and barking the way cornered wolves do because, for her, there was no difference between inside and out. She was trapped on both sides of her being. Everything was about rage and the futile fulfillment of the promise not kept. She believed this was to be a fight to the death. She was howling.

The therapist understood she was the other animal in the room and knew she was not afraid of the wolf-girl in front of her. She understood the girl to be thoroughly human, and her wolf part was just that, a part but not the whole. She called her own wolf part (an aspect of herself she had tamed many years earlier in her own therapy) to assist in managing the aggression of the raging wolf-girl so the child, caught between worlds. It would not be accidentally hurt.

And so, the grown-up human working in tandem with her wolf part, cautiously edged closer to the wolf-girl to try to comfort both parts of her client. It was a very dangerous thing to do because the wolf-girl's needs had been starved so long that it was possible if the child were released, she might be eaten alive.

The howling grew worse, permeating the office and waiting room walls and then escaping the building entirely as the sounds echoed out into the universe. There seemed to be no end to it, which in some ways was fortunate because, during this distraction, the human was able to surreptitiously move closer, almost touching the wolf-girl.

And as the suffering wolf-girl kept moaning and scratching, the pacified wolf gently joined her wailing. The two wolf voices started weaving sounds together in a kind of ancient harmony that was melancholic and saturated with grief. They sang for as long as was needed, and natural weariness set in, which had the effect of soothing the wolf-girl and diminishing her scratching and clawing. Then they sat in rich silence.

The human took the girl's hand, which had delicate fingers and was no longer furry. She spoke as she held her hand, holding within her own, "The child survived, and your promise has been kept. Both of you outlived your childhood. Thank you, Wolf."

Then the last remnants of the wolf part that had inhabited the girl took in a deep breath, swelling slightly with pride. The therapist assured them both they got to live, and they were surprised they both were allowed to be in the world. That's when Beatrice asked Morgan, "Am I real?"

She responded, "Yes. You both are".

At the close of the session, Morgan brought Beatrice some water and suggested that she relax in the waiting room (no one else was expected) so she could gain her composure before going out into the chill of the fall evening. Beatrice was actually feeling remarkably excellent, almost giddy. The furniture seemed brighter and more in focus. The art on the walls, magazines on the end table, and all the textures came to life. It was as if she had awakened from the fog of time, and it was morning, although it really was late in the day.

Morgan invited Beatrice to stick around for the next half hour to gather herself together before leaving. She left her inner office door open to keep an eye on her, casually checking in with her for the next thirty minutes.

Beatrice announced she was ready to leave at exactly half past the hour and reminded Morgan about the drawing she left on the floor by her chair. Casually, she offered it to Morgan. "If you want it, you can keep it." Then she left, quietly closing the door behind her.

Morgan picked up the drawing, unrolling it carefully on her

desktop. There, staring up at her in shades of deep browns and rusty reds, was a wolf's face. Its eyes held a penetrating stare that seemed to sink beneath her skin. Deep in her inner being, she sensed the eyes of this wolf piercing through layers and layers of her own story, directly reaching her own wolf, who gazed back in acknowledgment, understanding the moment they shared in ways that no other being could.

The light feeling did not diminish as Beatrice took the train home. When she stepped into her apartment, she immediately realized she wanted to repaint at least one wall, something bright and open. Maybe the color of a brilliant blue stream or new spring grass.

Then, as she stood looking out at the nightlights of the cityscape from her living room window, the thought crossed her mind that being a successful artist wasn't anything she aspired to anymore. She glanced around at her paintings, feeling a tenderness she had not appreciated before about them. The appreciation was more like gratitude. How lucky she had been to always have the creativity to turn to in times of need and despair. It was almost magical how the alchemy of art and soul had kept her alive and whole.

She longed for more meaning in her life though she could not imagine the journey that would get her there. At least not until two life paths crossed, ultimately guiding her to the same place.

Chapter Eighteen

Edwina Adella Borowski RN, Esq rarely met her proofreaders because she was far too busy burning the midnight oil strategizing the healthcare defense cases her law firm handled. She would have liked to have time enough to sit and socialize with them a bit because friendliness was in her nature, as was curiosity.

So, when she learned from her secretary that one of her readers who had been working there for about two years was an artist, she was intrigued and committed herself to making an introduction. Around 6 pm one evening, she ambled down the long hall lined with paintings of modern Mexican artists adorning the walls towards what she jokingly referred to as "the writers' room". She adored taking in the vibrancy and clever design elements of the art as she walked past.

Her partial Mexican heritage played an enormous role in developing her passion for art and music of all kinds – but especially those of the Mexican culture, which she remembered as a child where she spent her early years living fully immersed in local tradition and language. Later in life, she used to joke with friends that she wanted to sue her parents for neglecting to continue speaking Spanish in the home when they moved stateside. If they had, she would have been completely fluent. Even at the age of 77, she continued to take Spanish lessons, ever hoping to return to the effortless communication of her childhood.

As she crossed the threshold into the writer's room, she saw a sole reader intently bent over a legal document with a red pencil in hand. She announced herself, "Hi there. I'm Edwina." and proceeded to sit directly opposite Beatrice at the narrow end of the long rosewood conference table.

Not sure what was correct protocol when meeting the head of a highly successful law firm, Beatrice stood rigidly in her place and extended her hand. Edwina, not one for superfluous behaviors, smiled, nodded, and with a cheery lilt in her voice, said, "Oh, don't be ridiculous. Sit down!" as she was not a true believer in hierarchy most anywhere except in court. That was the one place where she followed the rules to the tee so as to not prejudice the outcomes of any case for her clients. Also, she secretly loved the ritual of the court and, in her dream life, often found herself in the role of Chief Justice, with all the robes and curtains and throne-like chairs and grandeur.

An awkward moment of silence passed between them before Edwina jumped right into her questions. "I hear you are an artist. Have you seen the paintings on our walls in the long hall? I'm a fan of the Mexican muralists, though, of course, I can't afford any of that, and we don't have the space. What do you think of Diego Rivera? As a child, I was transfixed looking at his work. What kind of art do you make? I never had any real talent – they told me after I got stateside in second grade that I couldn't draw. Can you imagine killing a child's spirit like that? I never made art again. It positively crushed me. Good thing my true calling as a child was to be a nurse for my menagerie of stuffed animals. I kid you not. They got excellent care."

Beatrice was amazed both that this renowned attorney was sitting there chatting up a storm with her and that she never seemed to come up for air – a quality that Bea admired because she, too, knew about not needing air to survive.

"Well?"

"I'm sorry, Attorney Borowski, but 'well' what?" This caused Edwina to release a belly laugh so infectious that Beatrice started laughing as well, and neither of them could reel it in for the next few moments.

"What kind of art do you make, Beatrice?" And from that question, the next 87 minutes were filled with a rich conversation that belied the economic differences in their stations of life. Out of this encounter, a blossoming occurred into the sort of adult friendship that was not so much social as it was an elder attending to the spirit of a younger person and the younger person valuing the wisdom and attention of the remarkable grownup in the room.

They chatted with regularity over the next few months,

spanning the generational divide between them with their different stories of life that reflected deeply important moments, thoughts, and feelings of their separate histories. Beatrice had never known such a relationship.

She felt comfortable sharing the disappointments she suffered living in the loft – the realization that her art never really took off in the art scene and the central role it played in her therapy. She spoke of Morgan, though she never completely opened up about that pivotal session in late fall when she met the wolf and understood it to be a real part of herself. Those details seemed too far to wander with her new quasi-friend and boss.

Edwina shared many of her life stories the way old people do as a form of inheritance for the next generation, so the remnants of their personal histories are not completely lost when that person is no longer alive. Edwina, having no heirs to bequeath such stories to, happily found Beatrice eager to embrace her words. This was the nature of mutuality they shared, delicate, balanced, and without a care to wanting more. Like an exquisite jewel, sitting unset in its pristine glory, waiting to be lightly touched but not converted into a piece of jewelry or moved beyond the spot in which it rested.

One evening, Edwina stopped by to briefly hand over an article to Beatrice. She knew she was unable to spare much time because she was prepping for a huge case coming up where a nurse was accused of patient abandonment – it was complex and represented a pet peeve of hers whereby systemic problems ended up being blamed on individual nurses.

She often pointed out, as publicly as possible, that the expectation of nursing perfection was an untenable perspective that was driving nurses out of the profession, crashing careers, and missing the larger point that the root cause of failures was where the real blame lay. As both a nurse and an attorney, she understood the importance of seeking the brutal truth of culpability.

She could go on about this topic for hours and had the admiration of both professions because of her intelligence, advocacy, and capacity to paint the errant logic of her opposition into the tiniest of corners while never once making anyone feel humiliated or defeated.

She tossed an article onto the conference table in front of Beatrice with the comment, "You mentioned a number of times about your quest for making meaning of your life. Check this out. I think it may be of interest to you. You can't be a proofreader forever." With that, she left the room, scurrying down the long hall, not taking any of her usual time to stop and admire her collection of paintings. There was too much work to be done.

Beatrice finished red-marking the legal document she had been pouring over the previous hour. Then she placed it in a wire rack labeled, 'Completed Edits' – a routine that always gave her immense satisfaction because she was part of a system dedicated to helping someone in trouble or in need. She sat down again and picked up the paper Edwina thought was so important. As she fingered its edges, the title came into focus, "Art Therapy: Soul Healing through Image Making".

Chapter Nineteen

Morgan had held off sharing "her interesting idea" with Beatrice for almost a year until she was satisfied that her client was stabilized. She was glad she had waited because, in hindsight, she grew a more developed understanding of her client, the role of art in her life, and how she might respond to possibly relinquishing her initial goals about art for another vision of her future. She viewed Beatrice as brilliant, creative, defiant, empathic, and in need of finding the means to a meaningful life – the holy grail for trauma survivors.

During the same week that Edwina gave the article to Beatrice, Morgan had attended a lecture on *Creativity and Trauma: The New Frontier* at the New School. She chose to listen to a panel that included a drama therapist, an art therapist, and a poetry therapist. It was moderated by a renowned psychologist and expert trauma practitioner who had started a collective of therapists specializing in trauma and resiliency. It was completely inspiring and set in motion Morgan's intent to bring up the topic of art therapy in her next session with Beatrice if it seemed appropriate.

So, when Beatrice came for her session that Friday and mentioned the article that Edwina had given her, it was all Morgan could do to refrain from saying, "Hey, I thought about this for you over a year ago and again a few days ago" because in some odd way, she felt a little competitive with the old nurse attorney who beat her out of the gate and planted the seed first.

"That's so interesting. In fact, I had thought of mentioning this profession to you a while back, but we've been working so hard on so many things it slipped my mind. What are your thoughts?"

Beatrice spoke eagerly with the fervor of someone just discovering an unexplored part of themselves long hushed under the constraints of convention and expectation. "It seems like we might have been doing a bit of art therapy in here though we don't call it that. I mean, I bring you my art, and sometimes it sets things in motion. Sometimes I don't even remember creating what I bring you. But the making of it calms me, and the sharing of it feels expansive and moves beyond the crippling critiquing of form and content.

The urgency I feel when one of my pieces reaches right off the page, grasping both of us with its need to be expressed and appreciated, is something I sense you feel as well. This kind of art is alive. It has a voice that radiates a kind of life force I never feel I attain when I am trying to 'make' a painting or drawing. There is no trying with this. It is pure. In fact, it is the purest form of creativity I've ever experienced, and you are with me, witnessing something almost impossible for me to describe and still sound sane."

She continued, "I feel more whole while I'm making art

from a place beyond intellect and training. I can't explain it except to say it feels raw and honest. And so, when Edwina handed me the article, and I learned about art therapy for the first time, and I read about the significance of making art for its own sake, for the value of pure expression without the gallery pressures and bullshit, I felt this shudder working through my body. This felt real. I felt real. And these past few days, I have been thinking deeply about my relationship with art, which had always been burdened with competition and angst. And I realize that is not what I want out of this relationship anymore. I want to go back to something I knew as a child where the act of making, the thing made and the purpose for it in the world were one and the same. And though I don't know exactly what I mean by all this, I think I need to find out. And so, I'm here, talking with you. And wondering what *you* think."

The room fell silent as Morgan thought about the outpouring she just heard. After a pause, she smiled and looked Beatrice straight in the eyes, "I think you would be a brilliant art therapist." then she fell into a rich silence again which was neither awkward nor impatient to be over. In fact, they both became synchronized in their breathing in a comfortable way, as if they were old friends sitting on a front porch listening to the sounds of nature.

Why?" She was open to the response. She longed for validation.

"Because, aside from the skills you have as an artist who has trained for many years, you are bright, curious, compassionate, and non-judgmental (except, of course, when it comes to you talking about the Troika!). You are working hard on your own healing journey. You have the capacity for empathy, and you are seeking to have a meaningful life. These reasons and others lead me to believe in your ability to become an art therapist."

They spent the remainder of the session discussing her feelings about possibly going to graduate school, starting a new career, and whether she was ready. She knew there was one more person she wanted to run it by. When she got home later in the day, she picked up the phone and made a call.

"Hey Vic, I have an idea…".

Victor was entirely supportive of her thoughts about training to become an art therapist. "Makes sense. And who knows what that may lead to?! Hey – let's aim for a playdate soon, ok?" and with that, he was off to some real estate meeting or other.

Beatrice chuckled at herself, wondering why she thought it was important to get his opinion and realized it was just the support of her old friend she had needed. She wanted someone who would still recognize her from the old loft days well into the trajectory of her future. The continuity of relationships for her generally was frail, and this one seemed worthy of maintaining.

Chapter Twenty

Beatrice did her research and decided there was only one art therapy program she was suited for, and so, one weekend in late December, she pulled together an art portfolio, an essay about her interest in becoming an art therapist, and a letter to the school in Cleveland asking for her transcripts and letters of reference to be sent to the graduate program director. Her living room looked like a hurricane had hit it from all the papers and art strewn about while she was putting it all together. She completed the required documentation, sent slides and application and essay for review, and waited.

It was unnerving for her because once she had decided to apply, she found herself wanting it more and more, which she knew was just her anxieties wreaking havoc on her body and mind. She had survived all these years of not being an art therapist. If this didn't work out, there would be something else (she'd say these things to herself in an effort to talk herself down from the cliff of worry that was keeping her up each evening in spite of the amazing bed she crawled into each night).

Eventually, a thin envelope arrived from the university, which panicked her because she had heard from folks who knew she had applied that a thin envelope was a rejection because the thick ones held paperwork related to acceptance, deposits, and other instructions around admissions procedures. She needed to calm herself down.

So, she placed the envelope on her pillow, drew a steamy hot bath, placed scented candles around the old 7-foot tub and set out a glass of shiraz (a special bottle Vic had brought one time a few years back). Her theory was to get as relaxed as possible and then open the envelope. Pampering seemed called for at a time like this when the envelope was so thin.

After her bath, she slipped on an oversized, old, clean, but paint-stained sweatshirt to honor her past and remind her of her artist roots. She told herself it was likely she did not get accepted. That would be okay. It had to be okay. And she still had roads ahead of her to explore. It would all be okay.

Beatrice wasn't sure why she wanted to be on her bed to see the contents of the envelope. She just knew she needed to be on her back with the ceiling looming above on the off chance she might drift up there as she had on so many occasions in her life when the stress became overwhelming (she knew more about this phenomena thanks to years spent with Morgan doing the therapy to better understand how trauma worked and what might trigger her into both floating above the scene and becoming invisible when necessary).

So, she climbed onto her bed and lay down dead center on the perfect mattress, which was adorned with earth-toned sheets and an off-white eyelet cover that let the brown peek through the holes. Her final thought before her index finger pried open the envelope was, “I love my bed so much,” and voila! She read the letter.

Dear Ms. Pons,

It is my great pleasure to inform you that you have been accepted into our Graduate Art Therapy Program. While this letter is but a brief note to congratulate you, more admissions and registration materials will follow in the ensuing weeks. They will include your student ID number along with other important information.

In the meantime, there is a required $500.00 deposit to hold your place for the next 2 weeks, which you will need to either bring to the Bursar's office or mail directly to the address below.

Welcome to the world of Art Therapy!

Sincerely,

Director of the Graduate Art Therapy Program

Beatrice Pons felt warm tears trickling down the sides of her face, landing close to her earlobes. She made it. She got in. She was still real. She told the wolf (who by now was part of her being as much as her hand holding the letter and for whom, thanks to therapy, she developed real affection) they both would be going to school, which made her laugh out loud because, as she thought to herself, "can you imagine if I showed up for classes the first day with the wolf next to me?"

She was giddy with delight and briefly thought to call Morgan but figured she would deliver the good news the next time she went for a session. She thought about calling Vic, which would have been okay, but he probably would have turned the thing into another reason to fuck, and that wasn't what she needed.

She also knew, with this next chapter in her life, she was in some way finally leaving her mother, who had NO PART in her future. And then she pulled her legs up to her chest, wrapping her arms around them and curling herself into a little ball as her tears descended into full-blown weeping because the one person on the planet, actually in the whole solar system, with whom she wished to share this news was gone. He left long ago and never tried to find her.

The next morning, Beatrice realized she had a problem which cast a pall over her excitement. She brought the letter to work that evening, and when Edwina jaunted down the long hallway with all the Mexican art and bounced into the Writers' Room, Beatrice told her the good news.

Attorney Borowski, famed for her advocacy, writings, public speaking, and overall character, reacted like a twelve-year-old girl who had just found out her best friend made it into the Junior Olympics. Edwina was definitely a celebrator and, as such, never let a reason for reinforcing the accomplishments of others pass unnoticed.

In fact, though her reputation was as a no-nonsense litigator and tough attorney to train under, all her junior associates over the years showed up for her *Winter Holiday Specials* – an annual party that was inclusive of staff, associates, folks from the mail room, proofreaders, and all their partners. She was known to have a judge or two, and some politicians showed up as well. The party was too large to hold in her offices, so it was moved to various hotel ballrooms over the years.

Edwina asked to see the letter and read it out loud as she savored every word like the most outrageously delicious spoon of chocolate mousse. When she got to the part about the $500.00 deposit, she moved quickly past that obstacle, sensing a bit of strain emanating from Beatrice. Before she left the room to go back to work, she turned to her and said, "Well done, Beatrice. Things always have a way of working out." And back up the hall, she went.

Beatrice talked about money in her next therapy session. Of course, she told Morgan about the acceptance, which was such wonderful news, but what dominated the conversation was her concern about paying the deposit and not losing her spot in the program. She only had another week and was able to piece together a little less than half of what she needed. She had thought about skipping therapy, but she needed her therapy. Then she'd see about scholarships and loans.

Edwina had been away at a conference for a few days, but Beatrice did leave her a note asking if she could put in some extra hours the following week to make up the difference she needed to get the deposit to the Bursar. Her secretary told her, "Attorney Borowski will meet with you Monday evening," which though not specifically a specific "yes", helped her hold on to the hope that she could get the additional hours.

Monday evening, while Beatrice was proofing a particularly annoying legal document with lots of footnotes and complex references, she heard footsteps in the hall and assumed it was Edwina. Instead, it was Miss. Moss, her secretary of thirty-some-odd years and, frankly, the most formidable guardian for keeping people from bothering Attorney Borowski. No one ever got past her.

"Ms. Pons, Attorney Borowski will see you now."

Beatrice's stomach curdled. She actually felt fearful going to her boss' inner sanctum and sensed this was not going to be a pleasant encounter. The long walk up the hall only served to augment her anxiety, so by the time she was ushered into the office, she was squeezing her hands to try to prevent herself from taking a trip up to the ceiling. "You can do this. You can stay for whatever comes. You do not need to take flight," echoed inside her head and for a moment, she didn't see or hear Edwina waving her to a huge red leather seat opposite her with a huge wooden desk actually carved by Salvador Dali (she had bought it at auction in Madrid decades ago) separating them.

"Please close the door, Miss Pons. Thank you. Welcome, Beatrice, to my favorite place on earth." This, of course, was somewhat of an exaggeration because Edwina was prone to hyperbole as part of her effervescent personality. But she did love her office very much.

She had all the awards, accolades, and degrees one would expect of such a luminary. But she also had two fountains (one in each corner of the room) with water delicately flowing down a pair of diminutive marble staircases, which she found soothing and calmed her down somewhat.

She loved the roly-poly art of Botero and had one maquette of a naked woman brushing her hair on a pedestal next to a rare etching by Picasso of sad people during his Blue Period. The light in the room was fairly low, though there were plants and books and an odd pair of ancient scissors on her desk. The whole place was eclectic, to say the least. It felt magical.

"I hope my calling you in here didn't scare you, Bea (she rarely heard anyone use that name and coming from Edwina, it was extra sweet), but I wanted to make this chat perfectly private." Beatrice nodded. She was at a loss for words.

"Ok, here's the deal. I'm the one who got the idea of art therapy into your head. I'm the one who told you that you cannot be a proofreader all your life. I'm going to be the one who lends you money to go to this excellent, albeit expensive, graduate Art Therapy program. You will pay me back after you graduate and have been working for a while. The interest rate will be zero – the ONLY 'interest' I am interested in is you keeping me informed on how things are going. And, if possible, and I'm still alive, I'd like to attend your graduation when the time comes. What do you think of that?"

And with the speed it takes a heart to beat, the deal was struck. Beatrice Pons was on her way to graduate school.

Chapter Twenty-One

Two and a half years flew by for Beatrice, the art therapy student. Her time was completely accounted for between classes, clinical training, proofreading work, therapy (though sessions were drastically cut back so Beatrice could save money and the initial crisis was well behind her) and making friends. She was devouring information, expanding her knowledge about psychology, feminism, humanism, art as an agent of healing, trauma, symbolism, metaphor, diagnoses, and cultures outside her own limited worlds of Ohio and New York. The list for growth was open-ended, and the possibilities were endless.

She took advantage of every opportunity to dive into the subject of trauma, which intersected substantially with events of her own life. To really treat trauma meant to deconstruct prevalent attitudes about mental illness – like being viewed as crazy instead of incredibly clever to, as in her case, adapt and become invisible, not needing to breathe and developing the amazing skill of flying to the rafters when necessary.

She learned that many esteemed healers had survived their own trauma and gone on to thrive. She was lucky enough to attend workshops and take courses with persons in her student years and beyond. Trauma training flourished in church basements, classrooms, living rooms, weekend retreats and other venues not typically meant for such purposes. Established trauma therapists, neuroscientists, art and drama therapists, psychiatrists, philosophers, and writers (especially feminists) created a culture of exploration, all with the goal of digging into the realm of restoring broken and dispirited souls. It was a vibrant time to become an art therapist.

Beatrice believed the work to be a calling. She was inspired to believe the intersection of art, trauma, words, images, imagination, hope, trust, safety, grounding, systems, relationships, and dignity were all available for the purposes of healing. The skilled practitioner needs only to be guided by the needs of the client. To understand the needs, it was crucial to listen, observe, and support.

Beatrice made lasting friendships during those days. Though she was older than many of her classmates, her cohort consisted of others equally devoted, seeking ways to bring healing to those who were suffering, helping to lift the darkness of emotional pain.

Her group talked endlessly about art therapy over chef salads, and tofu shakes at the local diner. There was a room in the back that rarely was rarely used. The 'Gal's', as they called themselves (there were no men in her year), then chatted up a storm about everything from the profession to family matters. Even decades later, when all had gone their separate ways and they really only saw each other at conferences here and there or when someone was visiting relatives in town, they'd pick up the conversation as if no time had gone by at all.

Twenty-five years after graduation, when one of their group had died after a long-drawn-out illness, the group met for a final reunion at the old diner, each woman bringing a 4" x 4" drawing to share with each other in honor of their missing classmate. Though it was a beautiful gesture, no doubt each was likely wondering, "Who'll be next" as humans cannot help but compare themselves to others under such circumstances.

By the time Beatrice was ready to graduate, she had actually quite an expertise in the field of trauma and, of course, believed she was prepared to begin working as an art therapist for real, for money. Graduation was a week away, and she knew the terms of Edwina's financial support would kick in with her first job. She was looking forward to paying her back and planned on telling her about an amazing job offer she got from a Catholic Hospital on the Lower East Side.

It would mean she could no longer proofread for a living, and she worried about leaving the shelter of Edwina's wings where she had been so safe and comfortable. But it was time to step fully into the profession, and she was certain Edwina Borowski would be tickled she landed such a great job.

Graduation for her college (the university had so many

students and colleges they held separate ceremonies on separate days) took place on one of those perfect May mornings when the sky shimmers electric blue and the perfectly formed clouds drift slowly across the sky. Beatrice Pons stepped onto the bleacher with tiny seats with cap, hood, and gown in hand and slipped on her graduation regalia.

Gigantic speakers were dispersed throughout the surrounding park. Guests with their required tickets were seated opposite the graduates on the other side of the fountain separating the two sections. Suddenly "Pomp and Circumstance" belted through the air, and people seated closest to the speakers felt the sound waves vibrate against their chests. Everyone rose as the administrators and faculty followed the trustees, who were led by the processional Grand Marshall carrying the mace emblazoned with the University seal. They marched around the fountain to the seating chairs between visitors and graduates.

For the next three hours, the graduation address was given, the name of every graduating student was read aloud, and diplomas were symbolically handed out (the real ones would be sent the following week when all the grades were entered and signed off on by the deans and president.)

As Beatrice heard her name amplified above the crowd, she thought she heard a gentle laugh, deep and oaky, emanate from the sky above. Her eyes darted upwards, and she searched the puffy clouds passing overhead. She felt a certainty her father had passed across the heavens and finally come to find her.

Chapter Twenty-Two

Beatrice had been instructed by Miss. Moss is to meet Attorney Borowski at the Peony Club for a celebratory tea at 4:00 pm after graduation. This was a highly exclusive women's club, initially created by some wealthy women in the late 1800s who were avid gardeners. All the decor sported themes of peonies, and of course, no matter the time of year, each table was set with fresh peonies adorning the white table linen and crystal glassware.

Edwina Borowski rarely used her membership as she found the environment stiff and elite. In fact, she only joined the club because, as a young attorney, she had been denied admittance. She had been walking down the street and, realizing she was hungry, figured she try this 'Peony' place. She walked in and, without having the proper identification as a member, was promptly walked out and left hungry on the sidewalk. Not one to let a rude action go unpunished, she vowed to herself that one day, she would join the damn place and force them to feed her.

Ten years later, after her magnificent rise to fame, she strategically befriended the vice president as well as the treasurer of the board. Then she applied for membership. Actually, she applied for the highest level of membership, the Platinum Watering Can, and when the president of the board seemed a bit hesitant, those two, whom Edwina had been prepping for this moment, said, "Do you know who you are thinking of rejecting?? She is Edwina Adella Borowski RN, Esq! Are you crazy?" and so as not to be shamed into exposing her own ignorance about the applicant, the president put her finger to her chin and stated, "Oh, yes, of course. I had her confused with and a woman named Bialosky who would, indeed have been wholly inappropriate. Yes, we certainly want Attorney Borowski. Splendid".

While brunch and a 5:00 pm dinner were only served on certain weekdays days at the club, the really big deal was to come for tea on Saturday afternoons. Seating was limited, and reservations were required for this feast of sandwiches, tiny cakes, cookies, cheeses, and bread of all kinds. A single flute of floral champagne was presented (gratis) to each adult at the table when they first sat down.

A long narrow pink leather menu (embossed with an engraved peony on the back) would be brought to each table with select choices of international teas listed and bits of history and taste descriptions next to each entry. The writing was in such a diminutive script that it was difficult to read, and more times than not, the server recommended one tea over another, and that was that.

Most interesting was the dining seating. Each table hugged the walls with the center of the room open to the clopping sound of ladies' high heels clopping against the highly polished parquet floors. Each wall had painted murals depicting different gardens of peonies. Edwina, not one to hold back, told Beatrice as she started sitting down, "Aren't the walls ghastly?" in fact, Beatrice had thought the whole place seemed to be in a time warp, ornate and slightly musty with time.

What was also odd was the chair Beatrice was forced to take, for lack of any option, was not opposite Edwina but right next to her. They sat side-by-side.

"I know this must seem bizarre sitting this way. It was a relic of the past when a lady's backside was not to be seen by the rest of the room. So, here we are, next to each other. You know, in spite of the silliness of this place, it is quiet. Also, I think it makes the president a bit crazy every time I come here. Do you know, she didn't want to admit me? Can you imagine?" and with that, Attorney Borowski let out a peel of laughter that turned a few heads in her direction.

The tea chart came and went. The tiers of miniature sandwiches, pastries etc., arrived. Butterballs were rolled with scored cross-hatching designs behind peony impressions stamped into the soft surface. The silverware was heavy and substantial. The fork, knife and spoon all seemed way too large for the food. Beatrice joked that she expected to see the White Rabbit scurry by their table "Late for a date".

After they ate a bit, Edwina folded her napkin, not because she had finished eating, but because she wanted a pause, a moment to bring some attention to their being together. "You know Bea (she rarely called her that, but this felt right for the moment), I really am so impressed with you. I mean, if you don't mind, I am *proud* of you. When I saw your class in the bleachers, about to graduate, that was just thrilling. When I heard your name...marvelous".

Beatrice was filled with something she imagined was beyond admiration and appreciation for this woman. It was more likely in the category of love though she was not sure what kind of love. Not that it mattered. Edwina had believed in her enough to invest in her education. Now she was about to work as an art therapist in a really good hospital in NYC. She was about to embark on the next chapter of her life, trying to help others heal from their wounds of trauma.

And she was going to be able to repay the loan to her donor in regular installments over the next three years. As she started to speak, Edwina made a signal to stop her.

Then she handed Beatrice Pons a white envelope with a tiny painter's palette crudely drawn over the seal. Bea opened it up to read a quasi-legal document that she had never seen nor proofread before:

'I, Edwina Adella Borowski RN, Esq, on this 10th day of May, do hereby relieve Beatrice Pons of any and all indebtedness to me

for any reason whatsoever. Having satisfied the terms of the debt, completing her graduate studies as an art therapist (with Distinction no less!), Ms. Pons is free to give her skills, heart, and gifts to those in need as she sees fit.'

Bea, I couldn't be prouder of you if you were my daughter,

Love,

Winnie"

Chapter Twenty-Three

And so, the years went by, though more slowly than those of her time in graduate school, and they were rich with opportunities within her chosen profession. She worked for three years as planned in the psychiatric unit of the Catholic hospital accruing the requisite hours and skills to become registered and then licensed as an art therapist.

For a number of years thereafter, she worked part-time from special grants giving her opportunities to work at homeless shelters, in school settings, at agencies serving people with special needs, and even briefly in a prison setting. She taught graduate courses in her alma mater and then was asked to teach at other universities. She published papers about trauma and spoke at conferences.

Over a period of four more years, she did international work in Europe, the Middle East and Thailand. On one trip, she made it to Bali and imagined Vic had visited the same open market where he found her carved headboard that he lovingly had brought back to her apartment. She loved traveling but found the remuneration erratic and insufficient.

With experience under her belt, she opened a private practice. She let her friends, the 'Gals,' know about her new office, and they celebrated when they met one Thanksgiving in New York. She informed her therapist, Dr. Fine, (whom she had not seen for a number of years but would return to after Jenna entered her life and sent her into a temporary tailspin – trauma is a pesky operator, and it can take a lifetime of vigilance not to land back in its clutches) about her practice opening. She heard back right away that she should expect to get some referrals for children of her adult clients who she thought might benefit from art therapy.

She kept Edwina updated. She responded that she was thrilled to hear the news and that she was retiring from the law and thinking about moving back to Mexico before she was too old to enjoy it. She hoped Bea would come to visit her there one day, though sadly, that was not to happen.

Her private practice thrived, and Beatrice found herself somewhat in a clientele niche. More and more, she was working with children whose parents sought her skills and discretion. Often the parents had experienced their own abuse as children and were in their own therapy. They were highly concerned about the well-being of their children.

Referrals for the children most frequently came from other therapists – many of whom Beatrice didn't personally know had heard of her. She loved her work and felt she was good at it.

As time went on, parents expressed they were less than eager to travel to her office. They had excuses about schedules and traffic. Mainly, the more well-known the parents were, the more concern they had about the loss of privacy and exposure to the public. "I wouldn't want people to learn the Emmy award-winning star of *No Harps for Harriette* has a child in therapy. Can we do sessions at home?"

Beatrice, at first, was ambivalent about going to private homes to do art therapy. She contacted the 'Gals' for opinions. Would any of them do that? Had they done it? How does it work? She also asked her supervisor of many years about the ethics of it. She consulted Morgan. It seemed fairly unanimous that as long as the boundaries were held, that the clinical time and space remained well defined, it might be the safest way to see children who, if they could not come without risk of exposure, would not have the therapy at all.

And so, she tried a few sessions in the homes of two young clients. It worked very well. In fact, seeing the children in their living environments gave her much information about their lives she could not otherwise glean. Over time, she shifted her work to home visits. A year later, she only took clients who wanted therapy in their homes and gave up the office entirely.

Chapter Twenty-Four

Beatrice, who had been lost in thought for heaven knows how long, snapped back to her 71-year-old self. It was not uncommon these days for her to lose track of time and catch herself drifting through thoughts and memories. She imagined this pause in her mind was a little longer than usual because she felt stiff from standing hunched over.

She took a final gaze through the sharp light of the open refrigerator and stepped back. Nothing was calling to her to be eaten. Even though she had a number of good choices to pick from, her appetite was gone. She shut the door, listening for the familiar whirring vacuum of the last air being sucked out, sealing the door shut to maximize the freshness of stored food (one of those quality-of-life improvements her reasonable success afforded her).

She looked over at the wall clock above the sink, surprised at how late it actually was. Now she was just too tired to eat or do much of anything else. Tomorrow would be a full day. She had three clients to visit, and their homes zigzagged across town.

Lingering a moment longer, she mused that she really did love her work, but she was getting worn out. Even taking a ritual bath before bed would take more effort than she could muster, So as she stiffly ambled down the long hall towards her bedroom, Beatrice peeled off her work clothes, tossing them in the hamper as she passed by the bathroom, and landed naked, dead center in the middle of the bed. She'd shower in the morning.

PART II

During

Chapter Twenty-Five

Darby lazily lifted his head as warm rays of morning light awakened him from a deep slumber. A 17th-century stained-glass window with the image of Madonna and child projected a brilliant collage of colors across his body, shimmering confetti flakes of light on every other object in the room.

His feline nostrils twitched as they were aroused by a teasing aroma wafting into the room from an unknown source nearby. He surmised something yummy was cooking on a stove. He inhaled, confident that his morning hunger would be satisfied soon. Stretching his legs until his sharp black claws protruded beyond the white fur of his paws, he rolled himself onto his feet, digging slightly into the silky cushion he had slept on, leaving tiny pin-prick impressions in the soft fabric. He arched his spine and checked out the four corners of the room.

Floor-to-ceiling leatherbound books smelling musty with age and probably barely opened for who knows how long covered three of the four walls – the window, recessed into a faux castle wall supporting a white marble windowsill, projected sprinkles of vibrant colors. The ledge was wide enough to support a spinning globe (Darby found it odd that the oceans were all painted black and imagined having some fun later turning that big ball round and round with his front paws), two medieval wrought iron lamps (16th-century

Spanish candelabras rewired for electricity) and a few curious looking hand carved Japanese ivory knick-knacks in shapes of contorted animals and rotund people. He envisioned, with amusement, what great sport it would be to hear the clack, clack, clack of each of them tumbling to the floor as he knocked them off the sill.

To Darby, a book room such as this seemed to be an unlikely choice for a cat bed, but bipeds were often coming up with weird ideas about things cats and dogs would like. The evening before, when the Lady opened his crate and invited him to make himself comfy, she ushered him to an ornate pagoda-style cat bed centered between four overstuffed silk chairs. Encouraging him to jump onto the bed for a photo of his first night 'home,' Darby simply rejected the invitation as he had no intention of sleeping on or even hanging about that thing. He preferred to choose his own spot for sleeping and decided that the big green tufted satiny chair was more to his liking.

The Lady instructed her person (not a fan of cats), who was clearly in charge of the downstairs (yes, there were multiple floors to this place), that Darby was not to be disturbed. "Give him the run of the house downstairs, and please make sure his box and food are ready for him now that he is home. He'll meet Lindy tomorrow." And with that, the lady passed through the oak-carved egg and dart door and sprinted deftly up the grand staircase to the upper floor.

The Lady person neither cared for cats nor liked the situation she was in. She had no idea how to restrict Darby from ascending the stairs. So, she decided to lock him in the library for the night and then open it very early the next morning when no one would be the wiser. Darby was tired, so he didn't care much about the closed door. He just wanted to curl up on the great big chair, which he did, falling asleep to the lemony scent of well-oiled wood and unopened tomes.

After his morning stretch, Darby wondered where the litterbox was located, so he sauntered to the great big door and, with a mighty scratch, pried it open and entered the grand foyer to find it. Impressed by the enormity of the space, he figured other cats must be living here as well since there was so much room. Worried about this possibility, he kept his guard up because stranger cats could be highly unpredictable. He much preferred the company of dogs as they were generally more afraid of him than he was of them. It was easy to make friends with dogs and gain their respect and even boss them around. It took much more effort to get other cats to know their place, and they tended to make the mistake of judging him to be aggressive or hostile because of his fur situation.

Nothing could be further from the truth. During times when his fur fell from his body, his muscles would ooze a bloody discharge. When the skin around his eyes was raw, he imagined he appeared like a wounded prize fighter he once saw on a magazine cover in some house he had lived in so long ago. All he had were hazy memories of horrified persons' faces as they remarked how disgusting he looked. They said he smelled foul which was something about which he had no control, and at those times, he would hunt for dark spaces to keep the indignity of his appearance and odor as far away from offending others as possible.

At those times, he would summon up the courage to try to ignore his suffering though he never really could get past the deep shame he carried about his disfigurement. When he felt an outbreak coming on, he did his best to tough it out though admittedly, the stress of it all was wearing him down.

It was during one of those raging episodes that the seemingly infinite depth of the black pupil of Darby's right eye took on the look of an exploding star spreading golden specks across the universe as its whirling center was being sucked ever downward into the deepest and darkest hole imaginable. Across his singular electric-blue iris, stardust seemed present, radiating in timeless swirls across its surface, which left many people wondering if he could see with that defective eye at all. Some folks reacted in horror when they looked closely at it. Others, who were less put off by it, found it mystifying and curious. Darby believed it was a sign of his magical presence in this world. It was a gift to have such an eye and an indication of the importance of his life. It lifted his spirits to imagine his little eye was like a map of the solar system, which was something he knew about from a story he had once heard on the radio.

Those people, not willing to care any longer for the ailing cat, decided one day to put him out on the street. They were not altogether cruel as they remembered their own affection for Darby as a kitten well before his condition rendered them unable to find their own compassion, which, having been pushed to an extreme, seemed to have evaporated with the messy challenges of caring for such an infirmed creature. They were completely overwhelmed, and he had to assure himself, "Not everybody can love a cat like me."

They expressed their sorrow that "it didn't work out," which left Darby feeling exceedingly upset and quite apprehensive about what was to become of him. So, finding a suitable cardboard box, they dropped him gently inside, tucking the flaps under each other to keep it closed. Then, with a fat black marker, they scrawled his name on top.

The Man of the house lifted the box onto his right shoulder and began walking randomly about the City for an hour. Chatting continually to Darby, who was queasy from the movement and concerned about his future, the man said trite things like, "Hey dude, you'll be ok. You know you are kind of gross. Ha! Great Halloween costume you got there! Anyway fella, good luck to you" nonstop until he appeared to have found the right spot. And with a final farewell, he lowered the box, with the abandoned and terrified tuxedo cat inside, next to a red standpipe. The man paused, having nothing clever or particularly kind to say at this point, and turned his back to the box. He walked away, muttering, “Take it easy, buddy.”

Fortunately, luck was with Darby that afternoon. The chance meeting with the young veterinarian altered the course of everything for Darby, and soon, instead of scorn and abandonment, the cat was treated with medical attention and kindness. New words were coming his way, helping him feel, for the first time in his life, valued. “He’s so brave,” “Look at his courage,” and “He’s a lesson for us all” made his heart sing, and he knew his life’s purpose was to bring comfort to others. No doubt he would be just the right cat for a little silent girl named Lindy to love.

Chapter Twenty-Six

Exploring across the foyer, Darby found a small bathroom hidden beneath the grand spiral staircase. Its oak door fit perfectly into the curve of the steps, practically disappearing except for a highly polished brass lock and handle contrasting with the heavy darkness of the well-oiled wood.

The powder room door was propped open with a brick wrapped in an embroidered cover with stitched details of ladybugs and leaves adorning it (something the Lady had stitched to give the place a more homey feel). A tiny, shaded fixture emitted light from inside a tiny room. Stepping through the opening, Darby noticed a diminutive golden porcelain sink to the right of the toilet. In between both stood an unused litter box freshly filled for his needs.

He was growing more confident he might be the only cat in the house because he neither smelled nor saw any signs of other cat presence whatsoever. "A whole box of my own! All mine, all mine," ran through his mind. This was far beyond his wildest dreams, and as he stepped into the center of his very own litterbox and relieved himself, Darby imagined he was a prince, and this place was his kingdom for sure.

How he landed in this home was plain good old luck. He had had his share of bad luck in his life (he believed both types of luck were randomly distributed without any plan or intention). The fact that his black and white fur would periodically fall right down to the muscle of his body, leaving him vulnerable to infection from the elements causing him to suffer painful sores and possibly die, certainly stacked up as bad luck.

On the other hand, he had tremendously good luck the day the young veterinarian, in a rush to get to work, happened upon the cardboard box propped up next to the sidewalk standpipe. Hearing a scratching sound and noticing the name "Darby" scrawled in huge black letters along the outside flaps, he peered inside and found a half-hairless tuxedo cat, hungry and shivering. The doctor gasped in shock and then cried out, "What the fuck is this?" immediately shut the lid and ran the two blocks to the animal hospital with the cat madly clawing and hissing inside.

Darby figured he was brought into the clinic just when he was about to use up another one of his few remaining lives. After being poked and prodded, having blood drawn, and being ogled and gawked over by the entire staff, it was declared he might do well living in the hospital basement, where he could be closely monitored. The dogs and cats who were in recovery from their operations and procedures might enjoy his presence. He would never be alone, and all the folks working in the clinic could keep an eye on him (mostly, they would pet him and bring him treats).

There, month after month, Darby survived and thrived. He

liked the basement, seeing everyone wake up groggy from surgery, visiting each animal, smelling who they were, rubbing the cages leaving a trail of his scent with each patient. It was warm, he had food, and he got a lot of attention.

Occasionally a mouse or two would show up, and a wild chase would ensue, which unfortunately usually ended in the demise of the terrified mouse. Darby's hunting instincts were truly fulfilled at those times. And though he never thought much about the plight of the mice, Darby's spirit swelled with a growing sense of purpose (something he had never experienced before) in bringing comfort to other dogs and cats who were healing and lonely.

All the docs, techs, and aides in the animal hospital loved Darby. Really the only problem he had was the issue of his fur dropping off his skin at random times and worries about infection. Everyone remarked that his eye had the darkest pupil they'd ever seen, and its sky-blue iris showered with golden specs like tiny stars inhabiting a universe on his eyeball was most unusual. Darby knew his defects bothered others more than himself. After all, he could not see his odd eye, and he did not need to look at his own body.

Sometimes a tech would remark, "Look, Darby's lost his whiskers again," and everyone would come running over to see the pitiful pile of his whiskers scattered on an examination counter or some other handy flat surface. For humans, such physical failings could be very unsettling. But such moments rarely bothered Darby, and his philosophy was 'be damned' for those who pitied him.

It did discourage him at times because the outbreaks could be painful, and they always made him tired. It was a disruption to his usual pattern of curiosity and playfulness. And though he was too proud to admit it, sometimes he felt embarrassed because he thought he looked weak.

During the ensuing year, the docs and staff tried to get to the bottom of his balding problem. Their efforts included changing his food multiple times (Darby hated the one called *Diet Plan Plain* because it tasted like soaked cardboard), injecting steroids into him, drawing blood to make sure he wasn't becoming diabetic, and exploratory test after test.

As a last resort (and in a moment of brilliance by the young doc who initially found him), they took Darby one hundred forty-seven miles upstate to Dr. Scales (that really was his name), *Fish and Cat Allergist*. He ran sixty tests on his body, blood, and fur. When the results came back, everyone was shocked. Darby was basically allergic to everything in the world. He would need immunotherapy for the rest of his life, and that meant he could never go outside or most anywhere else again. And he would need a lot of money to support his lifelong requirement for expensive medication.

The doc was depressed that there was no real cure though

there was a way to mostly keep the allergies under control. He felt it was a grim and gloomy future for this cat living in the basement of a clinic in endless need of costly medical support because, by now, their relationship was more than just patient/doctor. The veterinarian felt true affection for Darby, but he could not keep him for his own. His wife and son had their own allergies, which severely limited what kind of animals could be in their house. Years before Darby's arrival, it was determined that freshwater fish would be all the animal life the veterinarian's family could tolerate. But all that aside, the cost of medications would be in the thousands of dollars – a price nobody he knew could afford.

Just when the young doc had plunged into his saddest reflection about Darby's future, the universe provided a miracle that might also be considered a coincidence or happy accident that changed the course of everything for this tough little tuxedo cat. Because, as fate would have it, the 'Lady' who was extremely wealthy and lived in a giant duplex apartment a few blocks north of the clinic, had been thinking about adopting, on the recommendation of the art therapist with whom her daughter was in treatment, a tuxedo cat for her daughter who had stopped speaking for almost two years.

Chapter Twenty-Seven

The little girl had retreated into silence at age five, withholding speaking to anyone in the world except her mother and, only then, speaking minimally in a secretive manner with her hand cupped over her mouth so no one else could see her lips move. The art therapist, who had been working with the Lady's now seven-year-old daughter, Lindy, for one year, suggested, in her clinical opinion, that the child be given a pet to talk to and love.

And, because Lindy's art therapist, Beatrice Pons, had witnessed the child drawing picture after picture of a black and white cat, she suggested to her mother to find a cat with similar coloring and markings.

Beatrice wondered what meaning and possible clues the little girl's fixation on this image might hold held to her muteness. And so, not expecting an actual verbal response yet intuiting the cat image was very significant for the child. Beatrice asked, "Lindy, why do you like to draw black and white kitties so much?" The child looked away.

The minute she asked the rejected question, Beatrice internally admonished herself. This 'why' question held too many complex vulnerabilities for a child so young and fearful. Open-ended questions generally were effective in opening up the conversation. But, in this case, it was effectively no different than intrusively asking, "Lindy, why don't you speak?" which the child would never want or be able to answer. For Lindy, 'why' questions likely felt as if she were at the helm of a rudderless sailboat tossing about in a vast roiling sea of inadequate responses. How could she know why? Why should she know why? Beatrice had endangered the metaphor.

On her way home after the session, Beatrice thought to herself, "This is the nature of trauma. Words cease to have contextual meaning, they become weaponized traps to snare you and leave you for dead, but you are very much alive, watching, always watching, trying to out clever their subversive purpose, which is meant to appear innocent but beneath that illusion, they set out to destroy you and any remnant of your will to be whole". And then she conjured her mother's terrifying mouth, lies pouring out like bile staining her flashing teeth.

She knew her attunement was off. What was this child saying with her silence and the relentless need to draw these particular cats? What might help draw *her* out? There's a need she's trying her hardest to express.

In their next session, Beatrice let the art speak directly to her. She told Lindy she was going to listen very hard to what the cat wanted to say. The child was riveted on the therapist and the drawing in her hands. Beatrice sat for a good ten minutes in silence, just taking in what the drawing needed to say. Then, in one of those rare moments when a therapist plain old gets it right, Beatrice said, “Lindy, the kitty wants to know if you would like to *have* a cat of your very own?” whereupon, the little girl, who hadn’t spoken a word to the therapist since the day they met, took Beatrice’s fingers, and gave them a tender squeeze. She then moved her young hand to her therapist’s cheek and whispered near her ear, “Yes, please.”

Beatrice would never forget the warmth of her words that ever so slightly tickled the delicate soft hairs of her skin with her child's breath.

And so Beatrice advocated for her little girl and suggested to her mother that a cat for Lindy might be helpful from a therapeutic perspective, and added, “It has to be black and white.” Lindy’s mother readily agreed as she really did want to help her little girl feel safe enough to speak normally with others and loved her enough to help heal the wounds that silenced her initially. A pet for Lindy made perfect sense. It never occurred to the therapist that the chosen cat would need medical assistance for life and a sky-blue eye that resembled exploding stars floating about in a universe. But that was her mother – Astrid was not hung up on those kinds of details.

Chapter Twenty-Eight

Darby was hungry, so he followed the scent of the food, which led him back through the foyer, past the library, through a formal dining room, behind a tri-fold embroidered screen (he made a mental note about how well it would serve as a scratching post) into the butler's kitchen. There he saw the same vaguely unpleasant person he had seen the night before with the Lady. She looked up from folding napkins (this reminded him of the veterinary wear hospital staff folding kerchiefs with something calming sprayed on them for every patient who came there) and proceeded to inform someone working in another room next to this one, "Darby's here." "Go on, Darby, go see Cook. And stay off my counters, you hear me?" He really did not care for her much.

He entered the next space and saw a hefty woman (older than both the Lady and Cranky – he had decided on her name the split second she scolded him for something he hadn't even done yet) wearing all white, tip-to-toe. "Hello, Mr. Darby. Pleased to meet you. My name is 'Cook' though I should imagine that might be difficult for you to actually say!" and with that, she let out peals of laughter, and Darby found himself rubbing up next to her, circling her legs as she bent down and scratched behind his ears. "Oh, Mr. Darby, I have something I just made for you," and she scraped some perfectly sauteed chicken livers onto a plate with little posies painted around its edges. As she placed it on the ground next to a crystal bowl of water, she added, "If they are too hot, just wait. No one will ever take food away from you in this house!"

Darby stood completely still as he stared at the steaming hot food on the posy plate. This truly was the most amazing smell of his lifetime, and when he could wait no longer, he gently began to pull the organs apart. The scent rising from the plate in this palace was fit for a king – though he knew better than to allow himself to become too arrogant.

It was far better to be a prince, to have freedom and no responsibilities. Being a prince meant he could retreat into himself. He could come and go at will. He could have the good stuff and walk away from the burdens. A king could never fully trust anyone, could never be completely natural with others, or be assured of being king forever. Kings were always waiting to be de-throned. But a prince, a prince, could live the full range of life and not worry because others wanted to be king, not a prince. And that was Darby's intention.

Chapter Twenty-Nine

While Darby was exploring his new digs and being treated like a prince in the kitchen, Beatrice awoke from the kind of sleep resembling a jetlag stupor where the body is overwhelmed by inertia, and the brain starts to slowly take in its surroundings through sounds and sight. First, she heard the clanging and hissing of the radiator priming itself to start warming the bedroom. She'd forgotten to set the alarm or pull the shades, so when the sun began to rise, the soft light of morning dawn eased across her face, enticing her to open her eyes very slowly as they adjusted to the growing light of a new day. Her brain gradually informed her it was time to get up.

Sometime during the night, she crawled under the rose-pink floral duvet and curled into a fetal position to get warm. Now, she briefly pulled the comforter up over her face and took in the scent of her own naked body, which she found soothing, sort of grounding, in spite of needing a shower. "This is the way humans ought to wake up," she thought and, with that, tossed the duvet completely aside, rolled onto her back, and realized she needed to pee.

She wished she could put that off longer but knew that at her age, it was better not to wait. So, Beatrice slithered her body towards the edge of her amazing mattress (still in magnificent shape after all these years), lowered her feet to the parquet floor, slowly sat up so she wouldn't get dizzy, stood up, and stretched her arms above her head and walked over to the bathroom.

Her ritual was to let the water run a bit before washing her hands because the hot water pipes were still cool. The same technique was applied to the shower water, which needed to run for a few minutes to grow warm. Shivering, she waited to pull the terry shower curtain aside until she saw the mirror on the medicine cabinet obscured with soft clouds of steam. Then, and only then, was she assured the shower was warm enough to step in and soap up.

As she became more alert, her thoughts went to the clients she was going to see today and to which parts of town she would be traveling. While she dried herself off, she suddenly realized she was super hungry, having skipped dinner the night before. She wanted a real breakfast today.

Chapter Thirty

According to Lindy's mother, Astrid (second wife of Easton Sinclair), she had been a perfectly 'normal' child for the first four years of her life. She met all the usual milestones for rolling and sitting and talking (babbling), and walking, and everything seemed to be going very well for the only daughter of Easton Sinclair.

His first wife had died in a tragic skiing accident while vacationing in Grindelwald, Switzerland. Disastrously, the life of his wealthy young wife, whose years attending Swiss boarding school had prepared her for excellence on the slopes as well as trained her to develop an uncanny ability to catch an equally moneyed young man to be her husband, was lost when she dared to take on the advanced Black Diamond trail of the Jungfrau without determining if it was safe.

The day had been exquisite, with the snow glistening like jewels encrusted in the whiteness all around. She felt exotic and free and ready for the long descent down towards the tree line. The air was crisp, and she noticed the little hairs in her nostrils standing rigid. She adjusted her sunshades to protect her eyes from windburn, and though she should be wearing a helmet, she just didn't feel like it.

She had a certain defiant core that Easton found both attractive but also irritating. From time to time, he felt somewhat insecure, a little worried she might leave him because she (like him) had all the money in the world and could do so. She could take off any time without her depending upon him for anything, including love. He knew, at some primal level, that their attachment to each other was not equal.

He tried to comfort himself with the thought, "She's with me because she wants to be, not for my money," which was wonderful at first until the reality set in that she really could leave at will. This condition, along with the undeniable fact that he was more in love with her than she was with him, made him hesitant to set limits around her independence though she rarely pushed those boundaries too far. But just knowing she could promote fantasies of locking her away in his family mansion. He felt ashamed about such thoughts though he did nothing to discourage them.

This ski trip was one of those times he had directly requested that she not leave New York. He did not really have a good reason, and every time she asked, "Why," he came up with lame responses about family obligations, finance meetings, etc. – everything except the truth, which was he was afraid. He was experiencing a non-specific fear in his bones and did not want her to go. He was desperately afraid to lose her love.

And so, standing at the head of the icy trail on this most glorious Swiss morning, filled by the brilliant sun lighting the shimmering way, Easton Sinclair's first wife shoved off by herself, following the few other highly skilled skiers who had headed down the Black Diamond route minutes before her. It was all so wonderful, so magnificent until it wasn't.

The surreal cracking sound was unmistakable as it pierced the mountain air. Then all hell broke loose as a white-out claimed her vision, and the force of snow collapsing down and inward from the mountain's edge buried the few people who had come early for a magnificent adventure under more and more deadly snow until all that remained of Easton's first wife was the hope they would find her body in the spring.

Easton struggled with the guilt of a man who believed deep down he should have done more to convince his first wife to abandon to ski trip and stay home. He could have forced the issue, risked her displeasure or even anger. But she would be alive. She might have put up such a fuss that she would have decided to leave him, but she would not be dead. He believed he had failed her because he was a coward who did not proclaim, "Love me as much as I love you. Please stay".

And so, like a child's mind needs to pretend it has superpowers over things well beyond its control, Easton believed in the darkest part of himself that he had caused her death. In the heaves of private grief, he made two vows that he applied for the rest of his life: to never feel deeply again and to significantly add to his fortune and inherited wealth.

His family and friends tried to support him through those dark days immediately following her declared death. During the day, he threw himself into work. In the evenings, he socialized, playing the field with no intention of developing any kind of serious love interest. But mostly, in the short run, he was silently managing the agony of waiting until the spring to lock her body in the family crypt.

Chapter Thirty-One

Astrid, his second wife, did not come from money. Both her parents' families owned small apple orchard farms in upstate New York, whereas children, they grew up on opposite sides of the same country road. The landscape was bucolic, with the splendor of all four seasons played out year after year. Life was simple, predictable. The junior and senior public schools had days off that coordinated with the first day of fishing, hunting, or harvesting times. On weekends children did chores and then played outdoors until the sun went down. During rainy weather, they'd get together and build basement forts or put on plays. People really seemed to get along.

Nobody was particularly worried about what either of Astrid's parents did with their spare time. They had been playmates their entire lives, and so it happened that one day, while hanging out under an old craggy apple tree that produced the most succulent variety of "Upstate Reds," both sixteen-year-olds realized at the exact same moment that they loved each other.

Both shared the dream to marry and build a future together. Coincidently, they shared a similar vision of plans that did not include working in the apple orchards (though they really were super fond of the fruit and had tremendous respect for its cultivation). They anticipated this fantasy of leaving the farms behind might be a bit of a problem for both families as, no doubt, with their union, the expectation likely would have been that both farms would become one.

But their dreams were set on other horizons. Their wedding at age eighteen was witnessed by both families, including parents, sisters and brothers, aunts and uncles, and cousins, as well as some high school friends and two teachers who had known them since third grade. Shortly after the ceremony, the champagne, and cake, the newlyweds informed the celebrating crowd that when the harvesting season was finished, they would be moving away in order to 'start new lives together,' which was a notion unheard of for their parent's generation.

Even the siblings and cousins seemed confused by the thought of starting life over. It made no sense when there was a perfectly good life to be had here. The teachers and former classmates, while remaining silent, secretly were a little more open to the daring of their plan. In fact, there may have been an element of envy as they imagined their own exits from the idyllic and predictable life in beautiful upstate New York.

The shock of their plans brought the festivities to a standstill. The air became heavy with disappointment as the festivities lost all energy. The dancing ended, and partying came to a swift close. Folks politely excused themselves with one insignificant reason or another, exiting quickly and without fuss. Astrid's parents went to bed that evening, exhausted from the day, excited about tomorrow.

With enough money saved (and really not having much to spend it on) from years of small summer jobs, Christmas, birthdays, and envelopes from folks honoring their nuptials, they packed their bags and hitched a ride from a cousin to the bus station. They bought two one-way tickets and headed due west. Their goal was to move far enough away from the orchards to completely branch out on their own yet close enough to make it a day's ride to come back home in case of emergency.

Having secretly poured over the mail order atlas, *Ride your Way Across America*, for months in anticipation of their exodus. The happy pair agreed a reasonable distance to go was a border town abutting New York and Pennsylvania. So they boarded the bus with suitcases in tow and, after half a day's travel, disembarked in Penn View, New York – a small college town which, it turns out, they were to call home for the rest of their lives.

Chapter Thirty-Two

Penn View College had a lot of things going for it. First and foremost, it offered a first-class fabulous liberal arts department with all kinds of interesting programs for motivated students. Aside from the classics like English Literature, Romance languages, visual arts, music (including a very popular band that accompanied students to sporting events in which they were participating), criminal justice, and a host of other options, students could take drama, pre-banking economics, and specialty courses including Chinese cooking and film studies. Students from all around the country applied, and if accepted (admission was selective, and there were many spots taken up by legacy applicants), access for students to study with top-notch professors was guaranteed.

The highly prized Grant Warren Museum, which bragged a national reputation for housing treasured artifacts of early American culture and superb paintings ranging from early American Itinerant art to the more bourgeois yet romantic art of the Hudson River painters, could be studied as a natural part of the Penn View curriculum. Period rooms were set up to replicate the interiors of colonial homes. One scene depicted a kitchen/living room consisting of a huge fireplace with a giant caldron hanging from an iron armature that could swing the pot over the fire or away from the flames depending upon the meal being cooked. Another room, far more sophisticated and clearly on the wealthier end of life, had a long cherry table, waxed and polished with seating for twelve. The chairbacks, which gave the impression of a ribcage, had delicate spindles splayed slightly from a central post, and the legs, heftier versions of the spindle shape, seemed stocky and able to take whatever weight sat down. The table settings included scalloped white porcelain plates with tiny blue birds drifting around the inner circumference of each piece. Lead crystal goblets rested at the head of each place setting, along with individual salt cellars of hammered silver, which matched the style of the eating utensils. Five-armed silver candelabras adorned each end of the table.

On the campus grounds, just past the non-denominational chapel with a side cemetery available for elite emeritus faculty and administrators (no relatives included in the deal) whose lives, devoted to the college, were forever honored with a headstone and a small burial plot, was a historic landmark playhouse, the Black Box at Penn View.

The red brick octagonal building, partially modeled in a neo-classical Jeffersonian style, was erected for the college in the 1920s by two men with a superficial interest in architectural history. One was a local barn carpenter, and the other was his Saturday night drinking buddy who happened to be a foundation bricklayer whose most impressive contribution to the creation of the blueprints included knowledge of where to find a really excellent hidden homemade brewery (this was during Prohibition) and gain admittance as he had the secret password.

Handshake business being what it is, they invited their classmate from elementary school (now the finance person for the college after working in a bank in Rochester for a few years) to join them for a drink. As it happened, their classmate spilled the news after the second round that the college wanted to build a theater to attract students from New York City. It was all about enrollment.

Thus ensued the first of four business meetings (one on campus and two more at the brewery), where the men convinced the college finance officer they were the guys for the job. The carpenter and bricklayer spent the next few weeks designing an exterior worthy of the college. The financial officer brought the plans and cost information to the president, who has a significant interest in moving to a parallel position at a more prestigious east coast university. He was too busy to look past the façade drawings to even notice the lack of details, let alone the actual design of the interior space. With his help, they had a building fund capitalized by generous donations from three legacy families that could adequately cover costs. The deal was struck, their work began, and the president moved to Connecticut just as the first brick was laid.

From the exterior, the expectation was the inside of the building would continue in a neo-classical theme. Instead, after walking through the building's outer doors, the visitor was greeted with an ornate set of wrought iron gates set into a massive two-story cement wall. This was the grand entry into the cavernous theater space, more or less resembling a vaulted barn. At the far end, the men built a deep stage elevated four feet higher than an orchestra pit in front of it. There were two small rooms off stage, right and left. These would serve as dressing rooms and storage. A shallow balcony, tied into the outer walls at the opposite end of the building from the stage, was suspended over the last fifteen rows of seats.

The Black Box at Penn View celebrated its opening with an official ribbon-cutting ceremony exactly one year after work commenced. Young men and women from New York City and elsewhere across the country were attracted to the possibility of becoming famous through study in the liberal arts. Enrollment increased, and the new college president appreciated the valuable contribution the theater made to the whole community.

In the late 1930s and early 1940s, when so many were either in the military or out of work and struggling to stay alive for lack of jobs, the Work Progress Administration hired three talented artists to paint the huge walls surrounding the wrought iron gates. In an outstanding burst of art making, a WPA landscape mural was created for the inner entry into the acting space to become known as "The Black Box Theatre."

On one side of the image, farmers, some wearing caps, and other bandanas, with white, blue, and checked shirts slightly untucked from their work pants, were stooped over sacks of saplings for planting in fields. Women were depicted in heavy skirts with aprons folded to hold small tools for digging into the earth. Their work stretched all the way to the horizon where the sun was lower in the sky – an indication the long day of work might be coming to an end.

On the other side was a huge apple tree, gnarled and bent heavy with fruit, right in the very front of the picture plane. A pair of tired harvesters, a man and a woman, pressed their backs against the old tree trunk and sat admiring the apples they were about to eat. If one looked very carefully, it was possible to see a snake-like form twisted around one of the exposed roots. Legend had it that one of the artists added this detail after the project was finished and approved for public viewing. It represented his symbol of rebellion against upper-class oppression.

During the academic year, students had opportunities to perform amateur presentations of classic dramatic works such as *A Streetcar Named Desire* and *Spoon River Anthology.* They came from English, music, art, and drama classes to audition and received course credit for classes that in any way were associated with serious drama and even the lighter musicals like *Camelot* and *The Wizard of Oz*.

In the summer months, small professional theater companies and yet-to-be-discovered playwrights used the space as a venue for the experimentation of new works and opportunities to tighten production before taking the works on the road to the big cities. The opportunity to get onto the "Box" (as it was fondly referred to) summer schedule was highly competitive – so much so that once a play made it to full production, that initial opportunity was so highly valued that the receivers of the award always listed, "Recipient of the prestigious 'Black Box at Penn View' summer invitation" in the local Playbill magazine.

Chapter Thirty-Three

At first, Astrid's parents rented a tiny cottage a few blocks down from the campus chapel, whose spire stood as the tallest landmark around. Their first home was a perfect one-bedroom with a generous eat-in kitchen and lots of counter space for laying out the flour, kneading dough, and core apples. Astrid's mother started baking pies right away.

They smelled so good that the aroma enticed hungry passersby, especially students, to stop by the porch just to chat with the end goal of being offered a slice. Astrid made pie friends easily because who doesn't adore a plate full of steaming fresh homemade baked goods?

Her husband, a genuinely warm kind of fellow, loved to sit on the porch and chat with the students and faculty stopping for pie, curious about where they came from and what ambitions they had. It gave him the perfect opportunity to learn about the comings and goings in their little town and on campus.

When the initial money they had saved started running low, Astrid's father applied to become a postal worker, which was steady work and paid reasonably well. He started as an assistant to old Mr. Porter, who was the Penn View postmaster, until the day he died, which turned out to be almost the exact same story for Astrid's father, who lasted forty-seven years in the job.

From the beginning, he loved everything about it, especially the uniform and knowing almost everyone in the town by name. Astrid's mother became the chief pie and cake baker for Romey's Diner just past the college two miles down on Route 422. Her specialty naturally was apple pie which folks passing through claimed was the best they'd ever had.

Everyone wondered what the secret was to her exotically aromatic pie filling. She never did give away that information which was so simple as to be ridiculous. Curry powder and crushed ginger root. She hit upon that combination as a youngster when she was helping out her own mother baking pies. Instead of adding customary amounts of cinnamon to the apple mixture, she grabbed the curry powder by mistake, and immediately upon seeing her error as the color of the apples turned bright orange, she figured crushing up some ginger might help calm the mixture down. It took a few pies of trial and error, but she finally got a good balance of flavor enhancement with minimal color distortion.

Astrid's mother baked thousands of pies in her lifetime. So many that in her later years, she kept pushing through the pain as her fingers grew stiff and swollen from arthritis. Finally, she had to stop, which likely broke her heart, and with that loss, she let go of life.

In her parents' third year living in Penn View, Astrid was born at home without fuss. She was a healthy baby and, quite surprisingly, arrived in the world with a head adorned with fine strawberry blond hair that neither of her parents knew even ran in their families.

Her eyes, slate blue, gave her tiny face an other-worldliness like an angel. As far back as they could recollect, all their relations had dark brown hair and eyes to match. Most people who met Astrid as a baby commented those blue eyes would change to brown in a few more months because that's just what happens with infants. But they never did switch colors and, in fact, looked more and more like the electric blue of the sky on a brilliant spring day.

In toddlerhood, her locks turned copper-red like a newly minted penny. A soft spray of delicate freckles swept across the bridge of her nose. Sometimes her parents would stop cooing and chatting mid-stream as they stared down in silence at the sheer beauty of the child they had produced. She was, as they would often remark, a perfect baby who grew to be a perfect child. They never had another – why bother when this one was so excellent!

Chapter Thirty-Four

From an early age, Astrid showed an interest in coloring and singing, and telling stories. She loved to collect grasshoppers and gave them names such as Lincoln and Estelle. Once, she caught tadpoles in a paper cup and assumed they would love orange soda as much as she did. It became her first lesson about death and killing when she plopped them into the cup, and they expired almost immediately in front of her. Inconsolable, Astrid looked to her parents for succor. They ever so gently helped her manage her grief and guilt as she learned about burial and ritual. They lovingly prepared a full-on funeral, complete with digging a tiny hole in the earth and erecting a miniature headstone (a pile of rocks) in the backyard. As a family, they sang an original version of *Amazing Grace* as the little tadpoles were buried. Afterward, they sat on the front porch eating pie and making up a story about tadpoles swimming up to heaven. Though it was a sad day, it became a sweet memory of love that lasted Astrid's lifetime.

Astrid cared for others. She was quick to defend a classmate being teased or offer a piece of something delicious in her lunchbox if someone else came up short on their meal that day. She tried not to be competitive though she did give her all to at least come in 3rd place in the yearly "Math Countdown" and her very best effort to climb the rope to the top beam in gym class before anyone else got there. It was not so much to beat her classmates as it was that the first one made it to the top and got to write her name in chalk on the beam.

She understood from an early age the importance of being a 'good' winner rather than a winner who made others feel bad. From the time she was little, Astrid understood the feelings of others were important, which gave her a kind of humility not often seen in young people. She also knew she did a lot of things really well and nothing superbly.

One of her great joys was to read all the international addresses and study the stamps on the envelopes her father sorted at the post office. She'd imagined being a food writer traveling all over the world, trying famous dishes (especially pies and cakes) from each country she'd visited. Her father loved having her help in the back room of the post office. Just knowing she was near him made him feel fulfilled and grateful for the life he and his wife had chosen for themselves years before.

The family traveled back to the old homestead orchards from time to time, but they never really felt fully engaged. Both their families were polite and welcoming, but there was an edge to it all, which left Astrid's parents feeling rejected and depressed. The distance, not measured in miles, between their former lives on the old country road and their present lives in Penn View was like the difference between an empty house and a lively home.

With each ensuing visit, they felt less in common and less welcome until, during one of those visits when all the older cousins and Astrid with her parents were hanging out in the kitchen, one of them (now speaking as if she were one voice for everyone) asked out loud (the way people do when they are making a nasty statement which inhabits what appears to be a neutral question just to avoid taking responsibility for the meanness) "Where *did* Astrid ever come from? Seriously, she looks like NOBODY from around here let alone our family. I mean that red hair and those blue eyes? That sure has some of us real curious…" which meant this had clearly been the topic of discussion plenty of times before it ever reached the kitchen that day.

That was the precise moment that cut off any more visits from Penn View to the orchards. All that came to an abrupt halt because, if nothing else, Astrid's parents would never subject their little girl to unkindness of any form. On occasion, they got a holiday card, and out of politeness, they'd send a card back. But just to be a little devilish, they would slip in the latest color school photo of their girl before sealing the envelope. All through school, Astrid's red hair reached clear down her back, her freckles lightly sprayed across her nose, and her electric blue eyes flashed brilliantly against the photographer's white studio background.

Chapter Thirty-Five

By the time Astrid finished high school, she had memorized every inch of the Grant Warren Museum, taken sculpting classes in their after-school program, studied voice, learned to speak French with an excellent accent, ice skated well enough to spin once fully in the air, passably played the flute, and had a fetish for drawing pen and ink animals. Her 'good enough' gymnastic talents got her a place on the cheerleading squad though she did not really value that role as much as the other girls seemed who were determined to find boyfriends.

Mostly, she loved going over to the college to watch whatever play was being produced – especially in the summertime when the entire town opened up for a season of theatre supported by some pretty big names from around the country. During that time, the local children's theater program ran classes in acting, singing, and dancing. Her parents were more than happy to support her interest in anything done with the arts.

She was reasonably popular with both the boys and girls in her high school because she had a kindness about her that invited people to feel comfortable and safe. She had a soft spot for sad people and an instinct to befriend people who were a bit shy about socializing. She had a few dates, but because of the 'incident' with Lester Dimock one spring night in eleventh grade, she mostly demurred going out unless it was with a group of classmates.

Lester called to chat about this and that a few times, which was technically considered phone dating by the crowd she hung out with. The calls were becoming a nightly ritual about 'checking in' with each other. Astrid found herself looking forward to the attention. Then, one particular night when he called, something different happened. He seemed to have something on his mind, but the words stuck to his teeth. The conversation was stretching into pure awkwardness when he blurted out, "Do you want to go to the movies on Saturday night?" to which Astrid blurted, "With you?" which she realized instantly might have hurt his feelings, so she quickly interjected, "I'm just joking. I'd like that. Sure. Thank you. I just wasn't expecting to be invited." And once his question was out in the open, and it was such a direct invitation, they both seemed to be relieved, and the conversation moved on to other matters about classmates, school, and such. Asking for permission from her parents was, in Astrid's mind, simply a formality. They basically never said 'no' to her, and besides which, he came from such a good family.

Astrid considered calling her posse of girlfriends to consult about what to wear on her date with Lester, but, for some reason, she kept that news private. She found herself seriously concerned about his potential expectation of a kiss at the end of the date. She had zero intimate experience with boys though she had read some novels that alluded to things of that nature.

And so, in an effort to be good enough (though probably not superb) at the kissing part of things, she decided to ask an expert. She sought out her oldest friend (but certainly not closest), Beth Rainer, into her confidence (which she knew was one of Beth's finest attributes – she kept secrets super well) about the upcoming date and her lack of kissing knowledge. Beth immediately invited Astrid overnight on Friday to discuss the topic, which made perfect sense because people assumed Beth, who was considered to be a 'fast' girl, would have useful knowledge about the art of kissing.

Beth was not popular. Astrid heard nonspecific whispers about her in school, that she had 'done it,' which made other girls wary of her, but Astrid always got along with her the way she did with most people. She considered Beth to be worldly and interesting. While the two did not hang out, they lived near each other and saw each other around the neighborhood regularly.

In any case, Astrid figured she'd get the best advice on the techniques of making out, which was all she really was hoping for. She also sensed Beth was kind of sad about not having many friends, which was always the kind of feeling that drew Astrid into relationships.

On Friday night, Beth greeted Astrid at her front door with a homemade root beer float. The creamy concoction of root beer and vanilla ice cream was the most highly prized high school drink for socializing – plus. It was easily made at home. The evening was off to a great start. "My folks got us a Santorini classic pizza." Everyone knew they made the best pizza in Penn View with the thinnest crust and heartiest tomato sauce around. "They're going out to *Treasure Tom's* for seafood and should be home in about two hours. We'll have a blast."

And so, balancing their drinks and pizza on bamboo trays, they steadily ascended the stairs up to the second-floor landing where her parents and Beth's bedrooms were located. Astrid was certain if the other kids knew how cool Beth could be, they'd want to hang out with her as well.

As was trendy at the time, both teens had flannel granny nighties with ruffles across the front. Beth grabbed her grey Scotch plaid with a zippered front version and headed for the bathroom to change. On her way, she suggested to Astrid that she change into hers. For overnights, Astrid loved to wear her fuzzy Snowflake gown with the flattering stitching across the high-collared top. It felt so soft against her skin and never bunched up under the covers. When Beth emerged from the bathroom, they both started laughing simply because they were barefoot, gowned up, and free from having any parents around.

Beth's bedroom was large, and there was plenty of room

between her twin beds to really get hopping, so they began dancing to the 'A-sides of 45 after 45. Between the music, the pizza, and the root beer floats, they were having non-stop fun, though the gowns were getting a bit sticky from the heat their bodies were generating.

Finally, after they had danced so much that Astrid had to open her collar to cool off and Beth unzipped her gown down about six inches for the same reason, they both agreed it was time to settle down.

Beth turned off the music and, while turning on her desk lamp, lingered over a fluffy white feather-tipped ballpoint pen that was next to her diary. She loved that pen (a present for her birthday from her father) which had a peacock blue shaft holding the same color ink. Picking it up, she turned and shut off the ceiling light. The room was quiet, with the low glow of light barely illuminating the girls' faces. They both sat down on the floor, backs leaning into opposing beds, facing each other on the pink shag rug.

Beth broke the silence, coming right to the point, "So, you've never kissed a boy, correct?" Astrid blushed because though she had been fairly direct in confiding to Beth what was going on, directness coming back at her about intimate things in person left her tongue-tied, embarrassed, and feeling incompetent. She nodded.

Beth, on a mission to help, ignored the blush and continued, "Ok, listen. It's no big deal. Everyone starts as a beginner.

I'm going to help you so you'll feel more comfortable because I can guarantee you Lester is going to know what he's doing, and he'll expect that you know something about it too." For a split second, Astrid felt confused. "How would Beth know what Lester knows how to do?" but she pushed the thought away as quickly as it had arrived. It was just a turn of phrase. Anyway, everyone knows boys know much more about these things than girls.

Then Beth scooched over next to Astrid, rolled up her sleeve, and gently took her forearm. "Now A (she always called her 'A' ever since they were little), the lesson has 3 parts. Let me show you 'part 1". And with that, she took a peacock blue pen, which had been next to the diary on her desk, and began to slowly stroke the fluffy white feather part protruding from the top up and down Astrid's inner arm. "Close your eyes, yes, like that. See how soft that feels against your skin? Do you feel how light it is? How would you describe it?" to which Astrid responded (still without peeking). It felt "tingly" on her arm. Beth asked her if 'tingly' was an enjoyable feeling, and Astrid said it was. Beth whispered, "Very good. That's what lips feel like." and with that, she suggested they both lie down on the pink shag rug to make the lesson easier.

Beth then murmured, "Are you ready for part 2?" which Astrid anticipated was going to be the feather stroking her other arm, and so she responded, "Sure. Absolutely!" thinking this was so much easier than she expected. And so, Beth, understanding she had the go-ahead, said, "Let me be your teacher" and raised herself on one elbow and leaned over and placed her mouth on Astrid's forehead, kissing her lightly, slowly, delicately while her fingers caressed the curls of red hair surrounding the edges of Astrid's face and trailed along the outline of her eyebrows.

As gentle as Beth was being, Astrid stiffened slightly at the sensation of her friend's lips and fingers on her face. She suggested Astrid close her eyes and imagine Lester was exploring and touching her this way which helped release some of the tension in her body.

Beth moved her mouth down her student's face, kissing her cheek on one side and then the other. Her mouth hovered briefly, and then, lips met lips, and though this was not completely unexpected, it still surprised Astrid as it was happening. She felt the softness of Beth's lips which did give her the tingly feeling that she first felt with the feather on her arm – only this time, it had spread to other places.

"There is one more thing, A. Part 3, ok?" And Astrid, who couldn't imagine what 'more' there could be, felt her own body moving a little as she whispered, "Yes, ok." And with that, Beth slipped her tongue ever so slightly into Astrid's mouth, who, in response to the intense tingling now happening in other parts of her body, most naturally and with full enthusiasm, returned the kiss. They were kissing intensely when they heard Beth's parents ascending the stairs announcing, “We’re home! You girls having fun?”

Beth bolted upright and shouted, “You bet, Mom. How was dinner?” Her mom poked her head in the room, “My gosh, how can you see anything in this darkness? Anyway, time for sleep in this house!” and with that, she closed the door. Both girls took turns using the bathroom before they got under the sheets. They remained quiet until Beth broke the silence whispering, “You feel ready for your date?” Astrid sleepily responded, “Yes, that was quite a lesson,” to which they both started laughing until they heard Beth’s father shout, “Knock it off, gals. Time for your beauty sleep,” which was the last of what Astrid heard until she woke momentarily from a deep sleep to the pulsing sound of moaning coming from Beth’s bed.

Astrid had a quick breakfast with Beth’s family. She was in a hurry to get home and primp for her movie date. Also, in spite of having no regrets about the kissing lesson, she did feel some awkwardness about hanging around. So she helped Beth clean up the pizza plates and root beer float glasses and thanked everyone for a fantastic time. Beth saw her to the door and gave her hand a knowing squeeze. “If you get in a jam tonight, just pretend you’re me!” which was meant to be reassuring but had the effect of leaving Astrid with a feeling of incompetence and somewhat suspicious.

Chapter Thirty-Six

Lester picked Astrid up at 6:30 for a 7 pm show. The movie was being held in the Box, which meant they only needed a few minutes to get there before it started. The plan was to go out for a bite afterward in the restaurant side of the Santorini's, which was more or less charming and set up for quiet conversations.

The film was ok but nothing memorable, though truth be told, Astrid would remember few details of that night, which was her mind's way of sparing the details she'd rather forget. The dinner never actually happened, and the entire evening ended by 9:30, which made her parents curious since most dates these days seem to go much later. But always glad to have their girl back home, they never questioned her about her evening.

If they had, they might have learned what it was like for a sixteen-year-old girl to be tricked into going out on a date with a seventeen-year-old boy who had taken a bet with three of his buddies about the color of a redheaded girl's private hair. Two of them said there was no such thing as red hair 'down there.' The other one, as well as Lester, were fairly certain it could be possible.

And so, after the movie, Lester suggested Astrid, and he hang around to see what the Box looked like in the empty darkness before they walked over for dinner. Astrid, having little dating experience and even less knowledge about predators, agreed to wait while the last people left, and the lights were shut down. As they sat up on the balcony, she noticed her date seemed a bit edgy, which she figured was him just being nervous about things people worry about on first dates. She reached for his hand, but he pulled back, which made her instinctively respond, "Don't worry. We don't have to do anything. Maybe just talk".

That's when she heard snickering coming from somewhere else in the Box. Something seemed off, but she convinced herself her date was gallant and would certainly look out for her. Then was cooing and whistling, and just as someone said, "Shut up," the three fellows emerged from the shadows. Astrid recognized them as ones she had seen hanging around with Lester in school.

They walked towards her and Lester. Their faces, including his, were red and swollen. They were jumpy as they locked in on her like missiles on a lone silo in a field. Lester was smiling strangely. He put his hand on the back of her neck to hold her still.

What she remembered after that were just garbled words and cool air as his three friends lifted her skirt and pulled her panties down to her ankles. She began yelling for them to stop (or at least she thought she did, but her memory jammed up so badly that she was never sure exactly what she did at that moment).

One boy took out a flashlight, and while Lester held her steady, the two peered closely at her body. One of them warned her,

"Keep the fuck quiet unless you want everyone to know what you're doing with half the guys in school," which she knew was a lie but one that she could never overcome if it ever got out. The other one exclaimed, "Do you see that? Lordy, they really are red!" Now that they could see her nakedness covered with red hair, they had proof, and that would be enough to ruin her reputation forever.

And so she remained silent while they laughed and said nasty things and dared each other to touch. But Lester, who definitely seemed to be in charge, stopped their tormenting from going any further, "That's not part of the deal. This is just a look-see. Pay up and get lost." And the two who bet against red hair paid five dollars apiece, which Lester then split (he kept six dollars because he took the biggest risk) with the other one who voted red. Then those boys left the Box.

Astrid was leaning against the balcony rail, eyes glazed over, arms dropped by her sides. Lester stooped down and pulled up her panties, then smoothed her skirt over her hips. He asked, in the most normal tone in the world, if she was hungry. "Hey, there's still time to go for Italian."

Her eyes turned steely blue as she glared directly into his, speaking with a voice sounding distant and old, "Someday your heart will ache from what you've done. Then you will truly know disgrace, and you will remember this night as the beginning of your descent into the deepest loss" which were words that erupted from somewhere in her that she had never known before, and he did certainly did not understand at the time.

Only later in life, when his persistent habit of devious and predatory behaviors finally caught up with his sterling reputation as an honorable man, did he experience lasting consequences. Rolled into his assumption of never getting caught was the fatal hubris of a person supremely confident that he had all the power to silence the rage felt by so many young women who had experienced his abuse. The proof, in his mind, was that none had ever told (he counted on their shame being greater than their capacity to speak out) – except the last one, whom he misjudged as vulnerable enough to likely disappear after the awful event.

Instead, mistaken with the assumption that quiet people are generally weak, he later learned that after his assault, she walked straight to the police station and said, "I've been hurt. I'm only fifteen." and dramatically raised the bottom edge of her skirt just high enough that the officer behind the night desk saw evidence of bruising and bodily fluids reaching up and down her thighs.

Lester's wife only visited him one time immediately before he was sent to prison. She could no longer bear the sight of him but felt the urge to face him directly with the news she was divorcing him and taking their children as far away as she could afford to go.

Only then did his heartache with the deepest loss, and he became the sorriest and unhappiest of men.

Chapter Thirty-Seven

Astrid's teachers appreciated her polite demeanor and natural curiosity about the subjects she was learning. Her grades were not perfect, but almost so, and that made it obvious to the teachers advising students that she should continue her education and consider applying for colleges.

She discussed this possibility with her parents on a late summer evening while they were sitting on the wrap-around porch of what they referred to as the 'new house' even though they had been living there for twelve years. They outgrew the one-bedroom house just down the street from the college chapel and had saved the funds (they were excellent at saving money) to make a down payment on their two-bedroom house just steps away from the post office and closer to the diner (in good weather, walking there was a delight for her mother).

Her parents shouldn't have been taken off guard, but they were startled at the thought of her leaving home. As often occurred with her parents, they shared the same thought at the exact same moment, which was, "This is what our folks must have felt when we packed up and left! Oh, the sorrow…) And so, tinges of disappointment etched into their pride and happiness for their daughter. It was a bittersweet moment that Astrid understood leaving for college would be the true beginning of separating her life from theirs.

Astrid, being a person who dreaded causing sorrow in others, whose capacity for empathy only heightened in the face of other's suffering, immediately denied herself the vision of travel and adventure and reassured them, "Oh my gosh, no! I'm not thinking about going anywhere. I'm planning on getting into Penn View and sticking around here for four more years!" which she figured would give them time to adjust to the idea of her eventual parting.

Their relief was palpable. Then they asked if she was sure, which slightly annoyed her (an unfamiliar feeling for her because she always tried not to be negative) because it felt like an unnecessary demand for reassurance that this was what she really wanted, even if it was not. "Please, it's all fine" was all she could muster to say, putting an end to the irritation she was experiencing.

Her mother, hoping to eradicate the painful conversation altogether, shifted the subject as if nothing had transpired, "Let's eat," and then the three of them went in for dinner, which was, as always, delicious, having been made with an excess of love. In the meantime, Astrid needed to figure out a way to be admitted and pay for this prestigious and expensive college just down the street.

Chapter Thirty-Eight

In the fall of her senior year, Astrid applied to Penn View in spite of the recommendations of her college advisor to think about the local junior college. The odds were against her for getting in, but as everyone knows, the odds can be beaten. The last horse can run the fence to gain the lead. Exceptional results can happen, and for Astrid, such was the case. She had applied with strong but not superior grades. Her references were solid and varied. Her essay was engaging and smart.

But the oddest and most remarkable thing happened when she took the standardized tests competing with applicants across the nation. Without practice or any particular test-taking skills, Astrid received scores near perfect, which made no sense at all because a good part of the exams, she simply filled in rows of A's where she had no idea of the answer. This was one of those times when luck really did seem to have as much of a role in predicting her future as those exams touted that they demonstrated future college aptitude and success.

Always one to consider the feelings of others, Astrid mostly kept the good news about her scores private. She did the same when she received her acceptance letter to Penn View. It was only when the college advising counselor posted all the acceptances right before spring graduation that her classmates learned she had gotten in. A number of students got into other four-year colleges around the country. Most of those graduating went on to jobs. Some graduates joined the military. Others remained undecided about the future and figured they'd wait a year to decide, which generally meant they felt defeated even thinking about the prospects for their future.

Chapter Thirty-Nine

The day that Astrid received her acceptance letter, she marched into Penn View College's financial aid office to discuss options. They walked her through all the possibilities, which mostly meant she was handed a bunch of forms to apply for federal student loans. There was also a modest scholarship (hardly ever given) to help support a local citizen (literally the language used in the form) to attain a Penn View degree in Liberal Arts. It was looking like she was coming up short of money, which worried her because she did not want her parents to take on the debt. The counselor saw the concern on her face and asked, "Would you consider a work/study job?" she proceeded to explain what kind of time would be involved and the amount she would get paid. Astrid, not fearing hard work and really needing the financial help, agreed it was a reasonable plan.

Later that day, the finance counselor called her with good news. Astrid qualified for work/study, which, if she were willing, would actually begin early in the summer. She would be assigned to work in the advancement office, which the counselor laughingly explained was where "It's all about money, especially the old kind." Her comment left Astrid unsure about the meaning of old money and wondering if there was such a thing as "new money" as well. She felt like she was entering a whole new chapter in her life where words would take on definitions previously unknown to her. All would be clear enough in due time.

Chapter Forty

Astrid had a wonderful four-year college experience. She majored as a generalist in liberal arts, lived at home with her overjoyed parents, partook in all kinds of academic and social activities, joined the student government, and made all kinds of friends with different backgrounds and interests. She remained kind to all and intentionally obliterated from her memory the evening in the Box where, for the only time in her life, she leveled a curse on the life of another human being.

In fact, after that evening, she never spoke his name again. Her parents had naturally wanted to know how her first-ever date went with the boy, to which she responded, "We really had nothing in common," which put an end to their curiosity and any further conversation on the subject. From that moment forward, she only went out with groups of friends, which was rather conventional for her age group. Throughout college, Astrid continued to be sure she was in the company of multiple friends when socializing.

What she loved, more than any of the classes she was taking or student activities in which she participated, was her work/study position in the Advancement office. It was hard to describe the importance she felt in being the only student on campus who actually knew the ins and outs of how money was raised or how it was distributed to various projects to enhance the quality of what

Penn View could do for the students, faculty, and town. She was exposed to the power of big money, as well as the influence of multiple small donations.

At first, her tasks involved menial things like keeping the printer paper stocked, fetching files, or filling large envelopes with glossy folders containing mission statements, photos, and greetings messages from prominent graduates. As the years went by, she was taught about ledgers and grant writing, asked for foundation donations, and researched companies for potential alignments with Penn View's strategic plan.

In the summer between her junior and senior years, she was given special training to become an "Advancement Guide." It was considered prestigious to escort selected benefactors (it was never completely clear to her how they determined her to be a good match for any of the patrons she guided around the campus) so they could take in the latest Coolege innovations, see the "perfect space we hoped you might consider for a naming opportunity" and give the guests a real sense of the ideal Penn View student.

During one of the monthly calendar planning sessions, the Director of Admissions asked Astrid if, during the upcoming October fall break, she would be willing to do a morning campus tour with a legacy benefactor coming up from New York City. His wife died last year, and she was under the impression that he wanted to make some kind of memorial for her at Penn View. Astrid, whose heart was moved by this one-sentence story, was immediately transported to a fantasy of a lonely man weeping into his hankie with unbearable grief. Her genuine kindness and willingness to help out in a pinch (she really had no plans for the break, so why not?) prompted her to assent to the request even though doing her first tour of a legacy benefactor frightened her slightly. It was a big deal for the Advancement director to trust her with this mission.

Up til then, her tours were mostly with foundation representatives and people more or less adjusting to the responsibilities of having newer money. This heartbroken widower (she could only think of him that way since the image had formed in her mind) represented a whole new strategic guiding category. Astrid was emboldened by the confidence her director had in her touring skills. And thus, without the fanfare of intention or expectation, there began what could not really be called a courtship, but the merging of coincidence and luck creating an outcome behaving as if it had been one when Easton Sinclair was driven to upstate New York for a guided tour.

Chapter Forty-One

During the ensuing weeks before fall break, Astrid thought a lot about male legacy benefactors. Her imagination conjured images of up old, hunched-over, white-haired men walking with silver canes and smoking fat stogies. The Advancement director gave her some articles about Mr. Sinclair's family heritage (they made their money generations ago in finance – old money) and clippings from papers about the death of his wife. She saw a few photos of him, which seemed to make him look more youthful than she had invented in her mind. She saw no evidence of a cigar, even in the casual country club shots and images of him dining out with his elegant wife, who, at least in the photos, appeared distracted, like her mind was on something else.

In fact, he appeared ordinary, which subsequently led her to believe he'd be pretty boring, and the morning tour might be tedious because he was probably dull to be around. With those assumptions in place, she made a list of topics to keep the conversation going ranging from statistics about students, the history of campus buildings, and facts about the town of Penn View, NY. She also figured she could ask him about his student days but totally planned on staying away from the topic of his dead wife. She felt way out of her depth on that one.

Her parents were quite thrilled for her – they considered this legacy tour a big deal and hoped they would get the full rundown when it was finished. Her mother took it a step further and asked Astrid, "Why don't you invite the 'gentleman' over for pie after you see all those buildings?" Her father appalled that his wife would think someone of the 'gentleman's' stature might consider stopping by, shut down her suggestion with a cutting swipe of his hand in the air, which was very unusual for him because he was usually careful with the feelings of others. At that moment, he made his wife feel slighted, which was hurtful for Astrid to see because her mother, in her shame at having been so naïve, was just doing what she always did, offering pie to friends and strangers. What was wrong with that?

"Sure Mom. If there's time, I'll mention fresh pie. You never know." And with that, Astrid gave her father a look of 'hush,' which she rarely did, but on this occasion, it seemed appropriate.

Chapter Forty-Two

On the morning Mr. Sinclair visited Penn View College, Astrid noticed the air temperature outside had dropped considerably during the night; the clouds looked bruised and foreboding against the clear sky that was cool blue. Fall was definitely happening. On this big day, she opted for her red plaid kilt, a black woolen turtleneck, black tights, and dark brown leather ankle boots. The outfit set off her copper hair which she braided and then twisted into a bun at the nape of her neck. It wasn't quite cold enough that she needed a coat, so she left it behind as she sauntered over to the Advancement office to meet her very first legacy benefactor.

Since it was fall break, there were few students roaming about the campus. A few faculty and administrators were busily running errands, racing from building to building. Technically, only the students had the short academic break, though, by the looks of it, many faculty had taken advantage of the short holiday as well. Maintenance was mending cracked sidewalks and curb cuts– an effort more easily accomplished without a lot of people moving about.

The Advancement director waved at Astrid as she walked up to her office doors. "All set?" she asked. "Yep, I've done my research and read the materials you gave me." The director then whispered into her ear, "Just be you." Which helped Astrid calm some of the flutterings she was starting to feel build up in her gut.

"This morning, Mr. Sinclair is all yours. At lunch with him, I'll get down to his donor wishes and bottom line. You just show him what you love about this place." And with that, she scurried inside and left her standing to greet her future.

Chapter Forty-Three

Astrid had second thoughts about not bringing her coat as she stood outside waiting in the nippy air. The morning chill was starting to get into her bones. After nervously waiting about twenty minutes, a shiny black limousine with ES stamped on the license plate turned onto the college ring road and made its way slowly past the campus post office to the front of the Advancement Building. There was absolutely no mistaking the passenger in the car as anyone other than Mr. Easton Sinclair.

He rolled down the window and leaned forward, asking, "You Astrid?" the informality of which caught her off guard, causing her to accidentally respond, "Yup," which she instantly knew sounded so stupid and young. Worried she had just made a bad impression, she hurriedly tried to make a more sophisticated correction, "I mean, yes, it is." which sent the gentleman in the back seat of the car leaning slightly out the window into a gentle chortle. "No worries. I'll be there in a moment." And with that, the window rolled back up.

The driver, Mr. Smith (an older and very formal professional chauffeur), had driven Mr. Sinclair's mother, Linda Regina Tremont Sinclair, for half a century. She had been widowed in her forties after her husband, Randal Sinclair, had suddenly died of an unknown infection in his foot, which rapidly spread and turned his leg into gangrene. No one ever could figure out how the contamination had come into his right foot, but his fever shot up overnight while his leg started turning colors not associated with healthy tissue. It all happened too quickly to bring it under control. The doctors suggested removing the leg to possibly save his life, but he succumbed to death before they could find an available surgeon to take it off.

Linda Regina Tremont Sinclair became a widow three short days from the beginning to the end of the gruesome affair. Though in her own right, she had inherited wealth (her father owned the rights to an oilfield in Coalinga, California, that provided a hefty income to him and his progeny), she became all the more affluent as beneficiary of her husband's millions from his stock market investments paid for by the enormous income from the Grand Chew Gum Company which he founded at the turn of the century when he cheated a community of indigenous farmers in South America out of a massive swath of rubber tree forests.

His magnificent art and antiques collection, which included numerous Flemish Masters, Medieval illuminated manuscripts, French Impressionist paintings, antique tables (including a nine-foot refectory table of well oil-planks hand-hewn from an Elizabethan era walnut tree), and an original 15th-century wall relief crafted by Lucca Della Robbia, *Madonna, and Child,* adorned his grand foyer hall and massive living room. Of all the art and antiquities, however, his most prized possession was a stained-glass window he built into a faux stone wall in his library.

There, protected from the outside world, artificially illuminated, and timed to coordinate with the hours between sunrise and sunset, a shimmering window from the Gothic era of the 13th century glowed into the 21st century with as much vibrance as when it was initially created. The artisan and theme were unknown, as this window was merely a segment of a larger window. But none of that mattered because it was the movement of the colors that enthralled Mr. Sinclair. For him, it was divine.

She also owned the gigantic two-story apartment, peering down 10 stories from the top floor directly towards the grand staircase of the Metropolitan Museum. It was as if the building across the street were simply an extension of her own home. She was, simply stated, super-rich.

Linda Regina Trevor Sinclair remained a widow for the rest of her life. Her children, young adults at the time of their father's passing, included Easton and his twin sisters Elinor and Violet. She never became close to any of them, preferring to pour her affection into one black toy poodle after another (when one died, the next was always given the same name, 'Benny'). Mrs. Sinclair also kept canaries in her bedroom now that she did not have to share the room with her husband. At any one time, she had 4 or 5 songbirds living in an elaborate cage with swings and cuddle chips galore. She called them all by the same name, 'Johnny.' Other than her pets, Mrs. Sinclair pretty much kept to herself.

Elinor and Violet had never lived apart. After attending Miss Wheldon's Boarding School in East Everly, Massachusetts, the girls did a yearlong grand tour of Europe. During the trip, they met a pair of well-to-do Swiss brothers (born two years apart), and on a whim at the end of their travels, both couples married (without other family members present) in Torino, Italy.

The brothers, who were bankers, came from a substantial family that owned a residence compound in Zurich and a country mansion in Provence, where they usually summered. The girls' lives were set, and they had very little to do with New York or anything Sinclair related except their trust funds.

Easton remained in New York City, sharing the mansion home with his mother, her poodle, and the canaries. The place was so large it felt like separate domiciles, which was helpful because Easton was not a fan of having any animals around. He inhabited the grand main rooms of the residence, which were the epitome of upper-class taste and caste.

His mother sequestered herself into the 'back apartment' as she referred to it, which was no small by any means, but far less impressive in its grandeur. It was intended more as a place to hide from the world in the lap of cozy luxury. From her rarified perch at the end of the hall, Mrs. Sinclair could pick and choose the people and events she permitted into her life. From there, she remained a bit of a mystery to the world at large.

Easton's first wife had only visited her mother-in-law a few times during the first year she and Easton were married. His second wife spent six years trying unsuccessfully to get to know her mother-in-law. What she did accomplish was to help develop a small relationship between Lindy and her grandmother. Their special time together appeared to bring some joy to the grandmother before her death.

Easton eventually inherited the apartment and everything in it. He never planned on changing the downstairs floor with its grand staircase, dramatic library, oak-paneled living room the width of the entire building, fireplace large enough to stand inside, magnificent dining room adorned with a Steuben Christal chandelier, etc. This was the home of his childhood, and so it would remain except for the animals.

His mother's poodle, Ben-Ben (the third or fourth dog name derived from 'Benny'), was very old and blind by the time Linda Regina Tremont Sinclair passed. Her final wishes were he was to be put to sleep and placed inside the coffin with her. The 'Johnny" birds were given to another family in the building who loved their songs and were thrilled to inherit the elegant gilt cage as well. A few years later, after his mother's death, another animal, a cat named Darby, was to call the apartment home.

After his mother died, Easton inherited Smith. Even though he secretly thought he was the worst driver in the world – so old-fashioned and slow, he continued to employ Smith for special day trips for decades. He not only felt a family obligation to give him a few jobs during the year to help supplement his retirement income, he believed he was honoring the man's dignity.

Chapter Forty-Four

Mr. Smith opened his door and cautiously stepped onto the sidewalk adjacent to the front of the Advancement office building. He held a weathered chauffeur's cap in his gnarled fingers while smiling broadly at Astrid. Before she stood a completely charming man well into his seventies, dressed in the worn uniform of his trade, his eyes twinkling the most brilliant blue she had ever seen, with the exception of her own. Holding out his hand in greeting" Mr. Smith said, "Miss Astrid, it is a pleasure to meet you. Please call me 'Smith.'" With that, he turned around, moving to the other side of the limousine, and opened the rear door for Mr. Sinclair, who was perfectly capable of opening his own door but relinquished his capability to the chauffer's duty so Smith might feel like he was doing his job properly.

"Thank you, Smith. Please find a spot to park and, oh, Miss. Astrid, do you know where Smith might get a cup of coffee after his long drive?". She directed him to the library where there was a coffee bar serving light snacks, which was open 24/7, and requested that they both address her simply as 'Astrid.' Smith protested, thinking he should not leave the car parked where it was, but Mr. Sinclair assured him, "I wouldn't be concerned with that, Smith. Nobody will ticket us – right Astrid? I'm pretty sure about that! I'll come and get you when it's time to leave." And with that, the two of them watched Smith slowly head down on-foot across the grassy incline to the library.

"Welcome back to Penn View College, Mr. Sinclair. I'm here today to escort you around the campus, show you the highlights, and answer any questions you may have that I can." And for the next three hours, they walked around the grounds and into buildings. He had not been back to the college for at least twenty years. Some things were vaguely familiar, others new and impressive. He saw his dorm from freshman year and then visited the fraternity he had lived in (which he had forgotten was really just a rundown mansion located on the other side of the hockey field), the sports complex (now housing an amazing rock-climbing wall and half-Olympic size pool) and the cafeteria where he ate unimaginably lousy food for so many years (for his visit, an excellent lunch was being catered in the Advancement dining room).

Astrid's plans to direct the conversation didn't quite pan out. From the beginning, it was Mr. Sinclair who drove the conversation. Aside from his sharing some recollections and asking a few rudimentary questions about this building or that, he appeared more interested in learning about her. "What was it like attending Penn View as a first-generation student?" "How did she handle being local when most students came from other areas across the country?" "Did she have a favorite course?" "Professor?" "What concerned her most about after graduation?" The questions went on and on until the overall tone between them shifted to something more conversational and spontaneous.

She found herself speaking up in ways she never would have expected with a legacy benefactor stranger. “What inspired you most when you were a student, Mr. Sinclair?” “What did it feel like to live in a fraternity” “Did you have a moment when you felt most fulfilled in school?” “What were your dreams for the future?”

By 11:45, she had returned Mr. Sinclair to the steps of the Advancement Building for the noon presentation and lunch. She took him inside, where the Director was waiting to give him a tooled leather binder embossed with the Eagle logo of the college and filled inside with pamphlets, lined paper, and a tri-color combination pen for taking notes. There was also a typed page listing buildings, locations, and dollar numbers representing the costs of individual naming opportunities.

“Thank you, Astrid, for taking such good care of Mr. Sinclair. I hope you enjoyed your tour, Mr. Sinclair. Astrid is our best!” He nodded and, with a leather notebook in hand, began to follow the Director toward the special dining room.

Before completely disappearing down the hall, he took a look back over his shoulder toward Astrid and asked, “Would you mind finding Smith and asking him to be back here with the car by 3:30?”. She indicated she was more than happy to do so. “And oh,

Astrid, please stop by yourself so I can say a proper thank you and goodbye." which was really so kind of him and made her feel proud of the touring job she had done.

Smith and Astrid were at the appointed spot by 3:25. Mr. Sinclair shook the director's hand and waved goodbye. She went back inside to start a follow-up letter, and as he approached the car, he took a long last glance at the grounds in front of him, turned to Smith to get into the car, and then asked Astrid if she'd like to go for a brief ride. Having never been in a limousine in her life and frankly feeling pretty cold now that the sun was descending early as the autumn days grew shorter, she agreed. He held the door open for her as she climbed in, moving over to the far side of the car. Then he got in. There they sat, not moving, for about 5 minutes, which was a little awkward until she sensed he might be letting go of the formal lunch and afternoon sales pitch, which no doubt was, to a certain degree, tedious.

"Smith, if I recall, there is a lake lookout on Rt. 422, about 20 miles up the road. Astrid, do you mind if we head out over there? Then I'll bring you back." To which she nodded it was fine. She knew the spot. It was past the diner where her mother baked. The view was a bit overgrown, but it was quiet and nice, and there was a bench for people to take in the sight of the small lake. In the fall, the mirroring of tree colors by the water was magical.

A 20-mile drive on an empty country road should be a quick trip, but with Smith at the wheel, it took longer than usual, giving the two giving passengers time to start the kind of conversation destined to evolve into more deeply felt communication. Easton Sinclair pressed a silver button next to the unused ashtray that rolled up the privacy window between the driver and passenger sections of the car. They fell into each other's words, listened openly, and allowed the air to be filled with their stories. Astrid spoke of her family, her dreams, her lack of worldly exposure, and her having deferred going to college elsewhere because of the pain it might cause her parents.

She even very sketchily shared about the humiliation she experienced in high school, which (in his mind) explained why she ushered them past the Box without going in beyond looking at the murals. She could never enjoy that space without creepy feelings dominating the experience. Easton (he insisted she call him that now) was horrified on her behalf, but he tempered it so as not to overwhelm her with his disgust and rage at the boys.

He shared about his loneliness as a child and his sisters who, because of their twinship, left him feeling excluded. He revealed how his father was so distant and long gone; his mother was more able to shower her dog and birds with affection than her children. And then, in almost a dream-like state, he spoke of his wife. He harbored so much remorse at not telling her why he wanted her to stay, not go on that ski trip, and yet, he realized now, as he spoke about it out loud for the first time, that he had the kind of guilt often edged with anger that has more to do with resenting her for her not being who he wanted her to be. “How can I be so angry at a dead person?” Such were the conversations they shared during their 20-mile ride to the lookout at the pond.

When they arrived, the three of them exited the car. Smith pulled out a pipe from his uniform coat and leaned casually against the hood of the car while lighting it. Astrid and Easton walked a few yards stepping through scraggly bushes that snagged and pulled at their legs. There, deep into the path, was a once pristinely painted green bench, weathered and pealing and hinting at a history long forgotten. One of the slats on the back was missing, and another cracked. “Sit for a minute?” Astrid responded, “Sure,” and with that, they both lowered themselves carefully (they weren’t sure how steady or safe the bench actually was) down onto it.

Together in silence, they took in the reflected colors on the stillness of the lake. Rustling sounds of the fall evening wind passed through the bushes and across the lake, enveloping them in what seemed to be a timeless moment. Easton noticed Astrid, especially beautiful in the sunset light, red hair almost glowing like a crown of fire against her pale skin. Then he saw she was shivering and rising, took her elbow to guide them both back to the warmth of the car.

As they approached, Smith covered his pipe, stubbing out the ember with a tiny, monogrammed silver tamp, one the elder Mrs. Sinclair had given him for his birthday years before. The three got back into the car, and Easton said, "Ok, Smith, let's drop this chilled lady off home," as he handed Astrid a heavy gray woolen car blanket with the initials L R T S in the center made of stitched layered felt shaped like a shield. Astrid fingered the warmth of the cover as she wrapped herself in the fabric. For a moment, she imagined she was in a time warp and lost track of who she actually was. Without letting on to Easton, she pretended ever so fleetingly that she was Linda Regina Tremont Sinclair taking a country ride with her husband and chauffeur.

As they approached the town, Easton inquired which was the way to her house to drop her off. However, that was not to be the end of the story of that evening because Astrid, always kind and wanting people to feel appreciated, thought that Smith and Easton might really like meeting her parents but, more than anything, enjoy a warm slice of her mother's amazing apple pie. "Easton, you've just got to try my mom's pie before you leave. My parents would kill me if I didn't invite you to stop by." To which Easton responded, "Hey, Smith, we can't let her folks kill her, right?" "No, Mr. Easton, that surely would be impolite."

The limo pulled up to the modest house where Astrid and her parents lived. The white and gray home, with its wrap around porch, autumnal decorations, and comfy outdoor furniture, was welcoming in a way that touched Easton with a non-specific longing. Though Astrid wished she had been able to go away for college, she loved her home and took it for granted that most people felt the same way about theirs – especially rich people who could live any place and in any style they wished.

A year would pass before she would completely understand the depth of feeling Easton experienced during that first visit because it took that amount of time for him to reconcile relinquishing his 1st vow to never give himself fully again to another human being. As can happen, love came to him before he came to realize it, which was a good thing because had it been the other way around, he might have destroyed its possibility. It took a full year for him to declare himself to her.

As for Astrid, her pace toward love was more direct and conventional. During that first visit, she introduced 'Mr. Sinclair' and Smith to her parents. As they both stood in the doorway, the rich smell of apples and buttery crust filled the air. Her mother, with the promise of slices of pie, ushered them into the living room, where her father was adding a log to the fire. It was all so cozy. "Great to meet you, Mr. Sinclair. Please have a seat," as he waved him to the choicest spot near the fire. "Please call me Easton. Lovely to meet Astrid's mother and father! I hope we are not intruding."

The conversation went back and forth in that vein until, bit by bit. It opened up as Easton was genuinely curious about her father's work at the post office. He really didn't socialize with that many people who actually worked a job like that with real things like letters and packages. Mostly, Easton knew people who worked in numbers about things that were more theoretical than real. Just as Astrid's father was getting deeper into postal particulars, her mother stepped into the room carrying a tray with five large slices of steaming apple pie. "Anybody hungry?"

Astrid could tell Smith (who had taken a seat on the couch opposite the easy chairs) was definitely eyeing a piece, so she took one off the tray and handed it right to him with the gentle order, "Enjoy." Her father handed Easton a slice, and the family helped each of themselves to their own. For a few minutes, the only sounds were of people eating and the crackling of the fire.

Astrid's mother, never one to seek a compliment directly, derived the most pleasure from the silence that came as people enjoyed her baking. Of course, if they asked for a second helping, she was doubly delighted, but usually, the first helping was big enough to satisfy even the hungriest of appetites. Easton and Smith, while eating their pie, were smiling and complimenting and relaxing. Then, the hypnotic dance of flames in the fireplace dropped Smith right off to sleep.

Easton stretched in his chair and turned to Astrid, saying, "Do you mind if Smith dozes a little before he and I head back to New York?". "Of course, that's fine." Astrid's mother actually invited them to stay the night, but he graciously refused. "Maybe I could get some night air on your porch to stay alert?" and with that, he got up, thanked her parents for the pie and company, and with Astrid right behind, walked out onto the porch.

The night was clear and pitch black, the way it can be when one is far from the intrusion of city lights. Instead of sitting on the porch furniture, they sat on the steps to get a better view of the stars. Astrid had wrapped herself in a crimson shawl crocheted by her mother during her first year in college, "It keeps my hands busy when you're off doing college things with friends."

She was moved by the existential moment they were sharing and said, "It is amazing to think we are just now seeing the light of an exploding star billions of years old. That this is the time, the moment, we could be anywhere, but we are together here." And as she gazed towards Polaris, she imagined the journey of the stars, swirling through the universes across all time, guiding everything into forever.

And Easton, impressed with the depth of her reverie, responded, "Somethings are too brilliant to understand, too large for the mind. Everything comes from the stars, from an unimaginable beginning." Their conversation continued for quite a while.

After that night, they rarely spoke of such things again because, having done so once, both understood that there existed between them the capacity for a kind of thinking and feeling indescribable and overwhelming which, like an exploding star, only made itself known in the present though it is derived completely and utterly from the past. And the past had no business intruding into the here and now.

The next twelve months moved swiftly. Easton ended up driving Smith (who was too old and tired to be on the roads in such an exhausted state) back to New York after the pie visit. The following week he called Astrid's father, and after a long chat about respecting her boundaries and not taking advantage of her inexperience, he asked her father's permission to let Astrid take the train down to explore the city (of course, he would cover all the expenses) every few weekends. She would stay in a guest room in his apartment, and he would arrange for her to tour the museums, attend concerts, dine with luminaries, and generally have new experiences.

He promised his motives were on the up and up. Easton was very fond of Astrid and would take care that she was safe and treated with respect. She definitely would be home for Thanksgiving and Christmas, which he knew were such important occasions for the whole family to be together.

Then Easton asked, “Would it be possible to take her during spring break to Antigua for sun and sand and travel adventures with the purpose of showing her the kind of nature she had never seen?” – of course, he added he would be providing her with her own accommodations. He offered, “I would only broach this plan with Astrid if you and her mother approve.” Her father had one question at the end of Easton’s proposals, “And then what?” to which he responded, “Then, Astrid is free to define her own future. I’d support that 100%.”

Her parents talked it over. They knew Astrid, who was graduating from college in May, was more than old enough to make her own decisions about things and had no need for permission. They also knew their daughter well enough to predict she would worry about leaving them, and she might once again sacrifice her future for their needs. They were tempted to keep her in their small world while at the same time understanding the resentment that would be bred if they tried to keep her with them forever. Their thoughts were in one place and their hearts in another.

The deciding factor was they liked Easton Sinclair. He was a good man. He would take care of Astrid; therefore, she should be free to choose what to do.

Easton had the ‘big’ conversation with Astrid 10 days after his visit to Penn View College. She was astonished at the generosity of his offer and very impressed (at the same time a little embarrassed) that he had already run it by her parents. He had been smart in handling it that way, and their approval *did* make a difference for her and helped assuage her feelings of guilt about leaving home.

The plan actually helped ease the entire family into her ultimate emancipation as Astrid's weekends away were like practice runs foretelling the inevitable separation from the roots of her childhood. By the time spring break arrived, Astrid was accustomed to independently traveling roundtrip between Penn View and New York City as if she had been making the commute all her life. Her parents, recognizing their daughter was on the verge of stepping into her future, encouraged her to feel unencumbered by ties to the past. They listened with enchantment to her stories about New York, the details of places and people she was meeting. They grasped the joy she was feeling and encouraged her to reach for adventure and fulfillment in her life. They understood their job as parents were shifting and winding down. It all seemed more and more natural that she had wings to fly.

And so she did, as she boarded her first air flight to sunny Antigua, where she and Easton spent seven days in the verdant tropics at the five-star *Seven Roads Hotel,* which was known for beautiful beaches, outstanding snorkeling and delightful cuisine highlighting the renowned talents of 'Chef Maurice' who surprised guests with his culinary wizardry at every meal. His inventive combination of ingredients splayed in delightful patterns across one-of-a-kind platinum-rimmed porcelain tableware was extremely appealing to the eye as well as the stomach. All this fancy décor was not without some humor as one evening. The tables were set with dramatic stone plates shaped like clam shells and hand-hewn bowls resembling coconuts.

Easton and Astrid had separate rooms in the large ground-floor Gold Sun Suite located at the furthest end of the hotel. Theirs' were the prized accommodations attached to the main building and yet isolated in its distance from the restaurants, shops, and other smaller hotel rooms. At the *SRH,* as folks who returned year after year affectionally referred to it, only A-list people were ever considered for staying in the Gold Sun because it was booked so far in advance by returning guests and was so costly. Easton's family had been coming there almost every spring for as long as he could remember. He had childhood memories of playing on the pink sand, teenage badminton contests, arts and crafts, deep sea diving, and many other activities provided by the children's counselor, who was paid well to keep the kids busy (and tired).

The pristine beach was located just yards from the door to the suite. The modern designed living room was decorated completely in white though there were accent plants with huge leafy fronds that gave the space a distinctly tropical feel. The plantings outside their rooms were robust, with pink, red, and white flowers spreading a sweet fruity aroma in the afternoon breeze. Lizards scurried about in the bushes, and naturally, a number of them made their way into the suite, which was a good thing because they ate the mosquitos out of reach of the ocean winds blowing them away.

Though there was a fully stocked kitchen and bar just off the living room, they took their meals in the main dining room, where they had the opportunity to mingle with other guests (and Easton, in a nod to his own vanity, was proud to show off Astrid to whatever fantasy other guests might have about her). It was a festive atmosphere in the Conch Dining Room, which every other evening had a local music ensemble playing dinner music, more-or-less a blend of island and pop culture.

Up until then, Easton remained true to his word that his intentions were to give Astrid a taste of the world without any pressure. However, as intentions often go, circumstances change the best-laid plans. He never meant one evening to accidentally brush his hand against her shoulder ever so slightly as they sat down on the bench outside their quarters to look out at the rising moon over the ocean. He had no intention of delicately sweeping her red hair behind her ear off of her face. He certainly had no thought of moving closer to her and, much like the gentlest of breezes in this island paradise, whispering, “I’m sorry. I did not mean to do that”.

On Astrid’s part, she was experiencing feelings unlike any

she had had before. She tried to fight the word, which fought valiantly from being revealed but was fated to lose the battle. "Love, Easton. I love you." and with that declaration, she broke free from the emotional chains shackled on her by the cruel boys in the Box. And receiving her expression of love helped to diminish his memory of the unbearable loss of his wife (though at night, at times, it would come raging back).

Together, cuddling on an elegant wooden bench under the Caribbean moon, their mortal paths became most intimately entwined – especially since a month after their return to the States, she learned a baby was on the way.

Chapter Forty-Five

Astrid was unaware she was pregnant when she initially got back to New York. On the train headed home to Penn View, she noticed she was queasy but chalked it up to travel fatigue. Actually, her mother guessed first because she noticed her daughter's appetite had dwindled. She even refused apple pie. Astrid had been less talkative than usual about her adventures in Antigua, and her mother grew suspicious. Her father, scolding his wife, admonished her for 'interrogating the kid,' which naturally hurt her feelings a bit.

After breakfast the next morning, when she was alone with her daughter, she came right out and asked if Astrid was ok. Not one to withhold much from her family, her daughter burst out with, "I'm in love with Easton, and where the fuck can that go?" Her mother, startled by the intensity of the outpouring, tried to comfort her with advice about 'such feelings will pass, it's natural to feel grateful,' etc. And then, on a hunch, her mother asked, "Do you think you're pregnant?"

Astrid froze. "What do you mean, Mother?" to which her mother, unaccustomed to hearing Astrid call her 'mother' instead of more affectionately 'mom,' responded, "I'm just wondering. That's all." Astrid had not considered the possibility since she and Easton only had sex that final night. Then, she thought out loud, voice rising so her mother could hear, "Just once, my first time, it can't be. My life is over." And she proceeded to burst into tears because she was certain she would lose Easton forever and he would feel trapped by her, and she wanted to jump off a cliff.

The two of them spent the morning talking, figuring out the next steps (like finding out if she actually was pregnant, which she was for sure, no doubt, but it needed to be verified), and strategizing. They came up with a plan. First, take the home test, then, if need be, Astrid would go to New York and tell Easton. The two of them would need to come up with their own plans (which frightened Astrid, but she knew she had to face reality). If he didn't want to know her, be a father, or even a friend, she would need to make her own choice about what to do. But first things first. He had a right to know and be a part of the process. They agreed to wait to tell her father until Astrid knew where Easton stood in all this.

She wasn't due to visit New York for another week. They had not seen each other for a few weeks (though they chatted almost every evening about this and that) by the time she got to his apartment, unpacked, and met him in the downstairs library. She loved that room with all the leather-bound volumes, stained glass and giant easy chairs. It was cozy and felt much like one of the small private reading rooms in the 42nd St Library that he had shown her one rainy Saturday afternoon when they were killing time before attending a lecture on urban planning being given in the auditorium of the Arnell Building just down the block. That building, known for its inside art nouveau pillars and elevator decorations, was a frequent site for elite lectures.

She walked into the room, catching him a little off guard as he was reading one of the numerous financial trade journals to which he subscribed. Ever the gentleman, Easton rose immediately to greet her, giving her a modest kiss that likely would draw no one's attention if anyone happened to be looking. He grinned widely and, with that, said, "Hey, Red, I am really glad to see you." Ever since their evening of love, he had nicknamed her "Red." "I'm so happy to see you as well," she responded. Then they both sat.

There was a silence which he broke with, "I have nothing planned for us this evening. Maybe I should have, but I just didn't. I hope you don't mind. I thought tomorrow we could do the Cloisters and maybe catch a show. I've never taken you to the Twenty-one Club. Maybe we could check out the new Neo-Impressionist show at the Met? I also thought you might enjoy heading down to SOHO to see the goings on there." And as it was clear he was just going to keep throwing possibilities at her, she couldn't help but wonder if he was a little nervous around her.

"Easton, are you ok? You seem a little jittery. I'm perfectly ok just hanging out with you – no need to entertain." To which he responded with a large belly laugh, "I guess I am, which is not something I am accustomed to," and he got out of his chair and hovered over her for a few seconds before taking her face in his hands. What followed was a gentle, affectionate kiss. "Now I think I can calm down," and he went back to his chair and briefly gazed at her before adding, "I'm twice your age, but you make me feel young and real and alive. I never wanted to take advantage. I hope you truly know that. And if you tell me that what we did in Antigua can never happen again, I will totally respect that" (though it was killing him to make that offer because he certainly did want that to happen again).

In the other chair was a young woman who was in love with an older man, who was pregnant by this older man and who ran the risk of losing him once she told him she was having his baby. She and her mother had discussed looking for the right moment to tell Easton, but it occurred to Astrid there may be no such thing as a 'right' moment, so now might as well be the time.

She rose from her chair and walked over to his. She reached down and took his face, which was somewhat stubbly and in need of shaving, in her hands. She bent towards him and kissed his lips with a bit more oomph than the way he did hers. Then, with her fingers cold and trembling, she reached for both his hands which were so long by comparison to hers. She loved his hands and how they explored and learned so much about her body. She took them and kissed the tips of his fingers before placing his hands directly on her lower belly and holding them there while looking directly into his eyes, smiling. “We made a baby, Easton.”

He was silent. The antique grandfather’s clock in the foyer rang a hollow chime for the quarter hour. The odor of the old books hung motionless in the library. Easton felt like he was adrift in a cloud suspended over the world. Astrid returned to her chair. She wasn’t exactly worried, but she felt like she was experiencing vertigo and might fall over if she didn’t sit down immediately.

As with most fantasies between people, negotiations often are required to fulfill the actual needs of both parties. Easton had the fantasy of marrying this young woman and sharing a future wrapped in life adventures and endless nights of passionate lovemaking. Astrid had the fantasy of marrying this older man, having his child, making love as much as possible, and raising a family with maybe one or two more children.

And so it went that over the entirety of the weekend, they came to terms with most of their needs and wants. They both wanted to be married to each other, and they both wanted a lot of physical intimacy as the manifestation of the real love they jointly felt. The tricky desires were around the issue of children.

As an only child, Astrid longed for another sibling. She felt burdened as the sole focus and provider of her parents’ emotional needs and dreams. Plus, she imagined the joy and friendship of a sister or brother. Easton, a boy with twin siblings, always felt excluded and lonely by his siblings, even more so because his parents were distant and emotionally unavailable. He believed he only had enough love for one child.

What the couple ultimately agreed to was one child for now, but he would not completely foreclose on the possibility of another one in a few years, depending on how things went with the first one. Under no circumstance would he agree to a third?

But he would agree with his attorneys to have Astrid sign a prenuptial agreement. A man of his enormous wealth marrying a woman who had been a work/study in college, whose father was a postal worker, and whose mother was a baker of pies for the local diner, well, he certainly should protect his heritage. Though he wasn't entering into marriage thinking about endings, Easton had a lot to lose if it went belly up. She, being the trusting woman she was and soon-to-be mother of his child, had no fears that he would always take care of her. Signing the document took place without a fuss one rainy afternoon in his attorney's office.

Afterward, Astrid and Easton strolled over to L. K. Fenton's, the largest and oldest toy store that also carried high-end baby furniture in Manhattan. They spent three hours selecting a crib, pram, stroller, changing table, nursing rocking chair, storage bins, and other paraphernalia essential to welcoming a newborn. Not knowing the gender, they chose neutral colors for everything, including the giant teddy bear that was to become almost a member of the family sitting in the rocker when it was unoccupied.

Easton also decided to secretly put one million dollars into an interest-bearing savings account that was in his soon-to-be wife's name. He wanted to surprise her with it and tell her to do as she pleased with the money. What outwardly appeared to be a generous no-strings-attached gift for the woman he loved was, on its' underbelly, an insurance policy that his psyche needed.

If she stayed in the marriage when she knew since she had the money, she could leave, the proof of her love was evident. Ironically, giving her such a large sum of money meant, to him, that she was not staying with him for financial reasons. But as such duplicitous plans go, ill-placed logic warps the otherwise lucid mind of the schemer into assuming all scenarios have been considered. Easton still did not understand, even with the emotional distancing and then the catastrophic loss of his first wife, that walking out the front door was not the only way to disappear from a marriage.

And so, with ready hearts, Astrid and Easton married in a quasi-elopement in Lake George, NY, where his family owned a 'camp.' A local judge officiated, and Astrid's parents drove over, spending the weekend in the family retreat. Easton's mother arrived, being driven by Smith. She did not participate in any meaningful way in the ceremony; however, Smith bore witness and signed the marriage certificate along with the wife of the judge.

The ceremony was brief – Astrid was starting to show the pregnancy and insisted she not be fitted for an expensive wedding gown. She looked lovely in a champaign lace-covered dress that fit loosely and was comfortable. The meals were catered (by then, Astrid's appetite was starting to improve), and the festivities ended Sunday morning when Astrid's parents headed back to Penn View, Easton's mother and Smith headed south to New York City, and the newlyweds spent the next five days (until Smith returned to bring them back to New York) relaxing, sitting on a worn oak bench at the shore of the lake. They talked, held each other, and dreamed about their baby, who would make her appearance in a few short months. As husband and wife packed to go home, Easton placed the *Freedom Bank* passbook on top of her clothing in the suitcase. Astrid, without opening it, put it in her purse.

Chapter Forty-Six

Adele Linda Sinclair was born to her joyful parents between Christmas and the New Year. Astrid's mother stayed a few weeks after the birth to help her acclimate to motherhood and get to know her grandbaby. Her father could not leave the post office (the busiest time of the year) but called every evening to hear this story or that about what baby Lindy had done that day which always amounted to things most newborns do in those early weeks. When Astrid's mother wasn't sitting with her daughter or helping take care of Lindy, she was downstairs in the kitchen talking 'recipes' with Cook. While she was there, she learned how to make lace cookies, marzipan, and Baked Alaska (though she could never imagine an occasion to serve such an elaborate dessert!). In turn, Cook was delighted to learn how to make apple pie like none other. They got along famously.

Easton's first words when Lindy was pointed out to him in the newborn unit at West Bridge Memorial Hospital was, "Where's my little tax deduction? Which one is she?" to which a somewhat horrified nurse stood behind a tiny bassinette, pointed and spoke "Here she is. This is your baby, Daddy Sinclair."

Her words shook him to the core. The enormity of what they, his wife and he, had created, the responsibility, the intrusion, the delight all rolled into one moment of sheer panic. Suddenly his vow to never feel deeply about another human loomed large in his mind. How could he escape opening his heart completely to this tiny being that held such a firm grasp on his pinky finger? Surely he would fail at this fatherhood enterprise as his father and his father before that had so obviously done.

"Would you like to see Momma Sinclair (he momentarily got confused thinking she was referring to his own mother who was never called 'momma' by any of her children) now? I'll take you to her room." And with that, the nurse left the nursery and met the new father in the hall to take him to his wife.

Astrid was naturally exhausted from childbirth but alert enough to notice a strained look on her husband's face. When she asked him if something was wrong, he vehemently denied it, which concerned her more. But now was not the time to pursue issues. They had a baby to celebrate and welcome into the world.

For the next five years, they loved little Lindy mightily. For Astrid, the affection flowed simply like breathing. For Easton, his adoration was tinged heavily with fear of paternal failure filling him with so much self-doubt that he secretly wished he did not love his child so fervently. He was terrified his love would somehow bring about her destruction.

In his dreams, Easton frequently found himself to be in an avalanche of snow, tumbling round and round, losing all orientation of up and down. And in spite of the blinding whiteness surrounding him, all would go dark and soundless. Though he thought he was screaming, in actuality, he was merely whispering, "I am a bad man, I am a bad man," over and over again as he dreamed about plummeting down the slope of death.

Astrid would feel for him in the dark. His back was clammy, sticky to the touch, with the slight odor of worry lingering within the sheets. "My love, you are not a bad man. You are a good man. I know you. You are good." But he was not actually awake and could not really hear her words as he slept through the drama of his nocturnal agitation.

In the morning, Easton rarely recalled any specifics of his disturbing sleep, even though evidence of its presence left his body feeling pummeled and beaten down. The morning shower helped him regain the demeanor of control that helped him get through each day.

Astrid learned early on in their marriage not to bring up the night episodes as a point of conversation because each time she did, she felt she was losing him a tiny bit to the thief of depression and guilt. She had suggested therapy which he refused. At times she felt frustrated at his resistance to heal this old wound – as if holding onto it somehow kept the attachment to his first wife.

He began bringing Astrid gifts of all sorts to brighten his mood, and she quickly learned that her appreciative responses rubbed off on him enough to alleviate some of his depression for a while. He bought her jewelry of all kinds, among them, a Scarab necklace from Egypt (bought at auction in London), black coral earrings from Antigua (where they returned each spring), a blue star sapphire ring (mined in Sri Lanka, sold, and set on 47th St. in New York City) and silver bracelets galore from Mexico. Oddly, after she wore the jewelry once, he no longer enjoyed her enjoyment of them. Thus, he would feel the need to go out and find some new bauble to bring home as a gift, to stimulate an enthusiastic response, and to elevate his mood. But every time the spending cycle took place, his spirit sank a little more at night, descending into a brutal place lacking all forgiveness.

It slowly crept over Astrid's mind that her function, her reason for being merged with her legacy benefactor, was more about managing his suffering, staving off his very real depression, than building a life with him from the ground up. For Easton, the internal architecture of his spirit was built on a shaky foundation. His frail self-worth was constructed long before his first wife, Astrid, came into his life. And she, mother of his only child, remained as a permanent invited guest, a rescuer from the treachery of the downhill run of death.

Chapter Forty-Seven

Lindy was the heir apparent and, as such, was financially set for life. She also was a wonderfully happy baby, curious toddler, and charmingly sweet young child. All the staff at home (as well as Smith, who was still working on very rare occasions) called her "Miss Lindy," and for a time, when she first attended nursery and kindergarten, she told the other children her name was "MissLindy" because that's the name to which she had grown accustomed.

Her grandmother, Linda Regina Tremont Sinclair, for whom the child was partially named (the child's first name, Adele, was chosen just because both parents loved the sound of it), never left her suite of rooms in the upstairs right wing of the apartment. Lindy would be brought to visit her every few weeks and sit on her bed. But first, before anything else occurred, the child would help herself to a butterscotch hard candy or cinnamon ball from the porcelain goodie jar between the red leather wing chairs studded with copper nails.

Their conversations would always go the same way. Granny would ask the girl her name, and the child would give a spirited reply, "Lindy!" and then she would continue to ask her, "And whom are you named after, Lindy?" and the child would respond, "You Granny! You know me!" and the two of them would laugh and giggle as if the coincidence was the funniest thing ever.

Generally, Astrid took Lindy for visits during the day when her grandmother was alert. Easton missed most visits as he was at work. However, one day, he was home and decided to join the two of them to go see Granny. As the precious exchange of giggles and laughter between grandmother and granddaughter took place, Easton felt his head pounding and his vision darkening. He was uncertain of what was happening but just knew he had to get out of there immediately, so he turned and raced out of the room before tears gave away his emotions.

Astrid had been touched watching her daughter and her Granny's playfulness and thought it sweet until she was startled by her husband's hasty exit. Only then, as she looked towards the grandmother, did she catch an oddly broad smile creep across the old woman's face. Mrs. Sinclair, sitting erect amongst her satin bed pillows and starched linen sheets, stared deadly straight into Astrid's eyes. It all only lasted a few seconds, but strange cruelty etched a hollow feeling into the core of her being.

She reached for her daughter, announcing, "Time for Granny to get her rest." She took Lindy's hand and eased her off the bed. They walked by the table with the candy jar, and Astrid, sensing her daughter wanted a sweet to take back to her room, lifted the lid and pulled out a treat for later as they left Granny behind.

It all seemed weird and sinister.

Chapter Forty-Eight

That night in bed, both Astrid and Easton were restless. After tossing and turning and not settling in, she asked why he was so upset earlier in the day, watching his mother and daughter enjoying each other. Though he rarely let down his guard to anyone about such things, this time, he opened up. "She never once played with me, laughed with me, nothing. I wouldn't begrudge Lindy getting to have that with my mother. No, no. But suddenly, I couldn't stand to be in that room. I felt infuriated and wanted to scream 'Fuck you' in her face. I felt envious of my own child and felt like crying" Rant building, he spewed, "I know I can never have what I want and…."

Astrid firmly interrupted his outburst, "But you have me."

And in a split second, when emotions become so charged, they cannot help but escape any containment between thinking and spewing, Easton lashed out, "Do I?" which then cracked open the kind of fissure that draws all reason and caring down deeper and deeper into a cascade of bilious verbiage, smack into a roiling center of magma where all feelings melt into toxic truths.

The devastating truth Easton exposed was his emotional competition with his child. He could not bear watching and knowing that his mother could give generous love to his child, a generation of attachment skipped for this favored five-year-old.

He was equally jealous of the unconditional love his wife bestowed upon their child. In fact, he could not understand Lindy's natural right to expect closeness and safety, and it seemed intolerable to him that his wife provided these qualities unreservedly to their child. Clearly, for Easton, love was only acceptable if it was guaranteed only given to him. He knew he was an insane notion, but one he kept coming back to because, as people often do when they struggle to make sense of their own mess of thoughts and feelings, the words and their endless repetition represented failed efforts to convince himself he was rational.

Astrid attempted to reach through her husband's suffering (as was her way with all who experienced deep pain) to reassure him she was completely there for him, which only fueled the flames because his child part was now in control of his reactions and was spinning out of control, egged on by the familial ruptures of a lifetime. Easton was distrustful of the quality and quantity of Astrid's love for him and felt certain he was only second best now that Lindy was in the picture.

"You fucking got pregnant, and I actually never really wanted a child, even though I do love Lindy. I would have been perfectly ok never having a child, which I really did for you, and of course, now that she's here, I adore her, and I'll give her everything, and she'll never know…."

"She will know, Easton."

"She will never know the pain of having a parent who fucking doesn't give a shit like mine. I'll be careful of that, but I'll be goddamned if you think for a minute that I will ever bring another kid into this world that you can love more than me. We are NOT having another child. I can't deal with it."

And with that, Astrid came face-to-face with the abject depth of his jealousy, the fury of his wounding. She spoke barely above a whisper to both her husband and his child part, "Listen to me. Whatever problem you have, you better get it fixed. Lindy needs us both. I am not giving up on you, but I'm not going to love Lindy any less just because you can't tell the difference between love for a child and love for a grown man."

And with that, she turned her back to her husband and wept for his lifetime of emotional abandonment, the likely suffering this would cause her child because such wounds never remain contained but end up wandering and infecting intimate relationships everywhere they can, and for herself because she could see the long runway before her and understood her other children, the ones never to be created, would leave Lindy an only child who for Astrid, unable to make this right, felt like a failure.

Chapter Forty-Nine

Lindy mostly had the run of the house though she preferred to play in her bedroom with her extra-large collection of stuffed animals and dolls. She had an art table with ample supplies of every kind. Her canopy bed was covered with filmy pink tulle draped around the four pillars. Lindy loved her books which were scattered all over the place as she picked them up at whim and pretended to read them. Basically, it was a dream bedroom that any little girl in the world would love.

The staff working in the Sinclair household adored Lindy. Cook always had special cookies waiting for her when she would 'sneak' down the back stairs to the kitchen for a snack. Ice-cold milk was always ready to be given to Lindy in what Cook referred to as "Lindy's glass," which was blue and sparkly in the kitchen light.

Josie, whose thick German accent made her sound much more stiff and serious than she meant to be, had worked for Mrs. Sinclair since World War II, and for certain, there was some mystery about how she came to be in her household. One could tell she had an elevated status as she was not required to wear the obligatory black dress and white cuff and collar uniform of the other 'help' (the other exception was Cook, who was always in white). Josie would take Lindy into one of the back bedrooms in the apartment for staff and teach her how to sew straight lines with the antique Singer portable (first of its kind) sewing machine. They'd make row after row of lines just to practice 'getting them perfect,' as Josie would say.

Recently they hired Riva to aid in the household responsibilities as Josie needed assistance. Mrs. Sinclair, who was no longer doing much supervising of such matters, had left her interviewing to Josie, whose judgment of character she trusted implicitly. Riva was middle-aged and a bit hefty but was there to do light housework and straighten things up (though not much was ever really out of place) so Josie could spend more time with Mrs. S.

On Rivas's first day, she met Lindy in the kitchen as she was drinking milk and scoffing down a star-shaped sugar cookie with pink sugar crystals scattered across the top. "What's your name, little girl?" asked Riva. Cook looked on and encouraged the child to speak, "Go on now, tell Riva your name. You want to be polite, right? Swallow first!" all of which was said with a wide grin as both adults took in the preciousness of the child.

"I'm Lindy, after my granny, and I love star cookies. Do you want one?" Riva found the offer and the child irresistible, and so she accepted. "With pleasure. How lovely to meet you, Miss Lindy!" As can happen with children who have not lost the capacity to discern a trustworthy individual, they may extend an invitation for a grownup to enter their world as a partner in play. "Do you know 'Hide and Seek,' Riva?" "Why yes, Miss Lindy. It is one of my favorite games!" and with that, Lindy took her new friend's hand and pulled her through the pantry right past the 'grumpy one' and into the dining room. "Ok Riva, You're it! Count to 63 (which was the biggest number she could imagine at that time)" as she dropped her hand and raced into the foyer to hide.

"Ready or not, Miss Lindy, here I come!" Looking determined for the hunt, Riva moved through the library, muttering, "I wonder where Miss Lindy went." Then into the living room, which seemed such incongruous to play a child's game amidst the Flemish art and fine Russian porcelain. Then Riva heard a stifled giggle.

"I wonder if that child found a unicorn and flew away?" To which Lindy, whose imagination had few limits, shouted from the powder room under the magnificent spiral staircase, "Yes, yes, she's riding in the clouds on her unicorn, Puffy, and you'll never find her." as she broke into peals of laughter while at the same time, Riva slowly pulled open the bathroom door and exclaimed, "Oh my gosh, there you are! I would never have found you, Miss. Lindy. I'm so happy you've come back!"

And from that moment until two months later, Riva and Lindy met daily for cookies and "Hide and Seek," which always ended the same way, with the child returning from a flight on her unicorn.

Chapter Fifty

While Easton and Astrid remained on friendly terms, their actual friendship suffered a rupture that did not appear dramatic on the surface but, like a small snag in silk, could never fully be disguised or returned to the perfection of the weave. Sex lost meaning and became more of a habit than an act of love. He threw himself more fully into his vow of making as much money as possible. He kept buying her gifts which she accepted and then placed aside on her whatever table was nearby.

Astrid felt adrift except in the presence of her daughter; however, because of the pressures she had experienced as an only child, she knew better than to define herself through her own daughter. For Astrid, Lindy was the center of her breath, and she was devoted to her best interests, even at a cost to herself. For Easton, the little girl was loveable enough. He did adore her, but, critically, she was also a rival which made selfless love untenable.

Astrid was also well aware that the parent who cannot love their child unconditionally has a vicious advantage over the other. The advantage Easton had over his wife, who so desperately wanted him to show genuine fatherly love for their child, was the distance he could keep from the little girl and still give enough to stay in the game.

Chapter Fifty-One

Riva was resting for a short while in the family library with a book she had taken from one of the shelves open in her lap. This was her favorite spot in the entire house because the smell of it took her back to childhood and the little library in the primary school she attended in Millersville, Michigan.

Insomnia was a horrid thing that she just couldn't shake at her age. She listened for the grandfather clock strike at 3:00 am. She knew from watching it the past two months that the moon was almost fully showing above the 12, and that meant she would need to give it a wind in another day or two.

She found peace in this room that looked so out of place in the twenty-first century. At night the stained glass resembled pieces of a jigsaw puzzle outlined in lead. It was very pretty. She was getting tired and thought she might head back to bed. It was already the beginning of a new day, but she always found those two or three hours after the trial of trying to sleep the most delicious and peaceful. The chair felt good. It was so quiet. And still.

Chapter Fifty-Two

Lindy woke up extra early, filled with excitement because today was to be the first day of first grade. She and her mother had lovingly laid out her school uniform the night before on the pink velveteen bean bag chair she loved to cuddle into for reading; a plaid jumper and white blouse with a peter-pan collar.

Her expectations, based on conversations with her mother, were that she would be making new friends as well as reuniting with some old ones whom she knew from kindergarten the previous year. Together, mother and daughter would sing about "making new friends but keeping the old, one is silver and the other gold," which the little girl correctly figured meant both kinds of friends were valuable.

She was certain she would have a real gym class and art making. She'd heard from Granny there would be singing and dancing and a special time for cookies and milk every morning. Lindy had gone to visit the kindergarten the spring before. Outside the main entrance to her classroom grew a lilac bush in full bloom. The smell was intoxicating, and before going in, Lindy kept sniffing at the fragrant nectar to get a deeper whiff. She noticed that the more she tried to inhale the spring aroma, the less sweetness there was, which both disappointed and confused her.

Inside the classroom, the first thing she eyed was a lighted fish tank next to the teacher's desk with a sign she had to have read to her, "Fishes Wishes - Please Look - Don't Touch!". This was another frustration because she felt so tempted to pet the wiggly orange and black creatures swimming around inside.

There was a space called a cloakroom (Lindy was puzzled and asked, "What 's a cloak do?" to which Miss Van Arden, her soon-to-be favorite teacher, bemusedly told her this was where all the children would be putting their coats and galoshes (another curious new word but this time Lindy withheld her question).

And so, with exciting thoughts of worlds of adventure swirling about her mind, anticipation had awakened the little girl extra early, prompting her to tiptoe past her parents' bedroom and carefully wander down the spiral stairs in her nightie. In some misguided imaginings, she believed if she started her day early, the time might go faster to get the fun happenings. It was going to be an amazing day!

She was way too early for breakfast, the big clock in the huge hall had the long hand just before twelve and the short one almost touching the five. She knew that meant she needed to be quiet for a little while longer. She skipped into the center of the intricate oriental rug that she had often sat upon to play dolls in spite of its scratchy texture rubbing uncomfortably against her skin. Most fun for her was explaining to her dolls about the images woven into the carpet – a tree made into a forest, funny-shaped people, camels, and things she made up into stories that only children and toys could fully appreciate.

There was so much to be happy about that morning, so when she saw Riva sitting in the library, she was overjoyed and decided to run over and give her a big hug which was something they did from time to time when they finished playing hide-and-seek and other games.

As Lindy twirled into the library, she noticed dawn's first light turning the stained-glass shine all twinkly. She turned to Riva and exclaimed, "Look, the glass is starting to dance. Just like me! Did you see me dance, Riva? Maybe when I get home from school, we can dance together! And, hey, Riva…" for as the child faced her friend and placed her hand over the hand of the woman in the chair, the girl felt an odd and unpleasant coldness, causing her to quickly withdraw her touch.

"Riva, wake up. You fell asleep out here." The child felt confused because Riva was staring vacantly into the room and felt cool and was paying no attention to her whatsoever. Then Lindy noticed wetness at the edge of the seat under Riva, reminding her of her own nocturnal accidents from when she was younger.

There was the stillness. Nothing was making sense to her. And even though Riva had left this earth a few hours earlier, Lindy heard her hide-and-seek friend softly say, “It’s ok, sweetheart, but you better go tell Mommy.”

Chapter Fifty-Three

"Mommy comes" were effectively the last words Lindy spoke for the next year. Her mother was at first shocked and then deeply saddened to see Riva dead in the library chair, and she was heavily concerned that her daughter had been the one to find her. Easton's response was that of outrage, "Why the hell was 'help' sitting in one of our chairs when they have their own staff lounge back there?" which set Astrid off into a rage one of the few times in her life. Had he no empathy? But he was entrenched in his belief that Irene had transgressed by using his library (though he rarely ever used it as such) as if it belonged to her.

They bickered over the audacity of a person who, on the household staff, had the nerve to sit and die in one of the Sinclair chairs. Astrid couldn't bear the insanity and kept her interactions with her husband at a minimum, enough to give a civil appearance of things but far less than the warm and natural way they interacted in the early years of their relationship.

The old pair of stuffed chairs were both thrown out and replaced with a new set of designer overstuffed reading chairs which rarely, if ever, got used – that is until almost a year later when on his first night, Darby curled himself atop one of their delicious satiny cushions during his transformation into a prince.

It took weeks for the grownups surrounding Lindy to actually understand the silence that descended upon her was not going away anytime soon. Miss Van Arden sent a note home from school expressing concern that Lindy was not participating in activities and she was not speaking to anyone, ever. She was worried that if the problem didn't clear up soon, she might need to repeat a year.

Easton was annoyed because he regarded her silence as if she were willfully 'on strike,' to which Astrid retorted it seemed more serious a situation than that. She took her to the pediatrician to rule out anything medical, and the doctor found nothing physically wrong and suggested she be taken to a psychiatrist. His determination was to put the child on anti-anxiety medication, which Astrid refused to consider because of all the side effects. Cook tried to make special foods to help comfort her, and the other staff kept repeating, "She just needs time." None of the interventions seemed to be doing much except postpone dealing with the problem head-on. Then one day, the school sent a note with Smith, who was driving Lindy back home in the afternoons.

Dear Mr. and Mrs. Sinclair,

Lindy needs help. I am enclosing the name and contact information of an excellent art therapist for a referral to you. I believe she has the credentials and skills needed to help your daughter. We do not want to see her slip further developmentally behind. We also are concerned her needs may become disruptive to the others in the class.

Please rest assured we believe Ms. Beatrice Pons will be of help to Lindy. She has worked with a number of other of our children who have needed, from time to time, a little 'special' care.

We look forward to Lindy's progress in speaking again.

Sincerely,

Dr. Anita Grusen

Headmistress

And so, eight months into the child's silence, 'Ms. Bea' began art therapy sessions with Lindy Sinclair. For months the only words, judiciously chosen and softly spoken, came from the therapist. While the parents, the staff, and the school were impatient for demonstrable progress, the art therapist understood the work to help the child find her voice again would not necessarily be measured in spoken words, which, while critically important, were not their only means of communication. And while hearing the little girl chatter the way children generally do, was a primary goal, it was not the initial goal.

Nothing else could take place until the child, terrified by the trauma of her encounter with the death of her beloved friend, could feel safe again in her world. For it was one horrifying morning on the first day of school that Riva had turned into a stone tree, and Lindy, unspeakably alone with the corpse of her friend, became lost in a game of hide-and-seek in an impenetrable forest.

Chapter Fifty-Four

Darby slinked into Lindy's room – his black body in stark contrast to the range of pink hues on the furniture, wallpaper, and fabrics of the room. As she opened her eyes to adjust to the morning, he leaped onto the night table, knocking over a glass of water and spilling the contents onto the shag rug below. And then there was a squeal of laughter as Lindy, both startled and delighted, sent a full-bellied laugh out into the air of her bedroom. Darby, not easily put off by the unexpected, remained at her side. He, in fact, curled into her body, purring as loudly as he could, and instantly understood she was to be his person, and he was to be her prince.

Astrid appeared in the doorway, "Oh, I see Darby has found you!" and the little girl nodded because even though the presence of the cat was not a cure, it was 12 pounds of life, living, and breathing, that intuitively understood her in ways that words could not explain. Though unspoken, she understood he was there for her to share secrets, play, cuddle, and love. Darby understood this was to be his most important role in life and was willing even to withstand the indignities of being dressed up from time to time in doll clothing. There is something to be said about chemistry, and these two had it.

In fact, Darby would remain central to her life for the next twelve years until the fall of the year she went off to college. Lindy came home for the fall break in October when the leaves were turning orange in preparation for the coming winter's sleep. She saw her buddy-prince nestled tightly in a coil in the center of her bed. His fur was slightly unkempt (it never did fall off again once the two of them found their love) because he could not reach all the places to keep himself as clean as he once did. He tried as best he could to lift his head as he felt her caress his back. She felt the tips of his spine protruding against the blackness of his fur.

That night, under the silken covers of her bed, Lindy cradled her beloved and asked him to go ahead of her to find where they would be forever together. And then she thanked him, for truth be known, though a cat is not a cure, the relationship can be.

She took him in her arms and looked into the miracle of his eyes, staring at the infinity of the exploding star in his heaven-blue eye, and knew the time had come to let him go.

Chapter Fifty-Five

"Lindy, just a reminder that Ms. Bea is coming this afternoon. I'll bet she'll love meeting Darby!" which caused the child to look up at her mother and give a small smile. She and Darby had been getting to know each other for just a short time, so Ms. Bea coming over today would be extra special as they would get to meet as well. What a great day!

She looked around her room and knew that Darby was playing hide-and-seek with her just the way Riva had done before she left for heaven. She was still sad that her friend was gone, but the truth was her heart was so full of Darby's love that the gloomy space inside her had shrunk to make room for other kinds of feelings that were much more lovely.

Lindy had exhausted seeking Darby in the obvious hiding spots. He was not under the bed nor deep inside her closet. Just when she was about to call his name (a certain means for having him appear), she saw his paw poking out of a pile of pink and white feather boas she had tossed into a basket after playing dress up with him.

"Gotcha. You'll be mine forever!" and with a dramatic hug, the child and cat embraced.

Chapter Fifty-Six

Beatrice had appointments with three clients this afternoon. The first was with Lindy. She was aware that Darby the cat had arrived the night before and felt hopeful that his presence would provide the little girl with feelings of comfort and connection. Mrs. Sinclair, who preferred Beatrice to call her Astrid, was completely on board with her daughter having a cat to love. She wanted nothing more than for her child to be restored to full engagement with people. She hoped having a pet to love might dissolve the massive wall of silence that had isolated Lindy from others.

Lindy's father mostly expressed frustration with his wife, daughter, and art therapist. Why did his wife pour so much attention into the problem of Lindy speaking when, in his mind, the child was just looking for attention? Why wouldn't Lindy just stop the silliness and try to get back to normal? And finally, why spend so much money on a therapist when in her " clinical opinion," a cat might fix the problem?

After that session, Beatrice planned on hopping the crosstown bus to get to East End Avenue. There she would work with Nelson, the fifteen-year-old son of Dr. Avery Wilcox. She made it big in Silicon Valley a decade before her son was born.

Dr. Wilcox originally came from a military family stationed in Mons, Belgium, where she excelled in languages and science as a young student. With near-perfect grades and advanced placement in most of her courses, she topped off a stellar academic high school career by winning the prestigious *Presidential Scholar* 2nd place for her groundbreaking project titled, *Chips, Wafers and Conductivity Across Inter-Textual Mandate Materials.*

The crème de la crème US universities known for superb science programs were begging for her attendance, offering full-blown tuition, including room and board. Ultimately, her choice landed on the brand-new Institute of Cellular Inspiration in Paolo Alto, and thus, she made her move from drab Belgium to sunny California.

At age twenty, she snagged a significant position in nearby Vio Lab, where she worked for 10 years developing new technologies for micro-wafer transduction to be used in space missions for outer planetary exploration. Then, an amazing research position opened up at the influential think-tank at Drummond University in New York City. She decided to move to the East to become as highly celebrated in her field as possible and make herself wealthy.

She was also determined to have a baby in her belly to take the journey with her. Being fiercely independent, she had zero interest in having a husband or life partner tag along in her plans. She just wanted a child.

During her initial intake meeting with Beatrice, Dr. Wilcox was asked about the father of her son Nelson and if he might be available for a consultation as well. "That would be quite impossible, truth be told." Sensing the art therapist's curiosity (and confusion), she elaborated further.

"About a month before I planned to move to New York, I decided to invite three of the most brilliant scientists I knew from the Vio Lab to come over one evening for a homemade pasta dinner. Being an excellent cook, I remember my apartment smelled of tomato, garlic, and fresh basil. My plan was to invite all three gentlemen to join me in the bedroom as dinner was simmering on the stove."

She went on to describe the look of her bedroom decorated with candles and flowers though she actually had "no interest in any such adornments" (her personality was direct and awkward in utilizing the social graces). It was more like she wanted to give a modicum of caring to the kinds of details she imagined the men would expect from a woman.

She shared that she did not consider modesty whatsoever. She viewed the entire evening much as an experiment. None of it was about passion or love or even intimacy. It was all about getting pregnant.

As she dropped her dress to the floor, she noted the time out loud– precisely 17 minutes until the meal was ready. Then, with neither charm nor particular thoughtfulness, she encouraged all three to have as much sex with her as possible before dinner.

And they did. Never mind that in their wildest dreams, none of them could have imagined the rather stiff and formal Dr. Wilcox letting loose with them in such playful sexual behavior. They also found themselves naked in bed with each other, which, as the initial awkward phase of the first few minutes passed, generated a kind of unexpected excitement as well. They soon discovered their pile of copulating bodies helped keep the rounds of ecstasy with her going and going.

Had the buzzer of the dinner timer not gone off in the kitchen, Dr. Wilcox might have lost all track of time, an unusual occurrence for a woman tied to such scientific precision. But it did, causing her to stand and pull her dress back up. "You now have 9 minutes until dinner is served. Help yourselves to the shower," which the three did, though one quickly man washed up quickly and went to the kitchen while the other two lingered a little longer under the running water. They were exploring parts of each other that they had not dared to do in the bedroom. In fact, that evening of unexpected lust brought these two into a love orbit that was to last the next 42 years.

"The meal was delicious, if not a little strange in terms of conversation. All three excused themselves right after dessert, which was an exquisite tiramisu. It didn't bother me that they left abruptly though I thought it a bit rude after all the preparation I put into everything."

Nelson, (Neil, Evan, Liam + son) was born almost nine months after that evening in a hospital in New York where the birth certificate indicated a *sperm donor name unknown.* According to Dr. Wilcox, Nelson never asked about his father, so for her, it was a non-issue. She assumed if he was curious, he'd ask, which was certainly an assumption with which Beatrice did not concur.

Nelson attended a progressive NY public satellite school where he was encouraged to learn through doing. He had an education grounded in merging exploration, imagination, and reflection. Dr. Wilcox worked long hours between think-tank meetings and scientific exploration in her private research lab.

She hired a man-sitter, Ted, to take the boy to calligraphy classes at the Y, archery at the Eastside Shooters Club (they taught how to use guns as well, but he disliked such weaponry), and glass blowing at the Tinkers Studio on Staten Island.

His mother thought he was getting moody (adolescence was, as she referred to it, " the complete unhinging of the human mind") and learned about Beatrice Pons from a colleague whose child had worked with her after 9/11 and the world, especially Tri-Becca where she and her young family lived, was in chaos.

From their first session, aside from the remarkable collection of Outsider Art paintings hanging strategically around the living room walls with dramatic illumination highlighting the bold colors and lines of each composition, Beatrice noticed that Nelson was almost a work of art himself. That day he was wearing a Mexican sombrero and sported a multicolored shawl over his black shirt and pants. He was a real vision of creative essence.

She learned, thereafter, that he would constantly change his 'look.' She never knew how he might be dressed when he greeted her at the door. He was masterful at changing his appearance to suit his whim. One time he dressed as a hero from a Japanese Manga, another a poor waif out of East London. He had lacy dresses and thrift shop cardigans. He was playful about all his identities and enjoyed the shock value of doing something he deemed outrageous – like dying his hair blue and wearing heavy eye makeup. His goal was to attend the School of Fashion Arts though his mother, who rarely commented an opinion about his behaviors or outfits, was unhappy with his choice. She was hoping for a more science-based future for her son.

Beatrice and Ted, the portly man-sitter, frequently crossed paths as he hung out in the living room waiting while she and Nelson had their session in the kitchen. He seemed nice enough and truly cared for the boy. In the kitchen, there was an adequately sized table, water for painting, and great light coming off the East River through a wall of bay windows lining the room. She looked forward to their work together as he was bright, in touch with his creative spirit, and also funny, which he always reminded Beatrice was something he no doubt inherited from 'somebody' in his past.

To see her final client of the day, Beatrice would head back across town to the Westside subway. With her heavy art supply bag, this leg of her trip had become more and more challenging, and she was debating about cutting back her caseload. Her 71 years were taking a real toll on her body.

The ride underground to down the West village brought her within a block of the home of Emma Henkel, age 10. She was the younger daughter of renowned artists Raleigh Ventu and Mark Henkel, both highly successful abstract painters living in a renovated stable built in the late 1800s.

Their house was so large both artists had separate massive studios. The building also boasted a two-car garage and a single-lane lap pool in the basement. Raleigh and Mark were highly competitive with each other, which drove Beatrice crazy because the impact on the children was evident.

Their older daughter, Ina, age 17, was not in therapy, and as she would tell anyone who'd listen, her life was 'pretty perfect except for having an annoying little sister.' She was lithe and stunningly beautiful and was considered mysterious and brilliant though little evidence of that was apparent in school. Ina had to be better than her little sister at everything, which was not difficult given her seven-year advantage. The boys were all crazy about her even though she barely gave them the time of day.

Emma, on the other hand, was considered kindly and moderately clever but not especially talented in anything. She was a bit overweight, uncoordinated, and, by all accounts, unremarkable. She cried too easily when reading sad stories because she strongly identified with the loser, the one who couldn't finish the race. In her family, she was labeled as "interesting," which was about the same thing as being a failure or without real value. Her family did not hold out high hopes for her future even though she had barely reached her double-digit years.

Emma was actually terrified of Ina, whose favorite game, starting from a young age, was to sneak into Emma's room at night, pull out the half-asleep child from her bed and command her to address her as "My Queen" when they were alone. Ina referred to Emma as "My Servant" and made her swear an oath, sealed with a painful wrist-twisting rub to reinforce her authority and power, to always do as the queen told her and, of course, never tell anyone.

Emma felt humiliated and shamed in the servant role, but she did not dare disobey. Ina tested her control over her sister in school on two separate occasions. The first time, she instructed Emma to stand outside her classroom after all the other children went inside and count to fifty (no simple task for a 7-year-old at the time) before she went in. Ina watched from further down the hall and thought it was hilarious to watch her sister struggle to make the count and then go in late to class.

The other time was when Ina went into her sister's bookbag and pencil scribbled a curse word on her homework. Emma immediately recognized her sister's handwriting (and who else would do such a thing?). She erased the offending word just in time before having to hand in her assignment. Later that evening, Ina grilled her, "Did you tell anyone about it?" and of course, she had not because she knew better than to rat on her sister. It only took those two trials to convince the servant of the Queen's power.

In Emma's family, she was squeezed between the driving narcissism of her parents and the vicious temperament of her sister. She stood isolated and wilted in their presence, and, as clever children who are abused often do, she projected to others a kind of stupidity that belied the truth of her real intelligence in order to protect herself at all costs. This child was an expert at reading and adapting to other people's moods and needs. What was that, if not intelligence?

From the beginning of their art therapy work together, Beatrice was reminded of her own early years of loft living with the Troika. The self-centeredness, sabotaging, and conceits of those women felt oddly parallel to this other troika, Emma's family. There was a cruel edge to the energy of all of them, and she found it triggering to be around Ina and Raleigh, and Mark.

Beatrice was initially hired to do art therapy with Emma because her parents, according to them during the initial interview, expressed concern their younger daughter was not "living up to her potential, the girl made us nervous, she seems to be more and more fearful of coming into the room when we have company." They also didn't think she took sufficient interest in appreciating the demands their stature in the art world placed upon them as a family.

In addition, Ina had been filling her parents' heads with her own 'observations' about Emma, which they included in their litany of issues. "She sneaks food at night (no wonder she's getting so pudgy)." "Emma sometimes steals money from mom's purse (at the command of the Queen, who then spent the small change on gum and makeup from the local drugstore)." "Emma doesn't have any friends." The list was longer, but Beatrice indicated she thought it best to just meet the child herself. She didn't trust any of what she was hearing. Something seemed off.

In her first art therapy sessions, Emma generated stereotypes of rainbows, oversized flowers, and big hearts drifting casually across the pages. Happiness was on steroids (as was suffering, which Beatrice understood was disguised in these early works as a defense against internal collapse). Further into their work, the images took on more authenticity. The metaphors more directly reflected the emotional state of the child. Volcanoes were erupting, buildings were failing, and dragons were breathing fire at small owl families nestled among barren trees.

Beatrice recognized early on that there were major systemic problems within this family. Though she did not have firsthand knowledge about the ritual of "Queen and Servant" or the astounding depth of narcissistic abandonment by her parents, she surmised there were devastating truths inside this mansion. The scars and debris were everywhere.

And as is inevitable when the right brain wants to share its truths, the images of abuse were beginning to make themselves known through the child's art. Bit by bit, the deep slumber of protection gave way to representations of violent weather destroying skyscrapers and houses and a building labeled "museum." The images exposed the girl's inner world as in chaos.

Most recently, her art included a dog seeking shelter, huddling under a large broken tree amidst the wind and rain. Beatrice asked Emma, "Does the tree want to say anything?" to which the child responded, "You can stay here with me, Dog. I'll keep you safe" And does the dog wish to speak? "This is my dream. To be a dog and live under this tree." The art therapist contemplated if she should contact Child Services.

After that session, Beatrice took herself to supervision. She made a drawing of a burnt-out building, a shell of what it once was. Piles of rubble were strewn all around, and there, buried under the rocks and bricks, was a girl being pulled to safety by a shadowy creature with unusual strength and determination. In an instant, she was transported by memory back to a time with Dr. Fine when the same creature came to life on the paper for her. So many years had passed, but the feeling was unmistakable. She felt the wolf stirring and wondered if it had rescued the girl in the picture or had she?

She decided to wait for one or two more sessions before calling her report in. She was still on the fence. But, as things in life turn inside out at times, those sessions were not to be.

Chapter Fifty-Seven

Since Beatrice knew she would be trekking long distances across and then downtown, she double-checked the wheels on her fantastic art supply bag, which was worn with time and use. She wanted to be certain the handles and seams were all in good shape as well. The days of seeing six or seven clients no longer worked for her, and she considered three a full enough day.

She peeled open a raspberry-chocolate protein bar and took a healthy bite that at once felt too sticky on the roof of her mouth and had an overly sweet aroma that reeked of artificial flavoring. It was an unsatisfying breakfast, so she hunted for a bowl of leftovers from the fridge containing remnants of a spinach salad from earlier in the week. The lemon dressing was tart and provided just the right finish to cut through all the sugar.

Dressed in her New York black pleated pants, cashmere sweater, and flat leather walking boots, she appraised herself in the hall mirror and decided to re-brush her hair. Beatrice lingered, recollecting the mane of strawberry blond hair she once had while trying to ignore what was impossible to deny – she was getting older by the minute, and her hair was thinning out.

Not wanting to run late, she broke loose of these thoughts and grabbed her coat and supply bag, and was down in the lobby trying to get out of the front door. Unfortunately, Curtiss was positioned right there, which forced her to give him a weak "Good day" as she was stuck to pause for him to open the door for her way out. He wore a sickeningly sly smile while staring at her face with piercing persistence that gave her the creeps. She thought, "I'm old. What does he want?" Then she pushed through her discomfort, passing the man who seemed to inhale her very breath, and exited out onto the street by noon. First stop – Lindy.

Chapter Fifty-Eight

Aside from the general pleasure of working with the child clients (in spite of their troubles, they cling to hope) in her practice, what Beatrice also appreciated about her job was being exposed to so much amazing art in private homes. The Sinclair residence downstairs was filled with Medieval statuary, illuminated manuscripts, of course, that stained glass marvel in the library, and an eclectic assortment of small "objet'd'art." The Sinclair Collection was actually earmarked for various small museums around the country should the estate eventually be broken up.

The upper floor was surprisingly less impressive. There was little fabulous art on the walls, and the bedrooms were certainly well decorated but nothing too fancy. The rooms for old Mrs. S were paneled in dark oak and smelled strongly of oil and butcher's wax as they were maintained by the staff over the decades. A long hall ran the length of the rooms, which were lined up one right after the other. Family photos ran the length of it, which gave one a cozy feeling like a family really did occupy a place.

Near the end, opposite the quarters of Mrs. S, was a room Astrid used as her office, study, and quasi-studio (she loved to paint flowers). Lindy loved playing in there when her mother wasn't home, pretending she had a magic room where anything could happen. The one drawback was when she would forget to put on shoes because though the entire upper floor had wall-to-wall carpeting, this room did not, and the peril was accidentally getting a splinter from the old wood floor caught in a soft spot under her feet. When that happened, Josie brought out the needle, touched a flame to it, let it cool down, and then proceeded to pick away at the tiniest spot of wood under Lindy's skin until she was able to push the splinter back out of the way it came into her foot.

When Ms. Bea arrived, she left her coat and supply bag downstairs by the hallway credenza and walked up the spiral stair to the upper landing. From there, she made a left, walked past the family photos and the parent's bedroom, and knocked on Lindy's door. Before she could ask, "May I come in, Lindy?" the door popped open, and there was the child, smiling and clutching Darby under his arms. "What a fine cat you have there, Lindy! Can you tell me his name?" And though the little girl said very little for a very long time, she began with his name, "Darby," in the softest voice. It was a start. "What a clever name! Would you like to make a drawing?" And the little girl immediately got to work on a drawing that naturally had a cat but also included a child and a mother. Lindy was completely engrossed in her creative process, and Darby seemed to understand. This was his cue to give the child space with her therapist. He decided, being more than a little curious, to go exploring some more.

Chapter Fifty-Nine

As Darby wandered further down the hall, he spotted the office/study/studio. He was actually drawn by the smell of flowers and paints and some indescribable odors he could not name. He leaped up onto a vast wooden table supporting fancy cardboard boxes of all sorts of seemingly random things – parts of dolls, old books with pictures of paintings in them, train tickets (though he only guessed about such things because as smart as he was, he could not read). There was shiny jewelry peeking out from barely unwrapped packages, which made him wonder why someone would leave precious baubles only partially opened.

His paw instinctively took a swipe at some of the tissue wrapping papers and satin ribbons. The crisp sounds of his claws scraping across the little boxes were so satisfying to him. There was a woven brown and white basket filled with what looked like junk that he was just dying to pick at. And then, he caught the shimmer of a starry bit of light peeking out between all the bric-a-brac in the basket.

He crouched and slinked closer to get a clearer look until, even surprising himself, he pounced on the object as if in the hunt. In one swiftly skilled, unpracticed motion, with the steady confidence of a sniper, Darby found his mark. His paw plucked the star sapphire ring (one of the multitude of gifts Easton gave to Astrid for no reason except it fit his whim and to relieve him of some unnamed burden through the act of giving) from beneath the other things. After he batted it about on the table for a few moments, with feline precision, he grasped the stone prey in his mouth as if it were a tormented dead mouse, and he had made a perfect kill.

Chapter Sixty

By the time the art therapy session ended, Darby was also exhausted from his triumphant antics. He returned to Lindy's bedroom, looking forward to some sleep time. All the way back, he relived his adventure of carrying that ring around the house, pretending to show off his victorious winnings to throngs of other imaginary felines. Initially, the ring clenched in his teeth and hanging from his mouth. He strutted with it down the giant spiral staircase and into the library. No one was around, so he kicked and batted it under the giant chairs without fear of a scolding. His game was to re-capture it and begin the play all over again.

At one point, he lay down on his side, brilliant blue iris straining to see the magic jewel and challenge it to a staring duel though, the truth be known, he only had light and dark vision from that eye with its exploding star, which in a contest such as that was a distinct advantage. He refused to blink, but so did the ring, which eventually bored the cat into getting up. He attempted to count the number of arms of its star though he wasn't in the least skilled in arithmetic. He correctly guessed that there were six (a number he had heard the kindly veterinarian once say about the number of dogs and cats in the basement of the hospital) spidery white arms evenly trailing like delicate vines across the entire surface of the stone.

The blue of the highly polished stone was reminiscent of an

azure sky in the early spring he recalled as a kitten. His good eye was the one he used for experiences requiring precision and calculation. It was his good eye that identified color the best.

Before heading upstairs to Lindy's room, Darby jumped onto the antique credenza with his prize dangling from his mouth. This was the highest point in the room that he could reach and served effectively as the location where he could saunter back and forth across the velvet runner as if he were on parade. He was a prince of this place and had precious bounty proved it.

In an instant, Darby decided to bring the ring to Lindy as a token of their budding friendship. Swelling with pride and purpose, he was thrilled imagining the great joy this gesture would bring. However, in his excessive exuberance to prove his worthiness to be her heart's prince, the bauble loosened itself from his teeth as his jaw had grown a bit tired from clenching it with such fervor. In trying to maintain control, he stumbled over his front paws only to witness the ring tumbling wildly through the air, twisting, and turning this way and that. Both his eyes, though completely different in their manner of vision, watched for one coordinated moment in time as the star sapphire ring dropped right down into the opening of the art therapist's supply bag.

Completely out of sight, the ring landed between the crayons and the scissors, too far into the bag to be readily retrieved by the cat. Excavating through the layers of art materials constituted an insurmountable task for the already exhausted feline, who had a needy little girl waiting in her bedroom for his attention. With triumph deferred, Darby, in grave disappointment, slowly headed back up the stairs as his trophy lay buried among the chaotic tools of creativity and imagination.

Chapter Sixty-One

Lindy giggled loudly as Darby stood in the doorway to her bedroom. She skipped over, scooped him up into her arms, and plopped down onto her beanbag chair. Of course, she had no idea she was not getting a star sapphire ring that day, which made it easier for Darby to let the whole fantasy go. He moved on to other important business at hand – cuddling and purring with his special person.

The two of them were snuggling when Astrid peered into the room. "Everything all right in here?" Beatrice spoke first, "I think today was a great day for drawing." Pushing Darby slightly aside, Lindy got up, raced over to her art table, and waved a drawing she had created for her mother. "Oh my, I see Lindy, and Darby and me! Darling, I love this drawing!"

The little girl, who had not spoken to the art therapist in front of anyone before, softly said, "Family". Her mother responded, "Yes, Lindy. Darby is part of our family now. But I don't see Daddy anywhere. Maybe he's at work?"

Lindy chose to ignore her mother's comment. It wasn't that the child didn't love her father. She just wasn't ready to include him. Lindy was angry at him for his being mad at Riva for sitting in the Sinclair chair and somehow had it in her mind that had caused her friend to go to 'forever' sleep (a phrase which Beatrice advised the staff and the child's parents to avoid so as to not make Lindy afraid she might die in her own sleep. It was okay to say Riva had died and wait for Lindy to ask whatever questions about that she might have about the subject.).

After the session, Beatrice and Astrid walked down the hallway together, reflecting on the general progress of how things were going. The therapist offered, "The cat hopefully will serve as a special bridge to the world, supporting Lindy as she reconnects and practices communicating. She should be encouraged to take part in the care of her pet. Family and staff should ask her about Darby and encourage Lindy to speak of their relationship. We can keep working together, but honestly, I think giving her some space to adjust to Darby, inviting a friend or two from school to come over and meet him and having her dad play with Lindy and Darby would be a very natural plan for Lindy as she gently returns to regular functioning. I would also recommend asking her about going back to school in a few weeks. Maybe Miss Van Arden could come for one or two little visits, meeting Darby and lightly socializing. Lindy and I should keep working together until she gives the signal for me to come less often. For example, if playdates start happening and there is a conflict, let's take our cue from her that she's ready to be with friends. This process should be slow and natural. We can see how it goes to determine the next steps".

Astrid, whose empathy was genuine, appreciated the

openness of the plan for Lindy. She understood the process would take the time it needed. She was deeply grateful for the improvement she saw and the joy her daughter was experiencing. She appreciated that Beatrice was not the kind of therapist who saw clients as needing perpetual therapy. She respected Beatrice Pons for targeting her work to the needs of the client and then letting the client take more ownership of their progress. And she also found herself somewhat smitten with the newest member of the family, Prince Darby.

As Astrid walked Beatrice down the spiral stairs and across the hand-knotted rug of the grand foyer to collect her bag and coat, she instinctively gave the therapist a hug. "Lindy loves you. We both do." This left Beatrice feeling exuberant, tinged with embarrassment, for deep down inside, she knew Darby was really the most significant reason Lindy was starting to speak again.

To her, it had all been a bit of educated luck to figure out what might be effective in meeting the child's needs. For her years of training, knowledge of human development, and an array of clinical experiences with so many different populations, she imagined herself to be like the alchemist concocting gold. She was always a bit astounded by the success of the work but also never completely shook the tiniest feeling lurking in the back of her mind that she was a bit of an imposter, pulling off a sleight of hand that even kept her fooled.

Chapter Sixty-Two

Years later, as the future would have it, Lindy graduated with honors in broadcast journalism from Penn View College. Her remarkable language skills in French, German and Russian served her well in becoming a foreign television news correspondent (under the name Adele Tremont to keep people from assuming the Sinclairs had gotten her a free pass to fame). Her broadcast assignments in war-torn countries reached millions of viewers worldwide. She used her public platform for social justice purposes, rending scathing commentary about the perils of humanity's cruelties to oppressed women and children everywhere, inmates on death row, and climate change.

The only recollection Lindy retained of the almost two years she was a silent child was the arrival of her little friend, Darby, who she distortedly remembered arriving as a birthday present when she turned six years old. Beatrice Pons held no place in her memory. She never knew someone named 'Riva' nor found a dead person in her father's library chair. He was remote but kind. Her family was rich. Her mother was her biggest fan and dearest support. She had numerous friends and was treated with respect and appreciation across diverse social circles. The slumber of trauma erased the frightful memories of her childhood as if her life had been one seamless line of happy development.

From the first day when Darby and his princess instantly

bonded, the little girl rejoined the world, her heart opening like a rose blossom, leaning towards the light of the morning sun, becoming abundant in its fullness. And Beatrice, who was intuitive about the timing of starting and endings, understood their work together was soon coming to a close.

She lifted her coat and placed it in the crook of her left arm. Her right hand pulled the supply bag to the opening elevator door. Astrid stood and waved goodbye as the doors closed, and Beatrice disappeared from sight. Beatrice headed to the street to catch the crosstown bus for the trek across town.

Her back was aching, and her right wrist was getting numb in a tingly sort of way. She struggled more than usual, getting the art bag up the three bus steps even though the bottom one was lowered almost to the level of the sidewalk. Lifting with both hands gripping the handles, elbows out like bird wings, she heaved upwards one step at a time. "Old age sucks," she thought and then thankfully spotted an available seat for the rest of the ride. While staring out the windows in a daydreamy state of mind, she concluded the time had come to edit out art supplies that weren't really useful or desired by clients anymore. She needed to lighten her load. It would be a good weekend task.

Chapter Sixty-Three

There were other plans, however, developing inside the bag. The thump, thump, thump up the bus steps had driven Darby's trophy deeper and deeper into the chaos of supplies. While initially accessible by sight or slightly roaming fingers, the ring now had descended between the air-dry modeling clay packets, rolls of color tape and acrylic paint tubes. In fact, the swatches of felt for smearing oil pastels were in the same region, which basically was about halfway down the bag's interior.

Chapter Sixty-Four

By the time Beatrice reached Nelson's apartment, she was unusually tired. Her fingers had become especially swollen, which meant she was not drinking enough water. Having forgotten her thermos, she asked him for a glass, and they then set about their work.

She noticed his attire was preppy-looking, which was unusual for him. He had a haircut that was markedly conservative – also not his typical style. "Is something going on, Nelson?"

"I had to go to School Court today."

"What do you mean?"

"A few days ago, I made a drawing in my private notebook of an annoying teacher that made her look like part person and part pig in an electric chair. It was just a joke, but one of the kids saw it and told the vice-principal, and I got sent home, and then my mom had to bring me to School Court this morning for them to decide what to do with me. It's all fucking bullshit. She says she's going to call you later, but honestly, she doesn't think this therapy is working, and now she's got her mind on a military school in South Bend, Indiana."

This news was more than Beatrice could take in. Nelson was an amazing, creative, and talented kid who definitely should not be going to military school. She couldn't help but wonder about the motives of his mother. How could military school seem like a viable option to her? "Of course, I'd be more than willing to speak with your mother any time. Nelson, what are you feeling?"

" I feel like shit. I feel like I was a huge ass for getting caught with the drawing. I feel like the school is stupid, and the kid who ratted on me is a jerk. I feel like South Bend is at the bottom of the world. I feel like I wish I knew who the fuck my father was or is or whatever and that he would take me away from all this shit."

His last comment was no doubt the central problem in his life. He felt hollow inside. He needed the truth about his father (though one day, a few more years in the future when he was home from military school and about to apply to the Military Academy in Ft. Worth, he would take a home DNA test and actually learn to which of the three men he belonged. And a few years after that, he would meet the man who was his biological father, though sadly, the meeting was a disappointment, and it only happened once).

For the rest of the session, they sat in silence. He was not in the mood to make art or talk, so when their time was done, Beatrice reminded him she would gladly speak with his mother, and please give her the message, which he did later that evening when she returned from her research lab. But the conversation between mother and therapist was never to happen, for life has a way of stopping certain events from unfolding and the power to take control of the ultimate narrative.

Beatrice was so bothered by the developments with Nelson that she decided to treat herself to a taxi down to the West Village. She was feeling physically out of sorts which she chalked up to dehydration, agitation, and arthritis. The taxi driver was a large hulking fellow who insisted on tossing her supply bag into the trunk because the back seat was so narrow, there was no way for it to actually fit without the crappy (his word) wheels scraping the seat. The motion of the bag as it rolled onto its side pushed Darby's prize just close enough to the outer edge of the bag that when she arrived at Emma's house, and it was removed from the car, the ring slid down the narrow space of the outer leather and the two narrow tubes of tissue paper that clients used to make flowers and transparencies on top of paper images.

Chapter Sixty-Five

Last client of the day. Emma. Beatrice rang the bell and was buzzed in. The longest stairway went straight up to the second floor of the building where the family lived. Beatrice counted all eighteen steps up and down each time she came for a session. She glanced back and forth at the framed drawings lining the staircase – Rothko, Thursz, Cherry, Diebenkorn, Warhol – each signed and dated and clearly hung perfectly to set the stage for visitors to see an extraordinary display of modern art only found in museums and private collections of the super-wealthy.

It seemed odd to Beatrice that with all the money they put into the renovations of their 7200 square foot building, they chose not to install an elevator. Surely some visitors would appreciate a lift up. But Raleigh and Mark, both in great physical shape, never particularly considered the needs of others, so convenience never crossed their minds.

They also never considered giving Emma her own art supplies (and save Beatrice from having to lug her stash upstairs and down with each visit). In fact, they had no interest in the art of either of their children. Why would they, since they were the real artists living there? Such concerns simply never even entered the picture.

The art therapist had decided to see if the parents would consider some family sessions and intended to meet with them both after this session with Emma. She had expected to see Raleigh at the top of the stairs, chat for a moment to set up the meeting, and head over to Emma's room.

Usually, the home was noisy, with Ina's rap music, phone chatting, and exotic cooking going on in preparation for guests coming over later in the evening. Often people would be assisting in creating paintings and readying art to descend the stairs into trucks waiting to transport them for openings and museums around the world.

Sometimes Mark would be under the giant living room skylight, reading newspapers of all varieties. Emma generally hung back, waiting for Beatrice to come to her. Once when she came over, the 2nd floor of the loft was being set up for a piano concert (they had a 9-foot Martinsen known to have the sweetest tones, especially in its upper registers.). For those kinds of events, a caterer was brought in so the two hosts could focus on guests and interviews.

But the visit this day was completely different. Beatrice didn't even know who had buzzed her in. A tall person with a face mask on came out from behind the kitchen wall and stood 20 feet away from her. The reason became clear.

A raspy voice said, "Didn't anyone contact you, Ms. Pons? Oh my gosh, I'm so sorry you came all this way. We've got Covid in this house. You need to leave. Do you need a mask? Are you vaccinated?"

The conversation went back and forth for a few minutes longer. Beatrice was getting more and more uneasy about being there and stepped backward to get to the stairway. She barely said a word as she went down the stairs, this time slightly lifting the bag at the edge of each step to keep the bumping noise at a minimum. She wasn't concerned about being paid. That would happen session or not. But the trip from East End, climbing the stairs and back down again, had completely wiped her out. She did not remember being this tired in a long time, if ever.

Though she normally took the subway back up the Westside, she just didn't think she had the energy for the cement stairs, which were uneven, cracked and always crowded. Beatrice searched for a taxi. None around. And so, she fished for her cell phone in the top pocket of the supply bag. It was in a zippered pouch that also held her wallet. It was just too much to carry a purse and a giant bag at the same time.

She went to the car service app, tapped in where she wanted to go, heard a 'ping', and knew that 'Joseph' would be coming around the corner in 3 minutes to pick her up. He would be in a blue sedan with the number 380 in the window. And like clockwork, he arrived and carefully loaded her bag next to her in the back seat. He was charming and even offered her a bottle of water which she accepted because she was certain dehydration was why she was so worn out.

Chapter Sixty-Six

Beatrice rolled her bag behind her as she stepped into the elevator to go up to her apartment. Curtiss shouted, "Hold the elevator, please," as he sprinted to make it in before the doors closed. With exaggerated breathlessness, he huffed, "Just made it!" and pushed the fourth-floor button.

Beatrice was highly irritated to see him twice in one day and in such a state of exhaustion that she didn't even try to be animated. She ignored his presence. He sneered, "Cat got your tongue, Miss. Pons? How about a little smile for me." She looked away toward the corner of the cage and muttered, "Hello, Curtiss."

It seemed he was determined and pressed his intrusion further. "Want any help getting that big bag of yours into your place? A gentleman always offers to help a lady." This left Beatrice in the uncomfortable position of having to thank Curtiss for the offer, reject it, and somehow, by implication, assent to his being a gentleman – a notion that disgusted her.

He was getting off on the 10th floor, which meant he could watch her exit from the elevator. Her backside would be available for his scrutiny, which made her nauseous. At seventy-one, she should be free of animal instincts such as his. The odor of oil and disinfectant coming off him was making her more lightheaded.

The cage was a trap, and the lights, in need of changing, were flickering slightly. A dizzying feeling was "worming its way" up her body. Stealing a quick glance at Curtiss, she noticed pronounced furrows creeping down his face. His mouth seemed contorted, and his eyes fixated on her, were cruel and edgy. His animal part was in command of the cage. Hers was on high alert.

Thankfully, she reached her floor before an all-out battle ensued. She was primed for an attack. Curtiss, on the other hand, had been toying with her as a sport. He was not ready for the kill as he enjoyed the game far too much to end it.

As the doors opened, he said, "Have a great evening Miss. P" and began humming some sort of light-hearted show tune. She dragged her bag strategically right behind her derriere though it was awkward for her shoulder and back to do so. It was over.

She had not prepared to get the key ready during the car ride, as was her habit. She wanted Curtiss to know nothing about her rituals. Her fingers shaking, she had to hold it extra tightly so as to not drop it and have better aim getting the key into the lock and letting herself in.

She was home. She was really relieved to be there. She left her bag by the mirrored closet and briefly reminded herself about her intention to straighten it out over the weekend. That plan was very appealing to her now and felt like a cleansing ritual she much needed.

She draped her coat on the chair and kicked off her shoes. It was only dusk, but she was so weary she knew she just needed to catch plenty of sleep. The encounter in the elevator left her depleted.

And so, her final thoughts until Saturday morning when she awoke, refreshed and ready to take on new tasks, were, “I am safe inside my home. The beast is locked out.”

PART III

After

Chapter Sixty-Seven

Beatrice enjoyed her routines and, every six months or so, treated herself to a cleaning out and re-organization day of her traveling art supplies. Her ritual entailed digging deep into the bag and scooping out all the content, laying everything out on the foyer rug and taking inventory of what she needed to buy or replace.

She'd toss out unusable materials, realign packets of papers, check containers of tape and glue to be sure they were not empty or dried up, and generally put everything in top shape for the next six months. After she had cleared out the debris of the no longer useful materials, she daydreamed about her hopes for the good work she might accomplish in the months to come. What might seem like a chore to others was actually cathartic and renewing for her.

At a certain moment, she symbolically released her attachment to the work her clients had accomplished in the previous months. She'd close her eyes and mentally honor the images they had courageously created in therapy. Her actions of reviewing, sorting, appreciating, and anticipating served as her own 'art therapist's prayer". It left her feeling uplifted as well as grateful.

She also had sensual moments delicately fingering some of her more lasting items, ones with longer histories as part of her collection of art-making implements, like a pair of scissors given to her by a client who, decades earlier, had gone to China. The scissors came to the finest point she had ever seen and were superb for cutting silhouettes and flowers with tiny slits to make the petals stand up when they were pressed backward. She had sable paint brushes, some soft and bushy, others clipped into chiseled points for silky or fine wet work. Such special items were more like old friends than tools of her trade. She cherished them all.

Almost every time she "did her bag" (as she referred to it), she considered 'doing' the mirrored closet. It bugged her that she procrastinated so often over the years about attending to it and had become such a wreck.

She always ended up feeling overwhelmed at the prospect of going through everything, and now she knew the time had arrived to finally get to it. Her age played a significant role in pushing her to complete projects and simplify her possessions. So, that Saturday, something clicked inside of her, "Why should I live this way?" was the message that kept running through her mind as she placed her covered coffee mug on the floor and awkwardly lowered herself onto the rug, wearing just her robe and slippers.

The scent of freshly brewed French press coffee with just a splash of creamer wafted from the open hole of the double thermos cup next to her. "Ah, that first hot sip!" She was determined to dedicate this day to her bag *and* her closet! Fantastic! She would finally do this!

Chapter Sixty-Eight

Sitting within arm's reach of the mirrored door, she slipped her fingers under its bottom edge and yanked it open. From there, she took a long look at the disaster of her overstuffed closet, filled to the gills with clothing, cleaning items, parts of things like an old lamp, an oversized wooden bowl (she'd totally forgotten about that thing which would make a terrific giant salad container for when she had company over), boxes of all sorts, a tennis racket, and loads of other odds and ends.

Horrified at the almost hoarding quality of it all, she drew another sip of her coffee and exhaled, sounding exasperated with herself. She admitted out loud, "All this clutter, what the fuck Bea?" which caused her to then let out a short laugh as she figured her colleagues would no doubt see all this mess as diagnostic of some serious psychological disorder.

In looking at the insurmountable task in front of her, the words 'piles and bags' came to Beatrice's mind and she was transported by a memory. Years ago, a client had come to her for art therapy to process the trauma of a fire in her New York apartment. The woman's television had exploded (the firefighters told her that about 60 such fires occur every year, which seemed like an incredibly high number), and in the three minutes it took for the fire department to arrive, almost all her belongings had been destroyed, the bricks in the walls had popped out of the cement, and her little white dog Mollie (she survived thank goodness) had only saved her life by hiding under a stuffed toy bunny, a childhood present from when the client was born.

Mollie's beautiful white fur had turned completely gray from the surrounding smoke. When the firefighters broke in, terrified, she jumped from the bed out the second-floor window to the street below. From there, she raced down the sidewalk to the taco stand on the avenue only to be rescued by a friend and neighbor outside the building who witnessed the fire and chased after the terrified dog.

He called the client at work as he held the little dog. She worked nearby and ran home to find her apartment unrecognizable, as was her little dog, who was pressed into her neighbor's arms so she would jump away again, completely covered in soot and suffering from temporary smoke blindness. It took her a full minute to realize he was holding Mollie, which shocked and deeply saddened her.

The whole experience was devastating and required months of therapy to deal with all the logistical details, begin to repair the broken pieces of her life, and start to manage the PTSD. She lost family photos, her first-grade primer, letters from significant people, and so much more. Bun-Bun, the heroic stuffed toy that watched over her client as a baby, had protected Mollie at great risk of burning up. The bunny survived intact though his cottony fur did change forever from white to gray.

As Beatrice's client worked through her trauma over time, so too Mollie had to learn to trust the world again. For the client, losing her pet would have been unimaginable and the worst loss of all. Ultimately the client regained her sense of center, found the love of her life, and along with Mollie, set up a new home where all three lived for many wonderful years. Beatrice accidentally met her former client on the street some years back and learned that Mollie had lived to the ripe old age of 101 in dog years. She'd had a good life surrounded by love and security.

The words "piles & bags" were inspired by a story from that client with the fire. She had been so overwhelmed with the trauma, chaos, and damage of it all that she was at a complete loss as to how to sort through all the remnants of partially damaged, completely destroyed or even miraculously unharmed items in her apartment. Then her father flew in from Texas to help out and suggested a system to deal with everything.

"We're going to make piles. We need bags. Green ones for 'keep,' yellow ones for 'think about it,' and red ones for 'toss.' You decide what goes, what stays and what you can't decide and gets deferred to another time." His simple formula (he actually was a mathematician) made the cleanup not only possible but restorative for the client because she could have a process to see her way through it. Beatrice credited his intervention (which, aside from being practical, really cleverly underscored his support for his daughter) as what really helped her return to her pre-trauma functioning.

Beatrice, who was no longer limber enough to simply rise without some acrobatic help, rolled on her side, pushing her hand and elbow against the floor in an effort to stand up. She wanted a refill of coffee as well as find some plastic bags. She searched her kitchen, and while she didn't have red, yellow, and green, she did have large black and white bags on rolls, which she took back to the spot where she had been sitting on the floor. Black would be for things to throw out. White was for the keepers. That should be good enough for now. The organization would help make the process of sorting run so much more smoothly. She was ready.

Starting with the front floor of the closet, she dragged everything her hands could into the middle of the room. There were actually very few items she wanted to keep, which surprised her. They went into black bags. She reached further back into the closet and found two taped-up heavy cardboard boxes. One said 'studio stuff,' which excited Beatrice as she figured it contained supplies from when she was at the art institute in Cleveland.

The other box, a bit smaller but just as heavy, simply

said 'Mother' on the outside. This gave Beatrice a chill. She thought, 'My god, how long has that thing been in here?' Her hands trembled slightly as she hovered them over the box and delicately fingered the yellowed packing tape, which was partially dried and curled along the edges. With care, she moved the box aside, thinking, 'Later. I'll open this later because she wanted to push through her planned projects first. She wanted to procrastinate, which she also knew was an indicator of avoidance, but instead, she promised herself, "Everything will get sorted out today."

Chapter Sixty-Nine

With focus, one can accomplish more than anticipated - that was what Beatrice was thinking to herself as she looked about the room, which by midafternoon was teaming with black and white bags, odds and ends of her life that she either wanted to keep or try to give away to a good home where they would be used and appreciated. Tossing items into the garbage or down the incinerator chute was her last choice. Some things could be recycled and possibly even transformed into art materials. There was a lot of junk in the closet, which would be of use to no one. At any rate, it was all out. The closet was empty. She realized this was a two-day job and was grateful the next day was Sunday when she could take her time putting everything that she was keeping back in place.

Since the closet was cleared, she turned to the art supply bag. It seemed like she had emptied its contents days ago, but in fact, it was merely 5 hours since she reached in and pulled (she thought of herself as a midwife extracting a baby) everything out. She hadn't started examining the contents until now. Even though she was starting to feel hungry, she didn't want to stop to eat. After this bit of sorting, she would make herself a late lunch or early dinner.

Beatrice stacked all the paper items according to sizes and colors. The white paper was its own category. Small cardboard pieces were clustered and held tight with rubber bands. She kept a small wire-bound notebook and stubby pencil to record which supplies she needed to replace. While she seemed to have enough paper (she had found a half ream of typing paper in the closet, which also was good for drawing), she put it on her list. No need for other papers than buying a large package of origami squares which were useful for rudimentary folding as well as collage.

The colored pencils were in pretty good shape though she could not locate the silver hand sharpener. The erasers all looked tired. Replace them. Oil pastels also looked poorly – they were her most favored expressive drawing material and got used up quickly. They never made it back perfectly into the boxes with the ridges that held each stick in place.

She examined the boxes of sequins, ribbons, felts, and other craft-like materials, which were in good shape. Her scissors we fine, and even the child-size pairs were all accounted for. The watercolor tablets looked messy and awful. She could easily clean those up so they would be presentable for clients. Glue sticks were a mess – empty or dried out – she needed to buy a box of twelve to restock.

At the bottom of her bag were the oil-based and air-drying clays. As long as the air-dried ones weren't open, they'd still be good. The oil clays would never dry, which was part of their beauty. Sculptures could be transformed, added to, destroyed and re-born. She marveled at the metaphor of this material and reached for a sizable gray clump of the clay that had escaped its cellophane wrapper. Her fingers felt the usually sticky softness of its chemistry. But her palm immediately had an unexpected sensation. Something hard and unfamiliar was partially embedded in the gray substance, which she lifted off her hand and turned over.

There, protruding dead center in the middle and about half an inch above the surface of the clay, was a blue hue, a stone the likes of which she had never seen before. She was, to say the least, entirely confused at that moment as the stone, which was completely out of place sticking out of a clay mass in her apartment in New York City, was greeting her with its ancient and astounding beauty.

She drew her face as close as she could get without losing focus, and there, before her eyes, she beheld six white tendrils spanning the surface until they were interrupted by the body of clay into which it was embedded. She forgot to breathe until her body took over and forced her to do so.

Beatrice gouged the clay to excavate the stone with her fingers, driving the oily clay residue under her fingernails. When the object was freed, she placed it on the palm of her hand and rotated it around. It was actually a ring, and the blue stone was firmly held in a platinum setting. Small diamonds adorned the bezel as accents. The star, such a dramatic feature of the stone, varied in its visibility depending upon the location of the light and ambiance of the room.

Since it had been stuck in the oily clay, it lacked the true luster and needed to be cleaned before that would shine through.

Late afternoon was descending, and she was still in her robe and slippers. She slid the ring into her pocket and rose to go into the kitchen. With extreme care, she then took the ring out of her pocket, turned on the hot water of the sink faucet, and held it under running water. The stickiness would not disappear. She tried to imagine how to clean the stone without causing harm.

A friend had once been told to clean pearls in soda pop which was a disaster as the carbonation and brown coloring etched away at the soft surface of the pearls. She thought about lemons and was worried they were too acidic. Vinegar might be too harsh. And then she recalled an art restorer she briefly dated who shared her trade secret for old cleaning paintings without causing damage. Saliva. Good old spit (neutral ph. plus whatever else the body produces) on the cotton tip was used in museums all over the world to delicately clean dirty surfaces.

Beatrice reached for a fresh white kitchen towel, puckered her mouth and spit into the cloth. She began to rub the stone and immediately saw the oil transferred to the cloth, with tiny bits of gray clay sticking to it as well. Pleased at the notion this was working, Beatrice spit and spit again, rubbed and polished the stone, and the platinum setting it was in. She ran the ring under cool water when she was done and then slipped it onto her finger. Sparkling clean, the star shimmered as she moved her hand. It looked magnificent.

Chapter Seventy

Stray memories began weaving in and out of her mind. Simple remnants, threads of moments drifting randomly across time with neither cohesion nor regard for sequence and order. She is prancing on a dark and muddy beach, her father's firm grip lifting her above foamy waves that smell of briny sea life. She is in a cavernous garage, oil embedded into the cement floor, sooty work tools in a bright yellow bucket, old, cracked hula hoops, and some cooing pigeons pecking at kernels of raw corn. A picnic grill in an outdoor park smells of lighter fluid squirted on flaming coal sticks with marshmallows dropping from their melted weight. A chewed cigar embedded on a dirt path was newly carved for a country fair that only came to town in the summer. Napping to the rhythmic sounds of a pulldown shade driven by the soft, warm weather breezes slapping against an open windowpane. The scratchy feeling of ginger ale bubbles in her throat – medicine to relieve a sour tummy. Stray cats nesting on her father's car, her tricycle bell ringing with such clarity that it pierced the sultry summer heat. Fall leaves crunching, colors of rust and brilliant red. Daddy is humming. A sandbox he made by hand just for her. Winter snowsuit too stiff to let her move with child-like grace. Mother crying in her bedroom in the middle of the afternoon. The mother later cursed in the kitchen that their food was getting cold as they waited. Hungry, waiting and then watching perfectly good food go into the garbage. The room spinning. Hiding under the dining room table. Unused silverware feels cold to the touch. Time crawled so slowly that it seemed to have no beginning or end alone, though she did not know what that word actually meant.

Chapter Seventy-One

Beatrice drifted from the kitchen, through the hall, into the living room, walking past the remaining spillage of the closet, the art bag with its contents strewn across the hallway floor, the array of black and white bags with items sorted according to keep or not keep. Her body automatically gravitated to the couch where she had rested after so many long days she could not count their numbers. Her eyes, dully focused, wandered to the art on her living room walls as the late afternoon light softly stretched into the room.

Patches of translucent color quietly glided across the picture planes. Tiny prisms of painted light created forms through their proximity to each other and reminded her of shattered stars long ago lighting other worlds on their journeys to death. Once dead, only the eyes of those living eons later can experience their light. She looked down at her ringed finger and tried to imagine the world that had created such a gem and what message its star was meant to convey, like a note in a glass bottle, traveling on an ocean orbit to an unknown recipient.

She felt exhaustion seeping through her body and momentarily drifted off for one of those intensely unexpected naps, a micro sleep, that take a person by surprise, similar to jet lag locking the body until the will to rise outweighs the descent for a deeper sleep.

And as she released herself to the full sensation of endless falling without landing, she gazed at the ring again and wondered, "Why me?" which was an interesting question given up til now. She never really wondered how the ring came to be in her bag, what journey it had taken – which was probably a good thing because it might have been a hard matter to explain the transcendent dimensions of Darby and his sacred mission as the star-eyed prince of healing.

Chapter Seventy-Two

In actuality, only a few minutes had gone by when Beatrice awoke. The sun had not yet disappeared below the horizon. She got up, tightened her robe about her and went back to the piles of things scattered across the floor. Now that she was more rested, she was feeling curious about the box labeled 'Mother' and decided it was about time to go through the contents. Her back, aching from sitting so long on the floor, informed her decision to return with the box to the couch.

She had no need for a knife or scissors as the tape was fragile and falling apart in her fingers. The cardboard box felt dusty from age. She barely recognized her own handwriting on the outside – 'Mother' seemed alien, distant, from another universe. The open box had the vague odor of compression and airlessness. It wasn't altogether unpleasant, nor was it welcoming and warm. If one could feel or smell the stillness of time, this was the sensation she experienced in those first moments.

She reached in and lifted a few dried-out pamphlets of *Wildflowers Across America*, a rickety old flower press with some pieces of wax paper pressed down on what appeared to be daisies and violets. Their colors looked ancient and slightly out of register, giving the effect of a hazy red outline surrounding each flower image. There was a dog-eared copy of *The Divine*

Comedy with red markings and bright yellow highlighted notations her mother made throughout. An old stained tee shirt was wrapped around a pair of brown leather binoculars meant for birdwatching which brought back a visceral memory, the kind without words but ran deep inside a person, of sitting in the tall grass outside a back door with her father, looking through those lenses and trying to spot squirrels and whatever else in the foliage of a wild crab apple tree at the backend of the property.

In Beatrice's haste to make her exit from Ohio, she sloppily packed the box of her mother's possessions in a random, disorganized, and tossed-about manner. Now, decades later, she regretted her lack of care in selecting and packing things. As she explored further, she saw a few drawings she had made for her mother, once rolled and secured tightly with a green rubber band, now crushed and crinkled from age, and most of it was disintegrating on exposure to the room air.

Beatrice found an old pair of her mother's shiny black dress shoes which made no sense as she would never have worn them even if they had been the right size for her feet. They were in good shape, barely worn with heels shaped like thin wedges to give the person wearing their height and, she imagined, an alluring quality. She laughed at herself, "Whatever was I thinking?" for being so random about her choices. She spied a multicolor tile ashtray she had made her mother one summer at day camp under a pair of red and white mittens with the clips still on to hold them to her winter jacket. Though her mother was not a smoker, she kept it handy for folks who came over to the house with cigarettes.

As the rest of the box mostly had a lot of wadded-up newspaper filling the empty spaces, there wasn't too much left to uncover. It saddened her to consider what people leave behind and how little her mother had to show for her life.

Beatrice recognized the shape of the last item wrapped in another old tee shirt that was covered in drips and splotches of color - the top she used to love to wear when she was painting and making art. Her mother's wooden jewelry box was about the size of a loaf of bread and had been carefully tucked between the cotton folds of the fabric. Abstract carvings covered the entire surface of the box. As a child, it had been a special treat to run her tiny fingers over the bumps and swirls decorating the exterior and then to watch 'mummy' open the hinged lid to see the display of jewels inside (in truth, all that was there was costume jewelry though it was well made and worthy of admiration).

Over the years, when her mother became more and more difficult, resentful, and unpredictable, the sacred box was deemed 'off limits' to Beatrice. She never ventured to look inside after her mother accused her of being a sneak. Never again - not a peak, even when her mother was dead. She simply wrapped the thing to take to New York.

Chapter Seventy-Three

Beatrice drew a long breath, exhaling slowly as she centered the wooden box on her lap. It felt light in her hands, and she imagined it held a few tarnished pieces of junk jewelry and some random souvenirs her mother collected over the years. She had no real expectations and was actually kind of pleased with the maturity of her benign interest in the contents.

She closed her eyes for a moment and recalled sitting on the bow of a small fishing skiff that was rocking up against a wooden pier. She wore a bright orange vest that was all puffed out and tied together with a thick black ribbon. The vest also had a metal whistle with a ring and yellow cord pulled through it. She liked to blow the whistle while she was waiting for her father to get going though he warned her that once they were out on the lake, she could not blow the whistle unless it was an emergency. That was something else she didn't quite understand. What really was an emergency?

Her father, sitting in the stern by the engine, was preparing to get ready to go fishing. He told her he was setting up his tackle box. She was so little she didn't even know what a tackle box was until he showed her some tiny, brilliantly-colored, feathery objects he placed gently into the box. She reached to stroke them, "Careful Birdie, they are sharp. They have hooks inside under the feathers – Don't touch!" which made him sound harsher than he meant, which is what fear for the safety of a loved one can do to a person. He did not want her to get hurt even if, in the process, his words and tone startled her and stung her heart. "I'm sorry, Birdie. You didn't do anything wrong. I just was protecting you," which, because he had said this part with soft kindness, she believed, and the hurt receded as she forgot all about that lesson on love.

Beatrice tried to replay that memory as she sat with the wooden box, but efforts such as that could dimmish the recollection fading almost as quickly as it had arrived. She wanted to push deeper into that long-ago day. *We would be on the water. He would tell me stories about when he was little. We would cuddle.* But she had no fuel to run these fantasies. *We would try to catch fish with the most beautiful hook that he let me pick out of the box. He would reel in a 'big one,' and we would agree to take it home for Mummy to fry up for dinner. She would be so happy that we had such a wonderful day together on the boat. I would fall asleep in his arms as if I were being rocked in a boat by gentle waters, the sounds of gulls in the distant sky lulling my weary mind to dream.*

Chapter Seventy-Four

Time was passing at a peculiar pace. Beatrice knew it was evening, and buildings were lit up and down the street. Night sounds in the city had an enchanting echo about them. During the day, things moved quickly, and sounds seemed rushed and clashing. At night, sounds seem to take their time. She liked to sort one sound from another and pretend they were communicating with one another.

The living room was dark, so she stretched to reach the end table lamp to put on the light. She was startled by the glow of the star sapphire ring alit on her finger like some exotic iridescent butterfly. The light from the bulb hit the stone at the perfect angle to its perfection. Light permeated the blueness of the gem, which took on the color of the equatorial ocean, undulating its brilliant color without flaws.

She had a thought. She could sell the ring, or even just the stone, and use the money for travel. Take an amazing trip, well deserved after all the years of trying to help others. Why not help herself? Self-care was all the rage in the field of mental health. It was hard putting a lump of money together, large enough to really give one's self the trip of a lifetime. She figured (hoped) she had ten to fifteen more really good years left in her to keep working. She wouldn't retire (no way, but she did really want to cut back and have more time to read and take it easy). She couldn't afford to not work, but she also couldn't find the means to give herself a much-needed break. And here it was! Why else would the ring be in her bag?

Beatrice had skipped over the obvious steps in ascertaining why the ring landed up where it did or what to do about it. She did not, for instance, immediately contact her clients' parents to inquire if they had such a ring and it had gone missing. She did not report finding the ring to the local authorities. She did not even debate in her mind the ethics of not *trying* to locate its rightful owner.

She had no inclination whatsoever to return that which was not hers. She deemed this was not about possession – it was about opportunity. In her mind, therefore, it did not constitute stealing. She told herself she had been gifted the ring through an accident in the universe. How else could it have come to be in her life at all? The star had traveled all that way to be with her. Things people tell themselves can become truths if they can invent an acceptable intention.

Another memory visited her. She was sitting on the grass behind the house near a tree. It was a chilly night. Her mother had been extra edgy all afternoon, snapping at the child for this and that, then withholding and cold - not uttering a word to the little girl or her father throughout most of the dinner. The child, who was alone with the mother and the object of her torment all day, had been primed for anxiety.

She had accidentally spilled some cherry jubilee dessert from her TV dinner onto the black and white checkered kitchen floor. The red blob had landed smack in the middle of one of the white squares. "God damn it, Beatrice, pick it up before it stains. Stop crying, or I'll give you something to really cry about." shrieked her mother, but the sweet was too hot and gooey for the little girl's fingers to grasp. She kept trying to scoop it up without crying, and her father, who had been completely preoccupied with things of the future, only noticed the scene when it was about halfway over.

The mother, in full rage mode, turned, "You just really don't give a fuck, do you?" And her father, for the very first time in front of Beatrice, stared with dead eyes directly at the mother while whispering to his daughter, "Birdie, please honey, go outside to the apple tree. Wait for me. I'll be out in a moment."

A few minutes later, her father came outside carrying a blanket in his arms. Wrapping its scratchy wool around her shoulders, he sat next to her so they could snuggle and be close. "Birdie, let's take a good look at those stars up there." Together they took in the expanse of their tiny part of the universe. He told her about things she could not understand. The constellations, planets, the moon, the patterns of worlds they could not see and see things that no longer existed. He told her to pick one star to be theirs. She picked one that she thought was brighter than others around it. He told her that its light had come from so long ago that nobody really knew if it was still glowing. Time, he said, moves that way. “What we know to be true is only this moment. Everything else is just a guess or a memory”. She did not understand his words, but she felt their truth, at this moment, beneath their star.

The next day, he was gone.

Chapter Seventy-Five

Beatrice briefly considered taking a vacation using the sale of the ring to get the funds. She'd need to go to 47th Street to the Jewelry District to 'fence' it! She laughed out loud. "Listen to me, sounding like a regular crook" Then she worried, "What if the previous owner tips them off and she gets caught with 'hot' stuff?" Oh this was so insane. Who was she becoming, anyway? And then she pondered how easy it is to become unrecognizable to oneself in the face of the unexpected. Her thinking was swirling, out-of-whack, so she sharply pulled her hand away from the lamp light and pulled it into her chest. Her heart was racing. She needed to slow down. She touched the wooden box. She took a few focused in-breaths, counted to four, then exhaled to the count of five.

As Beatrice lifted back the lid of the box, her eyes drifted to a red satin lining inside. It was silky to the touch and in high contrast to the stark white pair of calf-skinned gloves lying on top. Picking them up to her nose (was it instinct that drew her to do that?), she smelled something old and familiar between animal and flower. The gloves had a slightly sickening odor though not really offensive, and she was reminded of being little and confused by the super soft texture of the leather, the smell and her mother's hands. She put the gloves aside next to her on the couch.

She next saw a number of faded photographs. She could

barely make out one with a little girl on a rope swing (presumably her?), a stone building with a young boy holding a spelling bee placard that said, "Winner #1," but she had no idea about the boy and wondered if he was a relative, perhaps her father, when he was little. There were no clues on the back, no words saying, "so-and-so age 9" or anything else. One photo definitely was of her mother, all dressed up, including white gloves and a pillbox hat. There was a truck in the background that was old and sported all the curves and bubble shapes associated with dated vehicles. Two pictures were of orchards – the trees were all aligned and ripe with foliage. Beatrice could make out a rustic house at the edge of a street and another house just opposite on the same road.

Beatrice opened herself to feel the nostalgia of her life's tale. All that in some way was gathered into the vortex of her mind, her history was becoming known in the absolute present she was experiencing. For all the distance and all the violence, it took to reach her, this moment of light was oddly tender. She was in the eye of her past, held together through the descent of time. Even without knowing why, all the parts of her had become unified fragments of her birthright in the present.

Chapter Seventy-Six

Though she had emptied the contents of the box to the bottom, she had not reached the end of the journey. The red satin lining, so pristinely attached throughout the inside, had a little curled-up corner that appeared to be ever-so-slightly detached from the rest of the interior of the box. With care and caution, Beatrice picked at the edge until enough fabric could be held between her thumb and index finger to pull back and away from the bottom.

And there it was. Truth has been waiting patiently from the time it originated to the immediate now. Though shut away in the darkness, its light was dimmed but did not die. Beatrice understood time moved that way – that distance and hiding it did not suffocate its reality. It just postponed its presence. The light now was real. This moment was not a guess or a memory. It was the truth, arrived, raw, and angry.

Chapter Seventy-Seven

She pried the letter tenderly from the box. Its envelope disintegrated into tiny yellowed flaky bits strewn about the red satin lining. The letter, written on tan onion skin paper, held together and was in pristine condition though it was tightly creased into thirds to fit better in the box. Opening it up required her care and patience as she did not want the delicate paper seams to crack. She noticed her fingers tremoring as they hovered over the surface of soft bumps and ripples. She recognized its texture as familiar and old. Bringing the note close to her nose, she inhaled more memories wafting in the air, swirling about and calling her mind into wordless remembrances of the past.

She felt breathless in proximity to the physical note she was holding. Before she began to decipher the contents of the letter, she experienced an extraordinary sense that something had traveled to her from galaxies far away where time had long ago been extinguished. And yet, as the weight of this ancient relic rested lightly on her palm, the heat it exuded, like the burning of the brightest star in the heavens, was meteoric.

In a singular instant, she felt the story it carried, like the message in a bottle drifting in an endless sea, escaping the great black hole and collapsing her universe. All while she was sitting alone in her apartment.

She saw their names at the beginning and end of the letter.

This was a communication between her parents, a single remnant of the fact of their relationship. Until she held the letter in her fingers, the reality of their having once been a real thing was only a murmur, a weak heartbeat in the background of her life.

For the briefest moment, like a child accidentally walking into a room where her parents are deep in conversation, feeling awkward, intrusive, and unentitled, she thought of putting the missive back, unread, into the box. Then her curiosity kicked in, and she assured herself she had every right to read the letter. It belonged to her by virtue of it having belonged to her parents. She inherited it.

She wondered why her mother had hidden the letter away in the old wooden box. She never thought of her as sentimental nor having attachments to anything about the man who had left her in the lurch with a child to raise. Perhaps it was actually a love letter that she hoped one day her daughter would find, just as she did, to confirm that, if nothing else, she was born out of love. There was some comfort for Beatrice in the thought that there was a time when her parents loved each other enough to have a child.

The letter was handwritten on both sides of the paper. Beatrice read it through carefully, trying to absorb each word, each sentence, the meaning of the whole. She repeated the process – '*take it slowly, don't rush it, you may misunderstand something.*' And while the individual words on the page were simple and direct, their meaning together became complex and distorted in her effort to comprehend its entirety.

Leah,

I just got back from my overseas assignment a few days ago and only got to reading my mail this weekend. I guess you've been waiting for my response to your telling me about Birdie's troubles and how I should stay away. So here it is.

You say that last fall (damn, I wish I had been stateside then because I could have come to visit and reassure her), Birdie started telling herself that I wasn't her father to make sense of why I was gone. That a doctor in Cleveland told you she has an illness of 'self-protective belief.' That she needs to "pretend this is the truth of things in order to not blame herself for my leaving so she won't have a complete mental collapse." That your "mother-daughter bond" must be protected at all costs.

The truth cannot be hidden away forever, Leah. Maybe she's too young to know the whole of it, but you and I know what really happened and how, frankly, you made it impossible for me to stay.

Each time you attacked me, you broke me further and further. You killed the love between us until the only proof left of it was our girl. Trying to calm your raging wasn't working, and you kept getting more and more vicious. I have the scars on my hands and back to remind me, every day, what made me go. You KNOW why I left. Birdie had become the only reason I stayed.

You tell me I have to be patient and wait until she is ready to let her 'invented story' go, But it seems to me it could be years, and it feels rotten to have to play this game without knowing that it will end. I hate having to trust you to let me know when that time comes.

I am her father, her Papa, forever and beyond. And that is the truth of everything.

Stephen

P.S. Did she ever get the Teary-Terri baby doll I mailed from Chicago or that crate of oranges I sent when I was stationed down in Florida?

Beatrice couldn't recall a crate of oranges from her father. She was sure she'd remember a gift like that since good citrus was hard to come by in their local produce store. There was that one time when she came home from school, and her mother had spread one dozen perfectly round oranges on the dining room table – lined them up like soldiers waiting to roll right off the edge.

She told Beatrice it was remarkable that Bennie's Produce had actually gotten the twelve in that day, 'unusual' he said and offered to sell them all to her mother at half price. In case the girl wanted them in the future, Bennie told her mother the delivery was probably an accident and didn't expect to get any more in the future.

Beatrice felt her mind twisting to balance on a knife's edge, trying to remember the details of those oranges, their smell, the bitter taste of the seeds against the incredible sweetness of the juicy flesh. "*The truth cannot be hidden away forever, Leah.*" Beatrice suddenly felt ravenous. She had not eaten much all day, and the oranges had triggered a intense hunger in her. Oranges can only be oranges. A crushing truth was prying her heart open - his words from the past were definitive, unambiguous, not nuanced. The oranges were a clue to her reality. She tasted that fruit which meant she had once existed as a child. She was real.

Her thoughts moved on to the *No Tear-Crying Baby Doll* but tried as she might, no memory came forth. Not even a fragmentary flash of it or a shadow of a thought. She knew, then, that though the reality of the gift doll existed through his words, it was never actually given to her. She recalled her mother's admonition, "You won't want to play with dolls forever."

The utter sadistic self-absorption, thievery, and manipulation which Leah perpetrated upon her daughter were so devastating that all of Beatrice's inner light was instantly absorbed into the blackest hole of the darkest night. Her mother's cruelty had permanently shattered hope, destroying any remaining assumption that she even had a father.

The evil truth about maternal betrayal is that it gnaws its way directly into the gut, heart, and brain. Children's survival is dependent upon the beneficence of parents, as well as other safe adults. Beatrice, having been denied any entitlement or expectation of safety and love, having no effective means to right the wrongs done to her, now had stunning awareness of the deprivations committed upon her child part which triggered her within the microseconds it takes for a heart to break, into a savage rage.

The mother's lie was so devious that both father and daughter spent their lifetimes grieving a loss between them that never was. And as valiantly as she tried to stay present with the internal chaos she was experiencing, she could not keep her body and mind from migrating into another part as she desperately longed to completely exit from the human world.

While she had been reading the letter, the room seemed to be heating up. Her arms and legs were growing sticky and clammy as a noticeable increase in body hair retained the wetness of her sweaty skin. She looked around and, squinting her eyes, gazed over towards her paintings. Little chips of pigment were breaking off the canvases – effortlessly floating about in the room, crystalizing colors like luminous stained glass chards capturing glints of light that startled her vision.

A burning sensation permeated her lungs, rendering her throat sore and dry. Words without context, like "fever," "rancid," trellis," and "vinyl," were exploding through her brain like detritus in a hurricane. Images in her mind of impoverished childhood, empty New York streets and dimmed rooms lighted only by a single source flashlight, all jumbled and pitched wildly into senseless conformations, kaleidoscopic, melting in the heat of the evening. Her yellowed eyes were stinging from the salty tears she had no means to prevent.

Instinct was taking over her remaining capacity for a reason. She swatted at the flying glass to protect her face and upper body from the sharp slivers raging through the room. Her wolf part had keen intuition and deft physical responses that swiftly shielded her from the onslaught of their attack. She became all animal in her ferocious dedication to survival.

Turmoil exploded full blast into the room. Eons of distance, gritty yet marvelous rocks and ruins were sucked into a downward swirl, vortex funneling glass and words, and images into a descent of streaming madness. Bits and pieces of music, art, and humanity were engulfed by waves of night rivers crashing into furniture and doors. The impact was so broad that the she-wolf could barely stave off her own collapse into the momentum of suction.

Suddenly, in the midst of her dodging the treachery of projectiles surrounding her from every direction, her gut was seized by a vicious cramp that nearly paralyzed her ability to react. As she looked about in desperation to avoid colliding into shatterings, her eyes momentarily dropped, and she noticed the claws of a fur-covered hand grasping onto the letter for dear life. She frantically wished she could manage her old trick of floating above whatever scene was destabilizing, terrifying to thwart the weight and wrath of worry. She felt desperate to get out.

The apartment had become unfamiliar, confining. She sniffed the paper, briefly considering eating it, but then shoved it back into the box. Her boney finger joints prevented the ring with the star from slipping off. She could not tolerate its presence and began tugging at it so roughly that her claws etched bloody tracks into her hand, dripping crimson tracks on the apartment floor. Finally, her body sweat made her fingers sufficiently slippery to get past the bump, which might have been painful, but by now, she was completely numb to physical suffering.

The ring and letter dropped directly from her hand into the wooden box. In one swift movement, the box was pushed under the couch. Since the she-wolf happened, there was no need for such possessions.

Chapter Seventy-Eight

She began panting and pacing the circumference of the room, ever widening the reach of her circle of tracks into the foyer. She understood her restlessness as an unrestrained desire to kill something. Frustrated by the absence of anything to slaughter, she searched around the apartment for the next best option. Her keen eyes zeroed in on the remaining untouched art on the hallway walls heading towards her bedroom.

The she-wolf had zero instinctive longing to protect her creations. None of the "They are my babies. " as is often expressed by former artist acquaintances in fits of narcissistic possession. In fact, the longer she gazed at her art, the less she was convinced any of it had ever been a part of her at all. They were as good as strangers. This stuff would make an excellent sacrifice for destruction.

Her claws slashed at the paintings, scoring one after another other until only shredded remnants littered the hallway floor. Old wooden stretchers, narrow and cheap from the days when money for such things was hard to come by, lay cracked in a heap under the wreckage of her rampage. Staples and canvas tacks were ripped partially off the frames. But instead of soothing her fury, the she-wolf only grew more enraged, which had the effect of desperately pushing her hunger to be immediately satisfied.

She trotted into the kitchen, mouth-frothing thinking about

swallowing the food inside the refrigerator. She knew there would be plenty to devour - all combinations of items. Which is what she did once she pulled its door open and dragged the chilly contents into a heap on the floor. She did not care which leftovers were mixed with others. She paid no attention to any loss of decorum in slopping down the food. She ate and ate until her gut was full, and she was feeling somewhat soothed.

Wolves belong in the wild, not in apartments. And so, with instinct driving action, with a belly filled and rage more or less calmed, she knew it was time to leave all the parts that had previously been her life in search of other parts yet to come. She did not experience fear or sadness, in the ordinary human sense, at this leaving.

Time was no longer burdened with nostalgia that often prevented people from taking action or moving on. Time was now an immediate experience relieved from the shackles of direct memory. Memories were wordless threads just stored in the body, reactions controlling behaviors ready to ensure survival.

With some awkwardness, the she-wolf turned the doorknob with the claws of both hands, twisting it just enough to unlatch it and open it. The building hallway smelled of good cooking, but because she was full, the aromas did not tempt her. The door to the fire stairs was wedged open with red brick, so it was no mean trick for her to squeeze out of the apartment and then into the stairwell.

She felt freedom loping down the seven flights. Four legs definitely had an advantage over two, and she felt a peculiar humor as she got closer to the ground floor. Who would ever want to be a biped when being a quadruped was so much more efficient?

The lobby was not her goal. For certain, she would be stopped if anyone saw her, and the likelihood of that was great. She kept descending until she reached the basement, which was dark, dank, and far less likely to leave her exposed.

Really her only concern was to avoid Curtiss, whose apartment was on the level of the building. She assumed, at this late hour, he and his wife were likely asleep and would remain that way as long as she made no noise.

As luck would have it, no one was around. No garbage cans fell open, making crashing sounds to catch people's attention. All appeared clear to go. She needed to reach the building's garbage door, and even that went without a hitch.

It was there, just waiting to be opened, but the knob was missing and in its place was a slot just for a key. This was an unforeseen obstacle in her escape. She'd come all this way only to be thwarted in her exit because the 'damn door' needed a key which, even if she had possessed it, would have been beyond her skills to maneuver.

But wolves are highly clever and brave. She searched all around in the darkness to locate another way out. And that she did, because around the corner, just above a sorting table for items fresh from the communal laundry room dryers, was a table just high enough for a wolf to possibly reach a window that had been cracked open by Mrs. Feldstein of apartment 216 when she last did her wash. The laundry room always sweated, which drove her crazy, so, unbeknownst to the super, she would let a little fresh air in, but she would always close it when she was done so as not to get caught. Today she had forgotten to do that in her rush to get backups stairs in time for her favorite soap opera, *Waning Times*.

This was all the opening the she-wolf needed as she leaped onto the table and angled her snout between the window and its frame. She delicately pushed and then crawled through the narrow space. It was easy. Her escape was all but assured, and in a matter of seconds, she would find herself walking on the sidewalks of New York, close enough to smell Central Park. Freedom.

She took one final look behind her through the street side of the window. There, in the pitch-black shadows of the laundry room, a pair of yellow eyes stared back at hers. White fangs flashed as the monstrous body of an alpha wolf lunged toward the window. His recklessness injured his front legs preventing him from making his way out. Curtiss retreated in defeat.

Chapter Seventy-Nine

She pressed close to the apartment buildings as she loped towards the avenue. Coming up to the crosswalk was the trickiest, most exposed part of her journey to the park. She was determined not to be noticed by passing traffic. As she reached its flashing walk light, she increased her pace.

Though she didn't know the exact time, she was aware that it was well into the deep of night, which worked in her favor, as did the oddity of anyone 'thinking' they were actually seeing a lone wolf in the midst of the City. Most likely, someone reporting such an event would likely be responded to with, "Sure you did, buddy," or "How ripped were you?" or maybe, "Wow, you saw your spirit guide." She increased her velocity (wolves move with so much more speed than bipeds) to reach her destination quickly.

She made it to the park entrance without being winded in the least. Lingering for the briefest moment, she took pleasure in inhaling nature and listening for the night sounds of raccoons and frogs and snakes in their nightly routines. As she moved further inside, she thought this was grand and felt her gut softening and her bearing loosen. Now she was breathing deeply, fresh air calming the last of the burning sensation she had experienced in the apartment.

She wanted to weep from joy as she felt the cool earth under her paws while moving closer and closer to the center of the forest.

The streetlights disappeared. She found a slatted wooden bench and jumped onto its planks. Though she had no real need for a bench, she hoped it might bring her closer to the stars, which were brilliant that night and seemed to be calling to her very soul.

She felt enticed to make a sound of her own though she had a slight worry of being caught. And so, for the first time in decades, when she had found her voice in the office with Dr. Marcia Fines, she wailed her song to the stars from the part of herself that had no words but understood all.

She sang as her tears flowed into rivers of memory though they had no specific shape. She sang in thanks for the beauty of the earth, for gravity, time, and distance. She sang until she thought her heart would burst as she absorbed eons of light rushing towards her with messages of love that did not fail to seek her but, because the journey had been broken and taken so long, had seemed unlikely to arrive.

And as the she-wolf opened her heart to the universe of her moment, she watched her body once more begin to choose its new being. The wolf felt neither sadness nor loss for its ending because her time was over, and she understood farewells in one form meant possibilities in another.

With generosity and kindness, the she-wolf invited the little girl over. “Come to the bench, sweet girl,” and though she was very young, maybe 3-4 years old, she was so brave that she sat right down next to the wolf and started singing alongside her. Her little hand petted the fur on the wolf's arm.

The last words the wolf spoke were, "Look to the stars, little girl," which the child did and when she looked back at the wolf, she saw she was alone, and her hand was empty save for the memory of touch left on her fingers.

Chapter Eighty

The child stared straight up into the night sky. She felt a little dizzy watching all the swirling and twinkling, so to steady herself, she tucked her legs under her and placed her right arm along the back edge of the wooden bench. It wasn't time for the birds to wake up yet, but she was excited at the prospect of being there at the exact moment they would appear.

In fact, she was feeling at peace because, though she missed her friend, the wolf, she expected new, unanticipated meetings and all kinds of friendships. She felt safe inside her being, and hope wrapped softly around her body.

And so, with joy in her heart, she began to sing her song while in the deepest darkness of the hour, between whirling universes colliding through time, before the light was even a thing here on earth, before the meekest of atoms formed into building blocks of life, and sounds became words, and thoughts became poems, there was no child.

She could not 'be' until so much of the work of time had taken place, and by then, when she had arrived, so much had already entered and left the vortex.

As her tiny chest expanded and her little voice grew, another voice– thinly at first like vapor lacing gently through the air joined in. She could not see the person behind the sound, but she could feel it. They were rhyming together, which made the song all the more delightful to continue.

Glancing back up at the stars, she felt a thrilling bond to all things visible and invisible. And then, in the way only children can observe and speak simultaneously without censoring the most challenging comments, the little girl asked, “Papa, is that you?” and the way only a parent can respond that reaches beyond all distance and time, “Yes, Birdie. It is your father. I’ve come to take you home.”

EPILOGUE

And Then

Chapter Eighty-One

The Medical Examiner held on to her body until it was formally identified and an official cause of death could be determined. Since the woman had died on a public bench in Central Park, in her bathrobe and without any identification on her, it took a little investigative work to find out who she was. Ironically, all her years of working with children paid off because she had to be fingerprinted years ago in order to do art therapy work in schools. The forensic technicians searched the data bank, and her whorls, arches and loops found a match. The official conclusion was Beatrice Pons, female, age 71, died of an aortic heart aneurysm.

Once she had been identified, it was easy enough to find where she resided as there were records of such things in rental buildings. The Examiner's office notified the building owner to see what to do with her effects and possibly find out if she had other relatives or friends on the lease they could notify. The owner was a big-deal real estate magnate who had multiple holdings dating back to the early 1980s. Victor Tibor had made such an imprint in New York as a major property owner and successful businessman that his name was synonymous with the Midas touch in that industry.

Victor was deeply saddened to hear about the death of his former F-Buddy (as he liked to abbreviate it in his mind once they finally parted ways as it seemed less crude and, on a deeper level, made their relationship seem more meaningful to him). Memories cascaded through his mind as he recollected their fun times, sexual escapades, and great conversations that continued into the early hours of the morning.

The special fondness he had for her prompted him from the very beginning of their relationship to the very end to help her out when he could, which even included knowing when to walk away when love started to enter the picture. He knew from a young age he was not going to be any good at old-fashioned love. He figured he'd be nobody's husband, and he never was.

When he got the call that Beatrice had died alone, half naked, on a bench in Central Park, he got off the phone and let out a roar of desperate laughter flanked by such a flood of tears that he canceled his appointments for the rest of the day because his eyes were so red and swollen. He was devastated because, as often is the case with humans who avoid considering the final cliff as an inevitable part of living, he mistakenly assumed she would always be around, even if they never spoke.

His memory brought him back to bartering for the amazing headboard in Bali, then the hours he and Beatrice spent locked in passion. Drifting into sleep under the carved decorations of elegant swooping mother-of-pearl inlay cranes and rare wood creatures hidden within the reeds around the pond. He pushed back into his plush burgundy leather desk chair and said to himself, "We sure played so well together, my B." And no doubt, had she been there to respond, she would have shared, "Every time I fingered that mother of pearl, I was stroking you as well."

Theirs had been a relationship uncomplicated by ambition and self-serving motivations. The beauty of what they shared existed because they both deeply appreciated each other. Also, they both understood that romantic love was something neither of them could really tolerate or admit.

Now that she was gone, Victor took on the responsibility of closing down the details of her life. He arranged for her cremation and planned to take her ashes with him on the next trip he made to Bali. Her modest bank accounts were earmarked to be distributed equally to various charitable organizations, including one for homeless women with pets in need. He contacted Curtis Cronkly, the super for her building, informed him of her passing and hired him to go into her apartment to clear out her possessions and clean up any messes that might need tending to.

Curtis was instructed to ship the headboard back to Victor. He was to box up the clothing for a local women's shelter. The art supplies should be wrapped up for *The Little Children's Art Day Camp* located in Harlem, which had an art therapy program year-round serving children struggling with traumatic histories. As for the other furniture, odds and ends, etc., Curtis should let him know if there was anything of real value, and he would decide the next steps. Finally, he should give the apartment a good cleaning and paint job so they could get it back on the rental listing as soon as possible.

Chapter Eighty-Two

Curtis had no idea about the condition of Beatrice's apartment. Since the door had been left slightly ajar, he certainly could have looked sooner, but it was the kind of building where people felt safe and sometimes did leave their doors unlocked or even opened a crack if they were expecting company. He wasn't the nosey type, so he never looked inside.

Now he wished he had because when the door was wide open, the stench from rotted food strewn across the apartment was fairly nauseating. This job was going to need more than the typical apartment cleaning. He muttered, "What a shit show," as he considered the amount of work ahead of him.

Mr. V (he always called Victor that) gave him clear instructions on all that needed to be done. Curtis went for the headboard first, which in the overall scheme of things, was a simple task of unscrewing, bubble-wrapping, and creating it for shipment. Over the next few days, he brought in heavy-duty bags for the rotten food and garbage to be cleared out. He figured with that done, being in the space would be much more tolerable.

On the fourth day, he packed up the clothing and other items to be distributed as Mr. V had asked. The art supplies mostly looked like junk to him, but he figured he would box everything up and let the camp decide what to keep and what to ditch.

On the fifth day, the apartment smelled fine and was looking vastly better. He inspected all the furniture to get an idea of where it should go. Most of it was shabby with age, but the couch seemed pretty solid. He briefly thought of keeping it for himself but decided it was too large for his place, and though his wife might have liked to have it, she would have to make do with the one she had. It would all be picked up by the Rehome Furniture Store, which specializes in fixing up and finding new homes for cast-off furniture.

As he shoved the chairs and couch back against the living room wall in an effort to organize things, he noticed a small carved wooden box that he had somehow missed when he had picked up all the other debris earlier in the week. With mild curiosity, he opened it up to explore the contents. Propped on top was something that looked like an old letter or bill with writing he could barely make out, so he figured he'd send it to Mr. V along with the headboard. Beneath the document, staring straight up at Curtis was a ring with a blue stone mounted in a delicate diamond setting. It was the bluest color stone he had ever seen. To get a better angle on it, he aimed the gem towards the light of the window, causing a brilliant white six-pointed star to dance across its surface.

The exquisiteness of the jewel was dramatic, especially in contrast to the mediocrity of everything else in this apartment and his life. Its glow seemed timeless and otherworldly. Curtis believed the ring was almost vibrating though he understood, of course, it was not. He immediately knew he was in the presence of something valuable. It was unmistakable. A ring like this had to be worth a lot of money.

In a stunned state of mind, he pushed the ring over the thick knuckles of his greasy pinkie finger, twisting it round and round like a nut on a screw to force it all the way down. Curtis took a moment to admire how it looked on his hand, even though it was meant for the slender fingers of a woman. For a few minutes, he pretended that it made perfect sense for him to wear it.

Then, he brought it to his face and rubbed the stone back and forth across his upper lip, noticing its' coolness against his facial stubble. Instinct drove him to start licking the star, taste the ring, as if in some perverse initiation ritual. His saliva made slipping the ring off his finger much easier.

Laying down on the couch, he closed his eyes while fondling the jewel between his fingers. He thought about Beatrice Pons for a moment and tried to imagine what she looked like half-naked on a park bench. He never knew quite what to make of her. Then he muttered to the ring, "I'm sure you could bring in a pretty penny."

His fantasies moved on to travel to an exotic beach, opening a swank bar, or even leaving his wife. He opened his eyes, rubbing both thumbs back and forth over the stone, playing peek-a-boo with the star. He whispered out loud again into the emptied apartment as if to convince himself, "Mr. V could not have known about you. Mr. V would have instructed me to keep it safe and send it to him insured, no doubt, for a bucket of money. Nope." He was certain this was a secret find. His secret find. The find of a lifetime that he could cash in at any time.

He found it. Finders' keepers. He did all the work to find it. If nobody asked for it, nobody knew about it.

Curtis got up to his feet and, in a grand sweeping gesture, raised his arms above his head as if stretching for the sun. Then, almost immediately (perhaps fearing the grandiosity of his own sense of entitlement), he shrank like a desperate squirrel hoarding an acorn and plunged the ring once again directly into his mouth as if to store it for another day. With his secret well hidden on his tongue, he defiantly thought, "You're all mine."

His declaration, driven by conceit born of a misplaced sense of possession, buoyed his confidence. He spit out the ring with the stone that took thousands of years to grow into a star to be mounted with diamonds and caught by a cat who tossed it into the bag of a woman in search of her father, directly back into his hand. And then, humming without a care in the world, he shoved the treasure into his pocket for another day.

About The Author

S. L. Wise has been known to tell people that creativity was embedded in her DNA. She would also share that the arts saved her life. Since childhood, when she participated in community theater at the Cleveland Play House, studied painting at Karamu House, sang in school choirs, wrote poems and short stories every chance she had, and hung out at as many museums as possible, the arts have been a wellspring of inspiration for her. They also served to protect her when the turmoil she experienced in her early years challenged her sense of safety in the world.

It is little wonder that decades into her adulthood, she 'discovered', as many who have suffered trauma and seek to make meaning of it often do, the creative arts therapies. She became an art therapist with particular interest in trauma and resiliency. After graduate school, Wise spent the next decades dedicated to attempting to ease the suffering of others. Her art therapy employment took her to every borough in New York City as she worked in homeless shelters, schools, psychiatric units, Veterans facilities, and recovery centers.

She was running her private practice in Manhattan when 9/11 happened. Because of her crisis intervention training, she co-facilitated group sessions and debriefings in office buildings near the Towers that had not collapsed from the attack. While these sessions did not involve art making, it was the work that needed to be done. She then traveled with other creative arts therapists to the Far East, Europe, and the Middle East to run train the trainer groups for teachers and social workers, working with children exposed to war trauma, who wished to bring or refresh how the creative arts were used in healing ways with students.

On a whim, Wise applied for an academic art therapy position in Pennsylvania and was offered the job. So, she turned to educating new professionals in the hope of sharing what she could about the art of art therapy. She ultimately became Director of the Art Therapy Program at Marywood University. Sixteen years after becoming a professor, she was honored with *emerita* status upon her retirement.

While Wise has authored numerous academic chapters and articles over the years, her writing always has the feel of narrative. She is, at heart, a storyteller. In the book she and clinical colleague Emily Nash co-authored in 2019, *Healing Trauma in Group Settings: The Art of Co-Leader Attunement*, Routledge, the writing engages readers because people and events are made real through story.

S.L. Wise's first novel, *A Vortex Tale*, is complex and engrossing. Themes of mystery, human nature, and the quest for meaning are wrapped up into one finely honed work where everything included in the story is present because it needs to be.

Everything has a reason for being.

According to Wise, "In some ways, all of our lives are mysteries - the ending of our individual stories, is not really revealed until the actual end."

She further states of human nature, "I believe we are made up of many parts - as an art therapist, I have been privileged to work with people as they meet parts of themselves that may, metaphorically at least, become characters in their own right. In particular, the creative arts allow us to explore and recognize the hidden parts of ourselves, the parts disguised that usually take background roles in protecting and guiding us or sometimes (when things are out of kilter) even aggress against ourselves and others."

"The quest for meaning demands the search for truth. As humans, we are compelled to make sense of things, to put things in order. When this is impossible, as in, for example, A Vortex Tale, the mind of a 4 year old child whose father has walked out of her life, drives her to invent a 'reason', something that makes sense, a story, to cover the wound. She is impelled to do away with the impossibility of her loss which is breaking her heart. So her imagination takes over providing a way that she can live with her suffering. Or so it would seem. Because for a child, rational thinking is not developmentally possible. Inevitably, there is an expiration date on the story the child tells herself as she out grows her own logic.

Wise adds, “Age provides the distance to make order of meaning and the proximity of urgency to do it in time. A Vortex Tale has found its moment.”

S. L. Wise resides in Bushkill, PA with her partner and wife of twenty-nine years, two dogs, and one cat.